A MUCH YOUNGER MAN

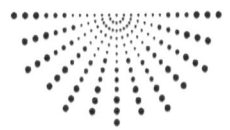

Z.A. MAXFIELD

This book would not be here without my shenanigangsters, Belinda, Linda, Morticia, and Sue. For all you do every day to make work fun again, I love and thank you.

CHAPTER ONE

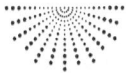

I FELL in love in St. Nacho's. It was a Tuesday.

At that point, my only real relationship was with the el pastor tacos cantina cook Oscar created on a vertical spit in the parking lot of Nacho's Bar. Outdoor cooking wound down with the light at eight—last chance to order tacos before going inside where the restaurant tables over the dance floor could be cleared away for an evening of dancing, drinking, and revelry.

Oscar created his tacos with fire and flash and tidbits of pineapple he flicked from the top of his spit into the tortillas he held at his waist. His partner, Tomas, bagged them up cheerfully while chatting with customers in a long, long line.

Every Tuesday, rain or shine, Tomas set my order aside precisely fifteen minutes before sunset.

Someone in line called out, "Hey, no fair, Dr. Lindy."

"Somebody has special privileges," someone else complained.

"Don't disrespect the doc," a third person said. "He orders ahead."

Most of the heckling was good natured, partly because Tomas did the same for several people with standing orders and partly because I did a lot for my adopted community and they seemed to like me.

I took the heavy, greasy bag onto the boardwalk and sat on the retaining wall next to the sand. Taco Tuesday at Nacho's Bar, Friday pie from Café Bêtise, the occasional poker game with off-duty firefighters on Saturday night—my rituals anchored me in time that would otherwise slide silently by as one season flowed into the next.

I loved my job, I owned a nice house, and the friends I'd acquired in quirky St. Nacho's made getting up every day easy and sweet.

Did I deserve that pleasurable life? Probably not.

I'd have to pay for my sins someday—ego, pride, and a few others—but apparently today was not that day.

"Nice night."

"Isn't it?" I turned to find Cooper Wyatt standing beside me, violin in hand as always, bow held loosely as if he couldn't wait to play.

"It's a little clear for June." A man of few words, Cooper. What he lacked in eloquent speech, he more than made up for with glorious music.

"I haven't been here enough years to form an opinion."

"Me neither, really." Brown eyes blinked against the red brightness of the sun as it settled into a fiery sea.

A large crowd of beachgoers had been drawn out by the fine weather. As the day waned, they strolled or biked or jogged up and down the boardwalk, some with children and pets I recognized from work. A few surfers still bobbed in the water, trying to get in one last ride before it grew too dark to see.

A feeling of contentment stole over me like sunshine, sinking deep into muscle and bone.

I belonged in St. Nacho's. Nothing matched its peace or beauty. Time flowed in a rhythm all its own as if progress, and politics, and the next new Instagram trend didn't exist there.

In what other Podunk town could you find an extraordinary violinist playing classical music on the beach because it made him happy, an award-winning pastry chef opening the doors to a quaint French-style cafe every morning? In what other town would a firefighter walk a cat down the sidewalk on Main Street?

I'm a pretty entrenched man of science and reason, but when I stopped to try the infamous brunch at Nacho's Bar, something about the town had caught me in an almost magical spell. I stayed for one night, then a second. I returned a month later and stayed for a week. The little coastal enclave drew me in and didn't let go. After months of thinking about moving, of dreaming about St. Nacho's and the people I'd met there, of pining for the way its waves crashed against the shore, I sold my veterinary clinic in San Diego and opened a practice here.

I moved for the view, the powerful feeling of community, the sense of belonging, and I've never looked back.

"You hear that?" Cooper asked once the sun had gone and there was nothing left but a glow on the edge of the world.

"The guitar?" Crystal clear notes drifted from farther along the boardwalk.

"'Asturias,'" he muttered. Like a dog scenting food, Cooper bounded away, following the sound. I wiped my greasy hands, tossed my trash in a bin, and followed.

He stopped near the small circle of people listening to a seated guitarist. Whoever was playing had skill—Cooper's rapt attention proved it. As I edged my way through the group to get closer, Cooper set his bow.

The guitarist glanced up in surprise, then delight, when he realized they were playing a duet. He followed Cooper's lead, handling all the musical transitions Cooper threw at him with happy laughter.

People gasped and several phones flashed up to capture the moment they shared.

I looked around to see if anyone else saw what I saw—joy, entirely unrestrained. Skill and passion. Creation in its purest, most breathtaking form.

Pure youth on the verge of magnificence.

The sight of that young guitarist felt like a wound, like a scar. Talent like his was rare. I also felt breath stealing sorrow, not desire or envy but a kind of despair, as if I'd lost something I'd never realized I'd had until it was gone.

Of course he conjured those emotions—it was nothing more than nostalgia for my own youth, a desire to be part of his, and the merciless inadequacy that is the human condition.

He held me in thrall, which was wrong, wrong, *wrong*.

Normally when faced with attraction to someone completely unsuitable, I forced myself to step back, congratulate God on a job well done, and walk away.

Normally.

But this Orpheus, this god-kissed boy with such rare talent, caught and held my attention like no other. How old was he? Twenty, maybe. I felt vivid personal shame just watching him.

Thank God that in the next second my attention was drawn to the chocolate Lab sitting patiently beside him. She, too, was a beauty. Healthy, yes, but on the thin side. Her coat was a little dusty, but her eyes looked clear.

Given the state of the musician's clothes and battered back-pack, the two of them were living rough. He didn't have the built-up grime or leather skin you saw in people who'd been in the elements for long periods of time, but his clothes were tattered in places and didn't look very clean.

Frowning, I turned to Cooper, but his eyes were closed. He was in his happy place where all that existed for him was music —the intersection of his art and someone else's. My compulsion to check out the dog rivaled my reaction to her owner. A gorgeous animal with rich brown fur, she had doe's eyes that radiated calm despite the number of people crowding around her seated human.

I'd wait and maybe ask a few questions after they finished playing—give him a few bucks along with my business card. Maybe I could get him to come to the clinic so I could make sure she was up to date on her vaccinations and free of parasites.

Cooper and his musical friend played until the song finished, their fingers finding the notes by some alchemy of instinct and motor memory. The boardwalk's electric lights came on, and the spell was broken.

After the last notes died, the boy held his instrument like a lover, and those in the crowd who were inclined to give him money dropped bills into his guitar case.

A sandy, shaggy-haired man climbed over the wall from the beach carrying a battery-operated lantern and a soft-serve ice cream cone. He sat cross-legged next to the musician on the boardwalk and offered him a lick with a grin. The guitarist leaned toward the newcomer and opened his mouth in invitation. As the man fed him, his eyes fluttered closed. Vanilla cream melted over his tongue and ran down his chin.

BOOM. Like a depth charge, heat and desire burst inside me.

My belly caught fire, and desire tightened my groin, making my blood rush south.

I wanted to be the one holding that cone, feeding that gorgeous young man, nourishing and nurturing him. Who was this other guy to him? They both looked young to me, but the grinning newcomer had a hard face. His skin was ruddy, and unlike the guitarist's, his nails looked none too clean. I couldn't help but notice that when he got too close, the guitarist's dog backed up to lean heavily against his human's side.

I exchanged a glance with Cooper. It was time to brush off my unexpected attraction or, at the very least, take a goddamn breath before my life turned into some Hallmark movie.

Cooper asked, "Where'd you learn to play like that?"

"My dad taught me some when I was little." His voice was deeper than I'd expected. Richer. "Later on, I picked up most of what I know from YouTube. I practice a lot."

"Beck's a genius." The friend threw the bottom of his cone toward the dog who snapped it out of the air.

"Beck?" Cooper asked.

"Last name's Beckett." Beck shrugged. "It's a nickname."

"Looks like you had a good night." His friend scooped up Beck's cash and pocketed it. "My boy here can play classical, pop, rock, Delta blues. He can play anything."

Beck glanced away shyly. "Not anything."

"Can too. I'll get us dinner and be back in a bit."

"Get some grilled chicken breast." Beck glanced up. "Plain. Don't forget."

"I've got it."

I added more cash to the case after he left before turning my attention to the dog.

"What's her name?"

Beck petted her ears gently. "Calliope. I call her Callie."

"May I introduce myself to her?"

Beck studied me closely while he made up his mind. I studied him right back. Hair like a rat's nest. Blue eyes. Scruffy, barely there beard. A lip ring.

Why was my heart racing?

Why did Beck hold me so entranced I could barely speak?

"Go ahead," he said.

"You're a beauty, aren't you, sweetheart?" I lifted my hands close to my body, palms up. The dog leaned over to give me a cautious sniff. She probably got a good whiff of the tacos I'd eaten. She licked my fingers. "You're a very pretty girl."

This got me a smile from Beck. "Callie's the best dog ever."

I held his gaze just a little too long over her silky head. Our hands met accidentally, and it was as if lightning snaked up my arm. He blinked the way cats do when they're displaying trust. My heart contracted with happiness. Or terror. I couldn't tell exactly which.

"She's pretty chill." I cleared my throat to hum while I petted her because usually that gets me the attention I want from a dog. Some people talk to animals, but I feel like a dumbass repeating stupid words over and over—*Who's a good girl? You're a good girl.* I get their attention by humming, or if I'm feeling jovial, singing out loud. It had become a useful habit and a bit of a trademark. In town they called me the singing vet.

As intended, my voice kept Callie still and alert. She was intelligent. Very receptive. Unafraid of human touch.

"I'm Linden Davies, and I've got a veterinary practice here in town." I took a card from my pocket and gave it to him. "Maybe you can bring her in and let me take a look at her."

He widened his eyes. "She's up to date on all her shots. I have the papers right here." I stopped him from scrabbling away to get them.

"I don't need to see them." I couldn't bear for him to be afraid of me. "It's okay."

"I take good care of her," he said defensively. "She's on a leash."

"It's all good." I lifted my hands in surrender. "It's just that I'm a hopeless meddler when it comes to pets. I like to check under the hood. No charge, of course."

"No charge?" He bit his lip. "Maybe that'd be okay."

"You know, I get lots of samples from distributors. Toys. Gear. Food. Maybe there's something in my stash Callie would like."

"Oh. Okay. Thank you." His smile slayed me.

"It's my pleasure." I wanted to keep staring at him but stood. Cooper promised to stop by for another jam session if Beck stuck around. As we made our way back toward the busy bar together, I couldn't help glancing back.

My gut said not to leave him alone like that. But he wasn't alone. He had that friend. Boyfriend. He may have been homeless, or he may have been having the time of his life. People weren't my *purrrview* as we say in the vet biz. I stuck to worrying about their pets.

Still, I asked, "You think he's okay outside like that?"

"I used to do it." Cooper's expression appeared thoughtful.

"What?" I asked. "Busking?"

He nodded. "Before I came to St. Nacho's, I never stayed in one place more than a day or two. Busking's how I made ends meet between dishwashing jobs or whatever."

"It seems like a pretty precarious way to live."

"Guess it depends on why you do it. Some of us have to earn cash that way to eat, but for others it's a big romantic adventure."

"I wish I knew which it was for him."

"He'll do okay, especially here. St. Nacho's loves to be entertained, and people are pretty generous with artists."

I saw Beck's friend leave the liquor store across from the cantina. He made his way toward us with a bottle wrapped in a bag. I wondered if Beck was even old enough to legally drink.

"Hey," he called in greeting. "Gotta get my boy some food. What's good here? Gotta be cheap."

Cooper opened the door to the cantina for him. "I recommend the carnitas tacos. They're three for five dollars tonight."

"Awesome. Thanks." We left him at the hostess station and made our way inside to get a drink.

Behind the bar, Jim, the cantina's owner, schmoozed with the denizens of St. Nacho's he knew and liked while another bartender did the real work. Cooper was a great favorite of Jim's. As soon as he saw us, he retrieved Cooper's violin case from behind the bar and handed it over.

"What put that big smile on your face?" he asked.

"There's a kid out there playing the fucking strings off his guitar." Cooper carefully put his instrument away. "Amazing fingers."

"That good, huh?" Jim's expression was fond. "Did you adopt him yet?"

"Ha, ha." Usually it was Jim doing the adopting. If the stories were true, he'd adopted Cooper.

"Looks like he's living rough," I said. "So maybe that's not such a bad idea."

"That's a rite of passage all up and down the coast," Jim said. "Kids hit the road with a guitar and a big dream. It's a rock and roll cliché for a reason."

"Hope it's just a summer thing." Cooper accepted his usual soda from Jim. I asked for whiskey.

"It's hard to see how he can care for that Lab properly." I took my drink and lifted it in thanks. "I need to make sure she's okay."

"You're such a softie." Cooper nudged me. "She looked healthy, didn't she?"

"The dog looked fine, but who drags an animal around without thinking about food or predatory insects or the fact that in the summer, the heat from the asphalt will blister her paws? People are free to put themselves through whatever adventure they want, but as far as I'm concerned, pets deserve better."

Cooper patted my arm. "C'mon, Lindy. Beck didn't look stupid. He'll probably come to the clinic, then you can make sure the dog's okay."

"I hope so." I wanted to help both of them and not just because I was a vet. There was something about Beck. It was that slow blink—that trust—as if he'd placed himself into my hands because he needed me. I couldn't get the image of him out of my mind.

Later, I saw Beck's friend carry his bottle and bag of food back to the boardwalk.

If I could have confined my compassion to the dog, I might have slept better that first night.

It was my heart that kept dragging me back from sleep, though. Emotions I'd never experienced before gave me dreams I didn't want.

I fell in love on Taco Tuesday in St. Nacho's.

Because it *was* St. Nacho's, the only person surprised by that fact was me.

CHAPTER TWO

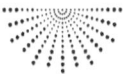

I NORMALLY DID surgeries between seven and nine in the morning. That Friday, I had my hands full. When I finally stepped out of the surgical suite at ten, my receptionist, Lena, flagged me down. I motioned her toward the recovery room where I discarded my soiled protective gear and stepped behind the curtain to change my scrubs.

"How's Maisy?" She peered into the cage of the dog whose malignancy I'd just removed.

"The surgery was a success. She'll be accessorizing with an e-collar for a few days." It was her second tumor removal, though, and sooner or later Maisy's owners would have a difficult decision to make. "What's next?"

"You were already booked through lunch, and Mylo swallowed a sock again. April's got him. She induced vomiting."

"Mylo, Mylo, Mylo. Goddamn, that dog is persistent. You could open a store with all the socks he swallows."

"The poor kids are crying, and Jill's a nervous wreck. They're in the waiting room."

"I'll talk to them. So far, he spits them back up like a champ." I stepped out feeling fresher and went to the sink to wash up.

"Anything else?" I rinsed off and dried my hands.

"I finished the summer newsletter for you to look over."

"Okay."

"Also, there's someone here who says you told him to come in so you could look at his dog for *free*."

My pulse rate kicked up. "Chocolate Lab named Calliope?"

"So you did tell him to come? He showed me her records. She's up to date on vaccines. I don't see why—"

"I want to make sure she's parasite free."

"Must you really tell total strangers you'll examine their dogs at no cost? Some of them could be looking for easy access to drugs, or—"

"Let me worry about that, Lena. It doesn't hurt to help people."

She *hmph*'d at me, muttering about how easy it was to take advantage of soft touches and fools.

"I'm both. I freely admit it."

She pushed her heavy glasses up the bridge of her nose. "You need an actual business manager, Lindy. You'd give the place away if I let you."

"It's my place. And I only give away my time." Which wasn't exactly true, but she understood.

"There's a finite amount of that commodity, you know." She handed me a stack of files. "And you volunteer enough of it without inviting people to come here for free examinations."

"I examine the pets, not the people." She flipped me off behind her back as she walked away. I stretched my stiff neck and raised my arms over my head. My vertebrae popped all the way down like corn. Hmm. It felt like a Queen day. I hummed a few notes of "Bohemian Rhapsody."

"We got it, but yuck." Vet tech April came into the room holding an emesis tray with a rancid sock in it. She slipped it into a zippered plastic bag, then removed her gloves and washed her hands.

"Mylo's a champ."

"He is. He's fine."

"That was quick. I was going to go out and talk to Jill."

"You have time." She wrinkled her nose. "He's spacey, and I need to get him cleaned up before I can take him out there."

"Thanks." I went to the human fridge and pulled out a bottled water. "Want one?"

"God yes." She took it from me. "Thank you."

"What's next?"

"Senior feline in exam one is listless. Owner says she won't eat or drink. Pebbles the pittie's in room two for her rabies vaccine. Oh my God, wait until you see the adorable schnauzer puppy in three. New client. He's so cute!"

"The client?"

"The *puppy*." She rolled her eyes.

"Can't wait. Listen, can you tell Travis to put the young man with the Lab in exam room four and make him comfortable? Tell him it might be some time before I can get in there." I took out my wallet and handed her a ten. "Have Travis get him a sandwich from next door and see that he has pop or something. Oh, and ask if the dog has eaten today. If not, get something from the back."

"You're feeding dogs and their humans now?" She studied me. "Something going on there?"

"No." I probably protested too fast, because she gave me the side-eye.

"It's one of your projects, isn't it?"

"No." I couldn't meet her knowing gaze. "Okay. Maybe. His name is Beck. The dog is Callie. They might be living rough, so they could use some help."

"Ah, gotcha. I'll tell Travis and then finish up with Mylo." She carried the baggie as if it was an animal carcass.

I left the safety of the back rooms to talk to Jill and her kids. They stopped crying as soon as they knew Mylo was okay. That dog was a lucky critter, considering every sock removal cost the family around two hundred bucks. It was hard on the dog too. I'd have reminded them not to leave socks where Mylo could get them, but Mylo was a wily creature. He'd been known to steal socks off a sleeping child's foot.

Outside exam room one, I pasted a smile on my face. "Hello, Mrs. Grimes. What's Misty got for us today?"

DUTIFULLY, I finished with the three patients who'd booked their appointments ahead before I approached exam room four. From outside the door, I could hear a distinct drumming rhythm. Fingers, probably, on the wall or the exam table. Like Cooper, Beck obviously made music wherever he could. The idea made me smile.

I opened the door. "Sorry to keep you waiting so long, Beck. Today just blew up out of nowhere."

He stopped his hands. "Beggars can't be choosers."

"Well, thank you for stopping by. I've been looking forward to seeing Callie again."

"Thank you. Your guy—"

"Travis."

"Yeah. He gave me a sandwich and lemonade. You didn't have to do that." Beck's guitar case and backpack sat against the wall. At his feet, a very patient Calliope leaned against his legs. "We make our way."

"I'm sure you do." I braced against the exam table with my arms folded. "But I kept you waiting for such a long time. I didn't want you guys to eat me when I finally came in."

His eyes sparked with mischief. "*Callie* wouldn't eat anyone."

Despite the AC, my face burned. "So, the reason I asked you here...Lena says Callie's caught up on her vaccinations, but I'd like to check her for parasites and make sure she gets protection."

"Parasites?"

"I'd like to see her protected from fleas, ticks, and mosquito-borne illnesses. A simple blood test will be necessary before we can give her heartworm medication."

"Oh."

"Did I ever formally introduce myself? I'm Dr. Linden Davies. My patients call me Lindy or Doc or any combination, really."

"Really?" His mouth curved impishly. "Hear that, Callie? Call him Lindy or Doc."

"All right, smarty pants." I flushed again. "My patients' humans call me Lindy. And you're Beck?"

As if I didn't know.

"Christopher Beckett. My friends call me Beck."

"May I call you that?" My throat tightened.

"Yes." Beck turned away to dig his fingers into Callie's fur. It startled us both when Travis entered the room.

"Need me?" he asked.

"Please. Help Beck lift Miss Callie up here." Travis and Beck got Callie onto the table. She kept her eyes firmly on Beck while she waited. "Do you think she'll need a soft muzzle while I look her over?"

"She hasn't in the past."

I hummed to get Callie's attention. Her head snapped up, and she stared at me with curiosity. She didn't mind my hands on her, so I checked her eyes, ears, and teeth. She was young and healthy. Good spine, hips, and paws.

She was such an easy blood draw I thought I could probably get away with anything, but when I went to clip her nails, she yipped and scrambled away. *Maybe not anything after all.* Of course, when she fussed, Beck's anxiety grew.

"She needs a nail trim."

"She hates that." Beck looked sick. "I hate to put her through it."

"We can leave it for now. All done, Callie." Beck and Travis helped Callie scramble down. "How long will you be in St. Nacho's?"

"I don't know. A few days?"

"Okay. Take this." I found a plastic specimen bag and wrote Callie's name on it with a Sharpie. "If you get me a sample of her poo, we can check for parasites. If all is well, we'll get you some chewies to give her once a month. They'll keep the pests away."

"What does that cost?" he asked.

"I have samples. Don't worry about it." I leaned against the table again. "But, Beck...Callie's a big girl. She needs proper nutrition to stay healthy. Are you able to consistently provide food and clean water?"

He tensed. "I take good care of her."

"I know you try, but life on the road isn't easy with a large pet, is it? Remember I said we have sample cases of the kind of food she needs? Do you want to take some with you?"

"They're samples? People give them to you?" Beck's eyes were an odd dark blue, like sapphires in water. They looked hopeful and frightened at the same time. Why the hell was he on his own at his age? "If you're sure it's okay? That'd be nice."

"She needs good balanced nutrition." I signaled to Travis, and he slipped quietly from the room to get her what she needed. The following few minutes were excruciating. Beck seemed to look in any direction but mine. I hummed. This time, the song stuck in my head was "Under Pressure."

A little way into it, Beck did a surprising descant *dee dee da da* before covering his face with his hands and giggling. He sings too. How...adorable.

"Do you always sing for the animals?" he asked.

"I do, actually. It's my secret thing."

He bit his lip. "Not so secret."

"Guess not." He cuddled the dog.

Callie had a good friend in Beck. He saw to it she got much-needed food, comfort, and companionship. Beck was the mystery. How had he come to be on the road like this? What could I do to help?

Travis returned with a medium-size bag of food and—to Callie's delight—an ultra-tough bat-shaped squeaky.

"Oh, thank you for this. She already loves it." Callie pounced and killed the bat over and over while Beck put on his pack and picked up his guitar. "Thank you for everything, Dr. Davies. I'll be back with her poop."

"I can't wait," I joked. "Please call me Lindy."

"Lindy." He nodded and left. I stared at the door he went through for a long time.

Travis lifted his brows. "Cute kid."

I cleared my throat. "Right. Let me know when he comes back with that sample. If I'm not here, give him whatever he needs for the dog."

Travis frowned at me. "What about him?"

"Beck? What about him?"

"Jesus, Lindy. Oblivious much?"

"What did I miss?"

He sighed. "You're a good vet, but where people are concerned, you miss the point sometimes."

"Well, tell me. I know you're dying to."

"You looked at that Beck dude like he was the last chocolate mousse at Bêtise. And he was right there with you. You totally dig each other."

"So what? He's a baby." I pumped soap into my palm. "He's a fetus. Do I look like Cher to you?"

"He's old enough to date."

"Is not." I washed my hands furiously. "And even if he were, I'm nobody's romantic ideal, least of all for someone his age."

No one believes me when I say I'm no good at relationships even though I prove it all the time.

"All right, then, if you're going to be a stubborn ass." Travis shrugged. "What Beck really needs is a job."

"You think so?" Would he want that? "I guess I could find a paying project or two around here."

"You could also ask around and see if anyone else needs a hand." Travis brightened. "Does Jim still have that room over the bar?"

Did he? "I should drop by the cantina and ask him, huh?"

"That's the spirit." He thumped my arm. "We'll make a real boy out of you yet."

"Thanks." I rubbed where it smarted. "But don't you think it's weird to do all this without asking Beck if it's what he wants?"

"It seems to me he might be happy to have somebody looking out for him."

"He has a friend he travels with. I think that's his job."

"Beck can always say no."

Animals gave clear signals, unobfuscated by subtext and subterfuge. People? Not so much.

Beck wasn't the first guy with a dog in need I'd pulled off the beach. He probably wasn't the twenty-first. I didn't begrudge anyone the love of a pet—even in dire circumstances. Life is hard, and the love of an animal companion could literally stand between a human and soul crushing despair. I'd never take that away from someone in need, so I did the next best thing. I stepped in on behalf of the animal.

If Beck came back with that sample, I could offer him something. If he came back. I'd given him plenty of incentive, but I'd never been good at knowing what people were going to do.

I wished I knew Beck's plans, and at the same time, I wished I didn't care so much. In my experience, caring too much led to trouble.

CHAPTER THREE

THE FOLLOWING NIGHT, Cooper's partner, Shawn, stood with Jim on his side of the bar opposite Cooper and me. This made it easier for him to read our lips. Cooper used either ASL or speech, but I was glad Shawn could read my lips because what little ASL I knew was limited to asking questions about cats or dogs.

We'd been talking for a while, but then the subject turned to Beck and his dog. I asked if they had any ideas how we could help them.

"Is the room upstairs empty?" Shawn asked. "Could they use that?"

"I can't have a dog in here." Jim slung a damp towel over his shoulder. "Health codes."

"Right." That made sense.

"Besides, Tomas and Oscar are up there right now until they can move into their new place."

"They're moving?" Shawn signed when he talked. I wondered if it was just habit or if he did it for Cooper since he was still learning. "They never said. Where? Out of town?"

"Just to a bigger house," Jim assured him. "I think Oscar has cousins from New Mexico who are going to stay with them, and they've been wanting a nicer yard for ages."

Shawn smiled brightly. "Glad they're staying. What would I do without Tomas's carnitas?"

"Is there anywhere else Beck can stay?" St. Nacho's didn't have a homeless shelter, per se. The local police and sheriff's deputies referred people in need to the appropriate county agency, who referred them to anyplace with available beds.

"What about the SeaView Motel?" Shawn asked. "Does Carl take pets? Maybe he'd discount a room, just until they get on their feet."

Cooper spoke and signed. "That's a big ask during tourist season."

"There's always our guest bedroom," said Shawn. Ken Ashton flipped houses, and he'd recently helped them buy a place large enough to accommodate guests. "I could see letting them stay as long as they don't take advantage."

Cooper's brows lowered. "I don't know about having strangers—"

"You talked about the kid for hours," Shawn teased. "He doesn't feel like a stranger anymore. Do you want to help him?"

"It's not the guitarist I'd have trouble with," said Jim, "but his friend. Seems to take the kids earnings for booze. Gets him food like it's an afterthought."

"Wait, what?" The behavior wasn't news to me, but I didn't know it was a pattern.

"Don't know about Beck's friend." Cooper nodded in agreement. "Hasn't made a great impression so far."

"Could we offer the kid and the dog a place without the friend?" Shawn asked.

Cooper tapped the bar absently. "What if that's why they're on the road in the first place? Parents didn't like the boyfriend."

"Obviously we need to know more about their situation

before we can do anything to help. If I see Beck again, I'll ask some questions," I said.

"He's probably out there right now." Cooper nodded toward the beach. "Want to look?"

"You go." Shawn came through the bridge and sat on one of the bar stools. "I've been on my feet since six this morning."

Shawn's work as a teaching assistant and the dance classes he led at Izzie's gym kept him in peak physical condition, but enough was enough, I guessed. I tipped my drink back. Cooper gave Jim a nod. This time he left his violin behind the bar when he went in search of Beck, Callie, and their shady friend, who pinged my radar all wrong.

OUTSIDE, instead of a brilliant sunset, there were clouds moving rapidly inland. A waning moon played peekaboo as they scudded across the sky.

"Might rain," Cooper observed.

"Smells like it."

He pulled his collar up against the brisk breeze. "Hope the kids have a tent."

I hoped so too, except there wasn't really any legal camping on the beach, and the SIPD might move them along if they made a nuisance of themselves.

We located Beck right away. He'd stationed himself under the light closest to the cantina, and he'd already drawn a small crowd.

"I played for cash when I first got here too." Cooper smiled at some memory. "Jim let me use his upstairs room and play in the bar. The rest is St. Nacho's history."

Lots of people drifted into Santo Ignacio and simply never left. Our little town had a reputation for collecting folks who felt like outsiders everywhere else.

Cooper met Shawn at the cantina, and the two had become a mainstay of culture in town. Things seemed to fall into place here. People slowed down. They took stock. They put things into perspective. Here, people celebrated their differences and found common cause in the natural beauty all around us. People met and fell and stayed in the kind of love most of them had only dreamt about before coming here.

Some said the town was mystical or built on sacred ground or enchanted.

I figured it was simply easier to find love when you were already happy.

As we watched, Beck's audience tossed cash into his guitar case. The atmosphere was festive, making larger tips more likely. We partied over the big things and the small—a ball game between the firefighters and the police officers, a new flavor of pie. We were too liberal to be called Mayberry, but we had traditions that went back to the founders. The drums we marched to played a different, more lively beat.

Look at me, a relative newcomer, going all squishy over my new home.

Cooper and I watched Beck play until the light faded. He finished his set with a Gipsy Kings tune that had at least two couples in the crowd dancing.

As he had the first time, Beck's friend climbed over the retaining wall when he was finished playing. He scooped up and counted Beck's cash without even asking him if it was all right. I resented this on Beck's behalf, but it was none of my business how they conducted their affairs. Obviously we weren't seeing the full picture. Maybe Beck's friend did day labor to contribute. Maybe he was the one who took care of all the mundane business while Beck thought only of music.

Beck's friend took off after promising he'd be back with food. Beck took his time putting his instrument away. The care he showed his guitar—and Callie—warmed my heart.

Once most of the crowd dispersed, Cooper and I stepped forward to say hello.

"Oh, hey, Dr. Lindy." Beck's face lit with gratifying, happy recognition. "Cooper."

"Hey, Beck." I crouched to greet Callie, who didn't seem to hold our earlier fracas with the nail clippers against me. "How's it going?"

"Fine." He dug through his backpack, found what he was looking for, and proudly handed it over. "Here."

"Thanks." I took it before I really registered what it was. "Ah."

"Callie's poop. You said you wanted it."

I *had* said I wanted it. "Thank you."

It wouldn't have come as a surprise to anyone who knew me that I simply jammed it in my pocket. Everything I owned was machine washable, and my jacket had been through a lot worse. I used hand sanitizer liberally while continuing to smile at Beck.

"Can I ask you something?" I waved my hands dry.

"You can ask." He tilted his head flirtatiously. "Maybe I'll answer."

"How old are you?"

That got me an eyeroll. "How old do you think?"

"I don't know. That's why I'm asking. I *hope* you're out of high school."

"I'm twenty." He huffed unhappily. "But I don't blame you for thinking I'm younger. You wouldn't believe how many cops think I'm truant."

Not legal drinking age. "What about your friend?"

"Callie?" His eyes held a playful challenge. "She's three and a half."

Cooper snorted. "Your other friend."

"His name is Tug."

"Tug?" I asked. "Like tug-of-war?"

"Exactly."

I tried not to let my reaction show. "How old is he?"

"Twenty-five." Beck's eyes dared me to question this.

"How long have you guys been living rough?" Cooper asked.

"A while."

"How long is a while? A few months? A year?"

"A while," Beck said evasively. "What is this? Why do you want to know?"

"Just trying to get to know you, Beck." I gestured toward the ground beside Callie. "Can I sit?"

Beck lifted a shoulder. "Suit yourself. But if this is the part where the town fathers ask us to move on, just get to the point."

"It's not." Cooper sat on the wall behind us. "No one wants you gone."

I gestured to myself and Cooper. "We only want to know if there's anything we can do to help you."

"You already helped with Callie. Tug and I are fine."

"I'm sure." There was a bedroll on Beck's backpack. If he and Tug had a tent, I hadn't seen it. "But maybe you need a roof over your head."

"Is that so?" He took a breath to say more, but right then Tug came back with pizza on a paper plate and another bottle.

"Got you a couple slices, babe."

"Thanks." Tug took the pizza and folded it like a New Yorker before stuffing the tip into Beck's mouth. *What the hell?* That was the second time Tug had hand-fed Beck like a goddamn baby deer. I got why Beck maybe didn't want to get his hands dirty while he was playing, but he'd put his instrument away now, and he could eat on his own.

I found it weird and distasteful, but fucking hell...*I* wanted to be the guy feeding Beck, which made me queasy and got me hot at the same time. This was so wrong.

Beck chewed thoughtfully and then took the plate and the pizza from Tug. "S'good. Thanks. But go get some chicken for Callie, please."

"I will," Tug murmured. "You eat up, and I'll go back for chicken and maybe find us some dessert."

My heart raced so guiltily I made myself turn away until Callie stood and sniffed at Beck's pizza eagerly.

He held her back. "Not for Callie."

Unhappily, she collapsed on his lap. He absently stroked her ears while he ate the rest of his pizza. Eventually Tug turned his focus on me and Cooper.

"You guys need something? This isn't a zoo."

"Don't." Beck shifted away from him. "This is the vet I told you about. He checked Callie over this morning. They just stopped by to say hello."

Tug's gaze traveled over me and then Cooper. He turned back to me. "Sure."

"What?" I snapped at him.

"Nothing." Tug leaned against the wall and pulled the cap off whatever was in tonight's brown-bag bottle. "You shouldn't trust do-gooders, Beck. It never ends well."

"It's my job to look after animals here," I said.

"Sure it is. You just give everyone free exams all the time." Tug had some kind of grudge; that much was obvious. *And nothing to do with me.*

"Let's go." I guessed Cooper decided an argument was not worth his time. He got to his feet.

"Stop by tomorrow for the test results. If she's good to go, we'll get some flea, tick, and heartworm samples for you." I let Tug warn me off for the time being.

"Thanks, Dr. Lindy." Beck's gratitude wasn't effusive, but at least it wasn't the outright hostility I was drawing from Tug. What kind of name was that anyway? Who called themselves *Tug?*

"Have a good night." Cooper took off toward the cantina, and I followed.

"I don't like that dynamic." I glanced over my shoulder and

found Tug glaring back.

"Judgy much?"

"Me or him?" I hoped Cooper was joking. "You saw how he takes Beck's cash and brings back whatever he sees fit. Two pieces of pizza? That's not enough for a twenty-year old male. Are they even getting vegetables? A piece of fruit?"

Cooper laughed at me. "They're kids. They're probably living off the food of love."

That irritated me further. "Musicians."

"C'mon. I lived like that. That Tug kid is probably protecting him from a lot worse things than malnutrition."

"But where will they sleep if it rains?" The sky was already spitting mist and the leaden clouds didn't look promising.

"Tug's got one of those two-man tents. I saw it on the beach a few nights ago."

"Is that legal?"

"No, but the local police won't move them along unless they build a fire. They might issue a warning."

"It must be awfully cold at night."

"It'll be okay, mother hen. They've got their love to keep them warm."

"And Callie."

"Right. That dog's probably like a furnace in a small tent."

I sighed and let him drag me back to the bar where Jim and Shawn waited to hear what we'd learned.

"Did you find them?" asked Shawn.

"They're okay." Cooper ordered another soda. "They're both adults."

"If Beck's telling the truth," I said.

Shawn grabbed my shoulder. "Say again?"

I repeated my words, adding, "I think Tug is taking advantage."

Shawn looked to Cooper, who shrugged. "It's Beck's life."

"So, you didn't offer them a room at our place?" Shawn asked.

Cooper shook his head. "Didn't have a good feeling about it."

"Tug seemed pretty suspicious of our motivation," I said. "Well, mine anyway."

Shawn never bothered containing or controlling his laughter. It sounded like pure happiness. "He obviously didn't realize your only concern is the dog."

"What do you mean? I'm concerned about the boys too." I was about to be ribbed. Again.

"C'mon. You don't even see people unless they're dragging around a pet," said Cooper.

"I've got lots on my mind, okay?" I downed my drink. "Speaking of…I've got to hit the road. Nice seeing you."

Shawn and Cooper hugged me. Jim waved from behind the bar.

I was on foot, so I took the long way home. It meant taking the boardwalk and possibly passing by Beck and Tug again. Was I already in too deep over a stranger?

Yes. Yes, I was.

They needed a roof over their heads. Nutritious meals. None of them were getting that. If money was as tight as I believed it to be, Tug had no business spending it on booze. I'd watched Beck with Callie. He'd never forgive himself if anything happened to her. Yet even though it made me distinctly uneasy, I couldn't tell him he ought not to have a dog in his situation. He and Callie were obviously devoted to each other.

I believed it was wrong to take on pets—or people—to whom you couldn't give one hundred percent. Who was I to judge?

Just someone who'd learned that lesson in every way possible.

CHAPTER FOUR

AT SIX IN THE MORNING, I unlocked the door to the clinic and killed the alarms. We took turns sleeping in the clinic—April, Travis, and I—but only if we had animals who needed overnight care. I'd toyed with the idea of adding another vet to the practice, but so far that hadn't been necessary. It would have been great to share my responsibilities with another DVM—especially on days after I'd been up all night—but it didn't make fiscal sense. The clinic needed to be a lot busier before I could seriously consider that.

I followed the sound of soft snores and found Travis asleep on the cot in my office next to our current box of abandoned kittens. We often found pets, especially kittens, abandoned outside our back door. The little guys' eyes were barely open, and for now, they required around-the-clock feeding with KMR —kitten milk replacement.

Travis had left unofficial feeding notes on the box, and I saw I could afford to let them all sleep for a while.

As I got coffee started, someone pounded on the back door.

I'd barely cracked it open when Beck fell inside with a

nervous Callie at his heels. His breaths hitched as if he'd run. Tears streaked his face.

"What is it? What happened?"

He swiped angrily at his eyes. "Tug stole all my stuff last night. My God. I can't believe he'd—"

"Slow down." I gripped his shoulders. "I don't understand. What happened?"

He sniffled. "I woke up this morning and Tug was just... gone. He took everything. He took my guitar."

"Okay. Take a deep breath." I locked the door and he let me guide him to one of the chairs in the waiting room. "You want coffee?"

"I want my *shit* back."

"Sit down and tell me what happened." I took one of the folding chairs and sat opposite.

"We got into a humongous fight last night." He drew in a shuddering breath. "He was high, and—"

"On what?"

"I don't know. Meth, probably. He used to have a...a drug problem." He glanced away, embarrassed. "I told him I wouldn't stick with him if he used, but he's been acting off lately, and I knew something was up. I guess he scored last night. We got into it, and I said I wasn't having it. When I woke up, everything was gone."

Shit. "Is there any chance he's just blowing off some steam."

He shook his head. Poor kid. "No."

His blue eyes, now ringed red with misery, streamed. I felt like I should smooth down his hair or something. I didn't.

"Does he even play the guitar?" I asked.

"No." Beck huffed a bitter laugh. "He'll sell it. I worked for a year to get that guitar, and he'll use the cash to get high."

"I'm so sorry."

"What will I do? That guitar is...everything. It's all I have."

"What about your family? Will they help you?"

He shook his head. "It's only Mom and my stepdad. They were adamant. If I didn't take Callie to a shelter, I had to leave."

"Oh, Beck. I'm sorry. But she's a beautiful animal. I'm certain she would find a loving home right away." My words were callous, but rehoming Callie had to be better than a life on the street.

"So I should just get rid of her?" he asked, outraged.

"Beck, God knows I love animals, but I don't think you being homeless because you want a dog is good for either you or the dog."

He put his head in his hands. "I knew you wouldn't understand."

"Then explain it to me."

"Why should I? You won't listen. Nobody listens." He rose and gave Callie's leash a flick. "C'mon, baby. Let's go."

"Wait." I caught his arm. "I understand you love her—"

"It's not about me." He pushed me away. "Callie was my half brother, Bryce's, dog."

"And your parents said he couldn't keep her?"

"Bryce died." He practically shouted the words. "Bryce is dead, and now my stepfather can't even stand to look at Callie—"

"Wait. What?" My mind reeled. "Your half brother is dead? What happened?"

Beck sank into his chair. "Bryce had acute myeloid leukemia. AML accounts for only about twenty percent of diagnosed cases, and it's tougher to beat than other types of the disease."

"I'm so sorry, Beck. That's awful."

He glanced away. "About three years ago, Bryce went into remission, and we all thought...I guess we let ourselves believe the danger was over, you know?"

I got up to get him a bottle of water because I couldn't bear the gut-level despair in his eyes.

"I'm the one who got the dog for him. When he was sick, we

had to be so careful of germs, and he didn't have much of a life. I mean, he did. He had the three of us and all the medical personnel. He made friends with kids in the oncology ward. But he didn't really get to play in the park, or run, or do Boy Scouts, or hang around with school friends. He was in pain. He had to live like that for so long."

I nodded that I understood.

"When he went into remission, I asked Mom and Roger if I could get Bryce a dog, and they said they thought it was a good idea. And it was. Bryce loved Callie. He spent every free minute training her and playing with her. He and Callie had two and a half good years together. Then some tests came back fucked up. He didn't make it."

"I'm so sorry for your loss."

"Not just mine. For a long time, Callie was devastated without him." He took a deep breath through his nose. "The last thing he said to me, the very last thing, was 'take care of Callie.'"

"But then your stepfather said you couldn't keep her?"

He nodded. "He couldn't stand to even look at Callie. Or me either, I guess. We'd never really gotten along. I was still there, but his son died. It wasn't hard to see that every time he looked at me, he wished it was me."

"What about your mother? Surely she'll want you back, even with the dog. She's had plenty of time to think about things. She's probably worried sick."

"I don't think seeing us is any easier on her, although I doubt she wishes I'd died. She says I'm an adult, and it's either the dog or me. I think she's just numb and doesn't want to deal with anything anymore."

"I think maybe you have no choice. At least with your guitar you were making money. Without it..."

He shook his head. "I had a *job*, you know. I was going to school. I had a life—well, as much of a life as anyone has when they have a sibling with a life-threatening disease."

"I don't understand."

"It's just...chaos." He frowned as if I was obtuse. "When someone in a family—especially a kid—is so sick, every single resource the family has goes to them. All the time and money and worry. Nobody can focus on anything else."

"Are you saying you felt ignored by your parents because of your half brother's illness?"

"No, it's not like that. You learn to do for yourself because everyone is in survival mode. Mom and Roger couldn't think about anything else. When things were going well, there was still the next hurdle, the next test, the next treatment. When they were going poorly"—he swallowed—"there was only the next minute. The next heartbeat."

"I think you must be very strong, Beck."

He shrugged. "I had to be strong. They needed me. That's why I assumed I could keep my promise to Bryce. When my stepdad kicked me out, I tried to get a place of my own, but any place that took dogs at all told me Callie was too big. Anywhere I could afford, you could only have small dogs. Fifty pounds, max."

"I'm aware of the problems inherent in trying to rent with a pet." I'd helped people rehome dogs and cats when they couldn't find rentals that would accommodate them. Some assholes simply left their pets on the street and drove away.

"I couch surfed for a while, and I got friends to watch her for me while I worked, but I couldn't do that forever. I was out of options." Beck swiped the hair out of his eyes. "I ended up playing on the street for cash, sneaking Callie into cheap motels when I could still afford it, and sleeping rough when I couldn't. But it was dangerous, and I was so scared. That's when Tug came along."

"Tell me about Tug." Why wasn't I calling the sheriff's deputies to come out and take a statement instead of being a nosy fuck? It would have been so easy to let Beck be someone else's problem, but I couldn't make myself do it. I wanted to be the hero, even though I knew it was naïve, and I'd probably get played.

"Tug is…Tug, you know?" Beck bit his lip. "When I first hit the road, I was pretty stupid. I practically shit myself if anyone even approached me. But then I met Tug, and he always knew what to do. He always had cash."

I hadn't missed the feral gleam in Tug's eyes when he looked me and Cooper over. I felt at the time like he was sizing us up, either to offer his services or con us. "How did Tug get money, Beck?"

Beck flushed. "Truck stops mostly. Rest stops. Parks. He said there were always old guys who wanted a quick—"

"I get the picture." Distaste turned my stomach sour.

"I never did that."

Did I believe him? I wanted to. "You're nothing like Tug."

"Don't judge. You have no idea what either of us is like."

"I apologize." I clamped my mouth shut. Even if Beck had accepted money for sex, I stood by my assessment. He was nothing like Tug. Not yet, anyway. But how long would it be before hunger and need and a society that didn't give a crap made Beck *exactly* like Tug?

"We hit the coast, and that's when I started pulling my weight. People on the beach tip good, especially here. I thought we were doing okay. That we could maybe even find a place and stay here a while."

"You said he scored here in St. Nacho's? Where?" We had a weed dispensary, and I knew there was always meth around, but I had seen very little evidence of its use among locals.

Beck glanced away. "Somewhere. I don't know where."

"And that was a surprise to you."

"Of course it was. I told you we made a deal. If I made it possible for him to stop selling his ass, he'd stop using. After we got into some trouble in Stockton, he was grateful for the break."

I was sure Beck believed that. Tug had seemed sketchy to me, but even I would've rather he had a better choice than to sell himself.

Drug addicts were a hard *no* for me. I always had the worry in the back of my mind that my clinic could be robbed and my staff harmed. I had a security system, and my pharmacy had a reinforced door and a deadbolt that locked from within. It probably still wouldn't stop determined thieves, but it would give someone time to call the police.

"So the first time you realized he broke your agreement was last night?" Travis came from my office with the kittens in their crate.

"It's feeding time—Oh." He must have sensed the tension between Beck and me, because he stopped suddenly. "Am I interrupting something?"

Beck got up. "I should go."

"Wait." I couldn't let Beck leave. Not when things were such a mess for him. If he took off, I might never see him again. I searched desperately for a way to buy time. "Do you want to help Travis feed some kittens?"

He froze. "I could do that?"

I read longing in his expression. "Sure. Okay, Travis?"

Travis nodded. "Sure. Of course."

"Beck, you need to call the police and report the theft. You can feed the kittens while you're waiting."

He raked his hair off his face. "I'm not calling the cops."

"Beck—"

"I'm not going to make trouble for Tug. I owe him, and he makes enough trouble on his own." He glanced away. "If it weren't for Tug, it would have been me selling my ass those first few weeks."

Travis looked utterly shocked, and I couldn't say I blamed

him. But I couldn't make Beck report the theft, and it would be a betrayal to report it for him. For now, I had to accept his decision.

"C'mon, Beck." Travis jerked his head for Beck to follow him, and I watched as they walked toward the supply room.

Beck turned back. "I'm sorry for just...dropping all this shit on you. I was upset, and I didn't know who else to turn to. I'll get out of your hair as soon as I'm done with the kittens."

"You don't have to go."

"But I can't stay either, can I?" He must have read the helplessness I was feeling, because he shrugged. "I'll figure something out."

I let him go with Travis, but I was determined to keep him in St. Nacho's.

I called Cooper, who answered on the first ring, and told him what had happened—including why Beck couldn't simply go home to his folks.

"Aw, shit. And of course Tug took the guitar. That was an expensive instrument."

"Was it?"

"It was pretty nice. All right. First, tell Beck he can stay in our guest room. Shawn already gave me a ration for not inviting him, but I had a feeling Tug was trouble."

"Thanks. I hope Beck will take you up on it. He can't go back to his folks."

"You'd think they wouldn't want to lose the son they have. God, people suck." He paused. "I'll bet we can get a line on local pawnbrokers and resellers. Maybe we can buy Beck's guitar back."

"We could try. I have a full day here. You think you could check that out. I don't have the first idea of where to go looking."

"Shawn's off today. I'll ask him to help. He can go online and make a list of likely places to search, and I'll do the calling."

"That'd be really great. If you find it, let me know, and I'll go get it."

"I'll be in touch."

WHEN I ENTERED the supply room, Travis and Beck each had a kitten and an eyedropper. I stopped in the doorway. My heart warmed at the scene.

Beck's eyes were on his tiny charge, an orange-and-white girl whose eyes had barely opened. I loved the way his messy brown hair fell onto his forehead and how gentle his long, delicate fingers could be. He looked underfed, and his hair wasn't clean, but my heart tightened painfully at the thought of never seeing him again.

Was I actually wondering what it would take for him to let me clean him up?

Oh, *drat*.

This was the same urge that made me keep water, food, and crates in the back of my SUV—the need to be ready for any animal rescue, any time. Beck was *human*. A nominal adult. My instinct to save him should have come with far less hubris and a modicum of self-preservation. He was a grown man for God's sake.

"That's right. I've got you." Beck sat on a stool with Callie's snout on his thigh, crooning to the kitten he was feeding.

I couldn't take my eyes off him.

Travis watched me watching Beck, his gaze subtly mocking when he glanced my way. I ground my teeth at his wry expression.

What the hell was wrong with me? My most recent failed relationship had accused me of wanting to be "everybody's hero." It was—embarrassingly—all too true. I loved the feeling of satisfaction I got from doing something good. My mother even made me scrapbooks full of newspaper clippings—success stories of animals I'd rescued, grateful pet owners, and volunteer work I'd done.

I told myself that's all this impulse to play knights and maidens with Beck was. I got job satisfaction from rescuing animals in dangerous situations. That had to be why I felt such a strong urge to pull Beck from the edge of disaster.

Beck needed me. He needed time and space to learn how to keep himself and his dog healthy and safe, and we—Cooper and Shawn and I—could give him that.

Beck must have sensed me standing there, because he turned to me with a smile that struck like lightning and left me dazzled.

I closed my eyes and counted to ten.

"Is something the matter?" he asked worriedly.

"No, not at all. Something's very good. I just talked to Cooper, and he and his partner Shawn say they have a guest room you and Callie can stay in until you find your feet."

I'd say nothing about his guitar for now. There was no guarantee we'd be able to find it.

"Really?" His eyes widened. "I don't know if—"

"You should definitely take them up on it," Travis told him.

"It's warm, and it's dry," I said. "Plus, I bet while you're there you can find some work in town."

"Maybe." His brows knit. "I'll need like, five jobs in order to pay for a place of my own."

"What if you start by offering dog walking?" Travis asked. "Pet sitting. That sort of thing. That way you can bring Callie along while you work."

Beck seemed to consider the idea. "I can do that. I'm pretty good with dogs."

"I could print off some business cards for you if you want," Travis offered. "You can leave some with Lena at the reception desk and give them to people you see on the boardwalk."

I did consider the possible ramifications of my clinic

endorsing a perfect stranger. I really did. I'd never have agreed to do it in San Diego. My lawyers were going to question my sanity at length. But the fact was the things I did—the things I felt comfortable doing—were different in St. Nacho's. And I wanted to help Beck.

"What should I do?" Beck looked up at me through thick lashes. Some weird, visceral pleasure flooded me—almost like a hit off a blunt or a shot of whiskey.

Put a fork in me. I was so done.

"How about you accept Cooper's help for now. Think of it like one musician reaching out to another." I swallowed hard. "They're good people. I think you'll like them."

As I turned and headed back toward my office, his voice and the entreaty in his eyes when he said, "What should I do?" kept coming back to me.

His panic when I opened the door earlier.

The absolute pain in his expression when he spoke of losing his half brother.

I was such a fool. All I could think about was how he'd come to *me*. How he'd known he could trust *me* to help him. What it meant to *me* that when Beck was in trouble, afraid, in pain, he'd come to my clinic for safety.

Beck's problem wasn't about me at all, but it was.

I *wanted* it to be.

I sat at the desk in my office considering what that meant and how I'd ever manage to hide it from the people who knew me best.

Then another thought occurred to me. Tug had to know he'd had a good thing with Beck. If we retrieved Beck's guitar, if Beck got work and had a place, would Tug come back? He might try if he sniffed out a steady flow of cash. Would Beck forgive him? Tug was already used to helping himself to Beck's nightly take. Coming back for more would be consistent with his behavior thus far.

In fact, he may have even done this before. Maybe they broke things off and reunited regularly. It wasn't unheard of for young couples to have Shakespearean levels of on-again, off-again drama.

The realization put a major damper on my enthusiasm.

Beck wasn't an animal I could control or pass off to a rescue organization. He was human, and as such he was as capable of subterfuge and deceit as anyone.

Was it insane for me to get involved or was I right? Had I read Beck correctly and all he needed was a helping hand?

My hand...

CHAPTER FIVE

Beck stayed around to worry over the kittens while Travis, April, and I worked our way through the patients of the day.

As a bonus, at lunchtime Beck and Callie were available to retrieve some really good salads from a new bistro situated a few streets away. We even got Lena to sit and eat with us at the staff table like we were some kind of family. That was a first on a day we weren't celebrating some holiday.

At least it kept Beck busy until Cooper showed up. He motioned me into my office to talk. "I called pawn shops and secondhand stores all morning. Glad we didn't just drive around looking. We found Beck's guitar at Secondhand Salinas. Tug sold it outright for a fraction of its value."

I accepted the news unhappily. "Aren't they required to see proof of ownership?"

"The kid had the receipt if you can believe it, and—here's where it gets weird—he carries an ID in Beck's name. I guess it looked legit enough. Guy said he wasn't the first kid to sell a nice guitar for drug money."

"Or even the hundredth, I'll bet. Fucking Salinas? That's two and a half hours away. Does it even make sense to go get it?"

"It's pricey, so it's probably pretty special to Beck. Finding it was the good news. The bad news is the guy who bought it paid a fourth of what it's worth and he's going to want to sell it for market price."

"What's that?"

Cooper winced. "Lots."

"What's Beck doing with an instrument like that?"

"It's hard to put a price on something that feels like one of your limbs." Cooper's lips curved upwards slightly. If the gossip was true, Cooper had traveled all over the country on a motorcycle with his expensive violin strapped to his back. "My instrument is a part of me."

"How much, then? What are we looking at?"

"Maybe two grand."

"Yikes." That wasn't couch change. It also made Tug's actions grand theft. "Beck needs to contact the police."

"I can promise you he won't do that."

"Why is he that loyal to the dude who stole from him?"

"If he calls the police the instrument becomes evidence. Then there's no telling when Beck gets it back."

I let out a sigh. "Can't we find him one to use in the meantime?"

"Probably." Cooper didn't look happy with that solution. "But a guitar like that? It's precious to him. Nothing else will feel right."

"Does it have to? Just for the time being, he—"

Cooper shook his head. "Beck's not just some amateur. There's real passion and skill and talent there. He could probably get into any music school in the country—even the one that starts with a *J* that kicked my ass out for fucking around. His instrument is his voice."

Ah, musicians and their mysterious touchy-feely ways.

Give me rational, talentless hacks any day.

"All right. Give me the address of this place. Are they at least

41

open late, or do I have to clear my schedule?"

"Till six."

"Aw, crap." I checked my watch and sighed. Together, we went to reception. "Lena, what's on the schedule for the rest of the day?"

"You don't have anything until five. Mr. Giordino and Muffin for a checkup and vaccinations, then you've got an ear recheck, and you're done."

"Can you please call them and tell them I have to be out of the office? Reschedule them for tomorrow or the soonest available appointment. I have to take care of something urgently, and I won't be back until late."

"Really?" She stared at me like I'd gone mad. Well, I guessed I had if I was planning on driving to Salinas to pick up a guitar some tweaker pawned to the tune of two grand.

"I'm afraid it can't be helped." I eyed Cooper. "Are you sure it can't be helped?"

"Yes." He shot me a stern look.

"All right then. Lena, would you be good enough to hold down the fort?" She nodded. "Beck's in the back with some kittens. Cooper, would you make sure he gets dinner?"

"Course." Cooper nodded. "Shawn will be by to pick him up later. I've only got my bike."

"Right." For some reason I'd yet to discover, Cooper didn't ride in cars unless the heavens opened up and lightning cracked the sky, and sometimes not even then.

I grabbed my wallet, phone, and keys and let myself out the back.

There are people who might say what I was about to do was unnecessary at best and crazy at worst. Those people would be absolutely, completely right.

What was it about Beck that got under my skin?

There was the talent, of course, which was not to be denied. And the dog. I can never resist rescuing a dog.

But I think for me it was that Beck ran to me when he was alone and scared. He'd been robbed, and instead of going to the police, instead of any one of a number of people who'd befriended him—Cooper, and Jim, and probably an SIPD uniform or two—he'd run to my clinic and banged on my door.

In a way, I figured that made him mine.

The drive up the coast was pretty, but the two-lane road between the 101 and Salinas was boring as hell. Because I don't pay for satellite radio, on that stretch of road, I had trouble getting anything besides banda; country; or endless, infuriating, Christian talk radio.

I barely made it to Secondhand Salinas in time, and Cooper was right about the owner holding out for a brain-boggling price. In the end, I got Beck's guitar. The dude threw in some sheet music he had like a party favor. I stowed everything in the back of my SUV, got a box of Popeye's fried chicken tenders, and started back the way I'd come.

Cooper rang me when I was about halfway home.

"Hey, Coop. What's up?"

"Beck's at our place. He looks like a zombie. I don't think he slept much last night."

"I wouldn't have." I couldn't begin to imagine how vulnerable he must have felt. "The boyfriend was a shit, but I get the feeling he looked out for Beck."

Boyfriend. I scoffed. Just more evidence that relationships were a sucker bet.

"Should I come by? I'm still about forty-five minutes out."

"You could wait until morning."

"I could." But I'd seen Beck's face that morning. He'd looked lost and hopeless and utterly betrayed. I didn't want him to have to spend a whole night feeling that way when it was in my power to help.

"You're really scaring me, Doc."

"What?" I asked. "Why?"

"I've like, literally never seen you act like this. This kid is way under your skin."

"Says the man who invited him into his home."

"All right. Fuck you."

Cooper was not a man to mince words.

"I'll be by before I go home. See you then."

Off to the right, the sun was falling into the ocean, leaving a long, glittering red path across the water. The beauty of the coast is something you can take for granted if you've lived alongside it most of your life, but I don't. To my left, a cargo train chugged along the railroad tracks going north.

For me, that's what it was like to meet new people—I'm going along one way, and they're speeding the other. Sometimes we slide by each other, but there's never a break in the momentum of our lives to really connect.

Yet somehow I'd connected with Beck.

Whatever that might mean in the future, right now, I was content to give him what he'd lost and make him smile again if possible.

CHAPTER SIX

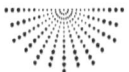

WHEN I KNOCKED on Cooper and Shawn's door, I was well aware of what I wanted to happen. I'd already shamelessly exploited the kitten situation to make Beck smile. I couldn't help imagining his smile when he got his guitar back.

Shawn came to the door with his finger to his lips, and as soon as I crossed the threshold, I saw why. Cooper sat in a recliner in the living room watching music videos with the sound turned low while Beck slept on the couch with Callie.

"Poor kid's exhausted," whispered Cooper.

Shawn motioned for me to follow him into the kitchen. Cooper joined us a minute later. He took the guitar from me and set it on the counter to look it over.

"He's going to be so happy to have this back."

"Yep. A total steal at full manufacture's retail price." I felt like an absolute tool, but I still believed it was the right thing to do.

Shawn, who'd positioned me to read my lips said, "You didn't bargain?"

"Sure. I got some sheet music as a bonus," I said dryly. "The owner of that shop could see how badly I wanted it. Dude wouldn't budge on price."

"Well, consider it your good deed for the year. Have a cold one." Shawn offered me a beer.

"Thanks." I twisted off the cap and took a good long swallow. The crisp bitter liquid totally hit the spot. I hadn't realized how tense I was until then. "Beck should still contact the police. If his boyfriend has some kind of ID with his name on it, he could end up in a world of credit trouble later when it's necessary to get a loan."

"That's not really our problem though, is it?" Cooper got a Coke for himself.

"No," I agreed. "We got the guitar back. He can deal with the ID theft on his own. After all, we don't really know him, do we? He could still be some kind of grifter."

From behind me, a rough voice asked, "Is that my guitar?"

I turned with a wince. I hoped he hadn't heard me, but it was obvious from his expression he had. Half-asleep with bedhead and flushed skin, he looked conflicted. He was angry because I was a dumb fuck, but he wanted that guitar like it was air and he was suffocating.

I wanted to ignore his shimmering eyes, but it was no good. "Beck—"

"We got it back for you." Cooper held the case out for him. "Call it a hospitality gift from the St. Nacho's welcoming committee."

Beck took it with a gulp. "How'd you even find it?"

Cooper explained, "I called pawn shops and secondhand places until I found where your guy sold it."

Shawn added. "Lindy drove up to Salinas and got it."

Beck turned to me, hugging his instrument to his chest. "Why would you do that if you think I'm some grifter?"

"You think you could give us a minute?" I asked Cooper and Shawn.

"Sure." Cooper touched Shawn's sleeve, and they left the kitchen. Beck set the guitar on the counter, but as though he was afraid it would disappear again, he didn't take his hand off it.

"I hope you're not a grifter"—I measured my words carefully —"but I can't worry about things like that."

"I don't understand what you mean."

I shouldn't have stepped closer because then I caught faint hints of the denim he wore, sweet tea, and salt in his hair. If he leaned toward me, I'd be able to make out whether there were other colors in the depths of his inky blue eyes. I'd see the exact color of his lashes. I could look for patterns in his freckles.

I cleared my throat. "I guess for me it's not about the outcome but the act."

"So you'd be okay if I played you?"

"No, I wouldn't." That seemed kind of obvious. "I'd be pretty sad, actually. But I hope it wouldn't change my future behavior. I want to keep doing the good thing, just because."

"Tug called you a mark." He pulled me closer by gripping the hem of my untucked button-down.

"He's probably right. I've been bitten by a drowning dog." I lifted my sleeve to show the lurid scar I'd gotten when I'd been young and dumb and hadn't thought things through. "I accept it's always a possibility that I'll get hurt. That doesn't stop me from pulling them out of the water."

"Thank you." He leaned his forehead against my chest. He had to be aware of my racing heart. "I need a hug."

I put my arms around his shoulders, and he slid his around my waist.

"Thank you." The words were a heavy sigh. "You smell good."

"I've been in a car for close to five hours."

"You smell like Popeye's chicken."

"Oh, yeah. I grabbed some on the way back." I snorted. "Probably smell tasty, huh?"

He breathed in deeply and straightened. "Thank you again, Dr. Lindy."

It wasn't his gratitude I wanted but his smile. I'd have torn the world apart to see him smile.

You could call my rescues a compulsion. A lot of the animals I worked with were taught to fear humans by experience, and I wanted to show them that despite their pasts, people could be kind. I didn't think I was some exception. Most people have goodness inside them.

My problem, obviously, was that even though Beck rang every bell and checked every tick box for me, he wasn't a lost pet. I had a crap track record with humans. My past relationships littered the field behind me like broken hurdles, and my exes all agreed that I was too emotionally distant to form a connection with anything but the animals I loved so much.

But I'd be damned if I started looking for trusting, desperate humans to adopt.

What if this is real? The emotional side of my brain wanted to know. *What if you're experiencing bone-deep human chemistry for the first time in your life? What if you've fallen in love, and you don't recognize it because that's never happened before?*

My rational mind shut that shit right down. *What if you're having a midlife crisis?*

"Well." I broke away. "I'll just take off, then. You have a good night."

"No." Beck seemed reluctant to let me go. "You haven't even finished your beer."

"Oh. Okay." I picked it up and chugged it.

"Who's looking after the kittens?" Beck asked.

"Tonight? Probably April, unless she switched with Travis." A cold nose burrowed into my hand, and I found Callie right beside me, angling for scratches. I knelt and dug my fingers into her fur. Her eyes drifted closed and she wiggled with pleasure. "Hey, sweet girl."

"I could help with the kittens if you want," Beck offered.

"You should get a good night's sleep, don't you think?"

"I had a cat nap." The pun made me smile.

"April can handle things tonight. How about you and Callie stop by tomorrow morning? You can feed the kittens, and if you're up for a little project, my supply room needs to be cleaned and inventoried. We've been so busy I haven't had a chance to check expiration dates for a while. Job pays fifteen dollars an hour."

He frowned. "I can't take your money. You got my guitar back for me."

"It's okay—"

"No, it's not." Hands on his hips, he defied me. "I'm not a con artist, and I don't want your charity."

"It's not charity. It's a legit job." I knew that guitar was going to come back and bite me. "Look, come or don't come. I can find someone else to organize that space, or I can put in the extra time over the weekend. You should still find a job around here. Plenty of people need help."

He glanced away. "You sound just like my stepdad."

"Great. Wow. On that note—"

He caught my hand. "I was doing okay until Tug screwed me over."

I couldn't bear the betrayal in his eyes. I'd have done violence if Tug was there, which was totally unlike me. "I know that must have hurt a lot. I'm sorry."

He lifted to his toes and kissed my cheek. "Thank you. You're a really good friend."

I coughed to hide the rush of...what? Shame? Embarrassed arousal? "It's been a really long day. I have to go."

"I'll see you out, Lindy." Cooper met us as we walked to the door. Shawn opened it for me. "We'll take it from here."

I made sure Shawn could see my lips when I said, "You guys are much better with people."

Shawn hugged me goodbye.

"Stop manhandling my man." Cooper pulled him away playfully then hugged me. As I left, I let go of all the unexpected emotions that plagued me.

Why wasn't Beck just another guy to me? He had parents, even though going through something traumatic had made them cold.

He heard me call him a grifter. He also said I smelled good. If he was up to no good, I'd feel it deeply. I'd feel it personally.

If Beck had been gone by morning, I wouldn't have been surprised.

DESPITE WHAT I'D SAID, I wasn't ready to face my empty house. My cockatiel Rico Suave would be there, but honestly, a bird wasn't going to be much company tonight. Pie was out because Café Bêtise was closed by now. Though I'd eaten earlier, I was hungry again, so I parked in the clinic's lot and walked to Bistro, hoping it was open until ten.

I got lucky, and there were still a few couples dining. Some I knew, like Izzie and her boyfriend, Andy, who was one of the local cops. I waved hello. The hostess showed me to a table by the window. I got out my phone and checked my messages, which seemed like the best way to avoid conversation. I liked dining alone, but people took it as a personal challenge sometimes.

The waiter offered me a menu. "Hey, Dr. Lindy."

"Hi." Did I know him? His name tag read Jeremy.

He must have seen my confusion, because he smiled. "I brought my roommate's white Himalayan to you for bladder issues last year. Pinky. You changed her food."

"Ah, right. Nice to see you again." I vaguely remembered a fat, fluffy cat with the air of deposed royalty. "How's she doing?"

"She's good. Beatrice loves that cat to pieces."

"That's what I like to hear."

"You got anyone joining you tonight?"

"Nope, just me."

"Can I get you something to drink?"

"What's on tap?" He mentioned several beers, and I picked a regional IPA.

"I'll get that and be back in a second for your order."

"Thanks." If ever a place illustrated life in a small town, it was Bistro. The menu proudly stated they served Yasha Livingston's artisan breads and Mary Catherine's pies. Everyone's business connected to everyone else's. You couldn't go anywhere without finding cooperative advertising or at least flyers for all the businesses on Main Street in a rack on the way out.

Jeremy brought my beer, and I relaxed into my chair. I gazed beyond the window at the boardwalk and beach. There was very little moonlight, so the sea was a blank, black void.

Sometimes I asked myself if these lonely, small town moments were how the rest of my life would play out. Would I still want to live in St. Nacho's when I was fifty? *Sixty?*

Was I content to be alone forever?

Normally, I'd have said yes, but the things I felt when I was around Beck made that answer feel like a lie.

Anyway, I was never actually alone unless I wanted to be. I could have turned around and joined Izzie and Andy. I could have walked down to the cantina and visited with Jim. I could have gone to the clinic and helped April feed kittens.

Hopefully Beck would stop by in the morning. Maybe I'd get that smile I wanted.

Jeremy came back. "What looks good tonight, Doc?"

"I think...a green salad, please, and the lobster mac and cheese."

"Ooh, that's luscious." He winked. "Good choice."

"I'll be taking a piece of pie home for dessert too. What's left?"

"Chocolate cream, coconut cream, apple, fresh peach—"

"Peach. Perfect."

"You want ice cream with that?"

"Absolutely. I'll just quadruple the cardio tomorrow."

He glanced over at Izzie, who happened to be the owner of the local gym. "You know it doesn't really work like that, right?"

"I'm not actually going to do it." I waved him in closer, like this was a secret. "I'm just giving the idea lip service."

"Lip service…" He deliberately dropped his gaze to my lips. "I could get behind that."

Shocked by his flirtatious banter, I fumbled my menu as I handed it back to him. I didn't flirt with babies. What were they putting in the energy drinks these kids chugged?

Did I have a sign on me?

Did I *need* one?

That made two times in one week I found myself focusing on someone nearly half my age and sort of wondering…What's the worst that could happen if I did date someone younger?

I was not interested in raising my next ex.

"Okay." My cheeks went hot under his scrutiny. "Wow, thanks. Can I have a water?"

"Sure, and I'll be right back with your meal, Doc." As he headed to the kitchen with my order, he glanced back with a cocky laugh.

Only teasing, I thought. He's only joking around. After he'd disappeared from sight, I sighed. Maybe it wasn't so comfortable living in a small town after all.

Taking stock, I'd spent a boatload of money on a homeless man's guitar. And for whatever reason, it seemed I'd started noticing—and being noticed by—men much younger than me. Which was just ridiculous if it was true. The last thing I needed was the kind of attention I'd get if I started going after twinks.

"Jeremy?" I called him over. "You know what? I think I'll take the whole meal to go."

"Really? Do you have to go?" I didn't imagine the disappointment on his face.

"It's been a really long day." The words were becoming my mantra.

"All right, if you're sure. I'll wrap that up for you then." His walk seemed a little dejected, but I didn't know what to do about it.

"Thank you," I offered, but he was already out of earshot.

I tipped well. Better than well. My wallet should bleed from the damage I'd done to the cards inside it that day.

I took my meal home and ate it standing at the kitchen sink as penance for the mess I'd become.

Tons of guys my age would take advantage of Jeremy's admiration. It was fair to say that. It was safe to say that if I laid on the charm, I could probably take my pick of the bright young men in St. Nacho's. But if I wasn't willing to find a partner on equal terms, I was less willing to take on someone who might only want me for my cash.

That would be a monumental embarrassment, and I was a pretty proud man.

Better to eat over the kitchen sink and go to bed unaccompanied.

Much better to take care of animals and leave the humans alone.

CHAPTER SEVEN

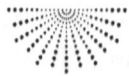

IT HAD TO BE ACKNOWLEDGED—PART of my job was euthanizing critically ill pets. It was never easy discussing the decision or seeing a client in distress over their loss, but some days seemed harder than others. Some days seemed agonizing.

For certain clients—those for whom it would be too painful to move the animal or those who preferred to undertake the act as a family rite of passage—I made house calls.

The day after I got Beck's guitar back, I had to put three pets down—two in their homes.

Children are my kryptonite anyway, but watching a parent explain that a child's pet was not simply going to sleep, that in fact their pet would never again wake up, was enough to scrape my heart raw.

I understood the instinct to acquaint children with the cycles of life. To educate them about the precious and finite nature of their pet's time on earth. I honored my clients' requests to allow children to be a part of the process when asked, but it was painful for me when I had to leave an entire family in tears.

At the end of the day, I accessed an emergency bottle of Jack I kept in the filing cabinet.

Lena tiptoed in. "You okay?"

"Sure," I lied.

She came forward and rubbed my shoulders. I tried not to flinch, but she had a grip like a mobster. I barely kept from screaming. Eventually her touch went from intrusive to soothing. Maybe it was the whiskey.

"Better?"

I nodded. "Thank you. Go ahead and take off. I just have a few things to finish up here."

"Beck's with the kittens until April gets back from supper. You skipped lunch, so make sure you eat something healthy for dinner, otherwise you'll be three sheets to the wind before you know it. And don't drive."

"I would never."

"No ramen cups. No protein bars. Cook or order actual food."

"Okay, okay." As she walked away, I lobbed a crumpled Post-it her way. "I have a perfectly fine mother, you know."

I immediately regretted my words when Beck appeared in the doorway with Callie at his heels. I resolved not to take my folks for granted. Beck held a kitten out for me.

"Blanche has got a gloopy eye," he said. "Is that a thing?"

"Well, let's take a look." I was pretty grateful for something to do and maybe just a little too relaxed. I swung up from my desk chair and had to shake my head a little to clear it.

"Have you been drinking?" Beck's eyes widened comically.

"A smidge." Looking back, I probably exaggerated every movement, but I felt like I was the epitome of cool professionalism.

Lena nudged Beck on her way out, and I saw them exchange whispers.

"Knock it off, you two. No chismes."

"Oh, there he goes."

"You speak Spanish?" asked Beck.

I thumped my chest. "Soy bilingüe."

"Okay. Bravo then."

"Night, baby. Don't be stupid.

"Lena," I whined before going to an exam room, where I could get good light on the kitten, with Beck. "Any of the others have eye gunk?"

"No."

"Not yet, probably." I had a bit of difficulty putting on my gloves.

Beck snickered. "You sure you're up to this? Maybe we should wait for April."

"Oh, please. I got this." I snapped the glove to prove I'd done it. "Most likely this is contagious."

Beck's eyes widened. "To me?"

"Nah. Wash your hands after handling them and don't touch your face. You should be doing that anyway."

He nodded. "Travis told me."

"The other kittens will get it, though."

He paled. "Oh, shoot. Is it because I did something wrong?"

"No, of course not." I held the little girl kitten while I collected some of her eye gunk for tests. "This is common stuff. The younger they are, the more susceptible."

He narrowed his eyes. "Okay, so how do I take care of them?"

"April will do what's needed. We'll monitor the others. They'll be fine."

"Okay." He relaxed a bit.

We took the kitten back to the kennel where he'd been feeding them, and I settled into a chair next to his.

"So, who's been fed and who still needs to eat? I'll take one."

"Rose is the only one left."

"Cool, which is she?" He handed me a mewling, tabby spitfire. "Ah, Rose."

"I named them in honor of the Golden Girls." He shifted in his chair to hold his kitten out. "Like I said, this one is Blanche."

"Ah."

Beck cradled his kitten after she finished eating. "Before I started helping out here, I didn't think I was a cat guy."

"It's hard to resist a kitten."

"Yeah, but then they turn into cats. I never thought I could like them as much as I like dogs. I didn't think they had much to offer."

I studied his forearms, which were streaked with tiny claw marks. "Besides scratches, you mean?"

He wrinkled his nose. "There's that."

"People think cats don't care about them or get attached to their families." I hoped I didn't sound like I was pontificating. "But honestly, most people don't know how to read a cat's little feline signals. If you expect it to act like a dog, then you'll be disappointed, but when you get to know cats, they're just as awesome."

"They have signals?"

"Sure." I finished feeding Rose and got us both warm, wet cloths to help them eliminate. "Cats blink at you, very slowly when they feel comfortable around you. They'll groom you with their paws and their tongues. If they believe they can trust you, they might relax and let their bellies show. Rubbing, head butting. Interrupting you to get your attention. All good signs they like you."

"I didn't know that."

"And if they like you but think you're kind of hopeless or you can't provide for yourself, they'll kill something and leave it for you."

"No way." He looked like he didn't believe me.

"Absolutely. They want you to learn to hunt." I made a funny voice, *"Poor ungainly human, can't even catch a lizard. So sad."*

He laughed. "That's hilarious. I'm glad Callie doesn't do that."

"She's got her little signals too, you know. Being adorably cute, she's helping you get bigger tips. Aren't you girl?"

Beck made a "speak" sign, and Callie gave a woof.

"Oops." My poor kitten jumped out of her skin.

"Rose! I'm so sorry we scared you."

I petted her soft ears. "She'll settle back down."

"Are you going to take one of the kittens?" Beck asked. "I bet Rose would love to go home with you."

"Can't. I have a bird that likes to spend lots of time out of his cage when I'm home. It'd be savage island if I brought home a cat."

"You think a cat would hurt it?"

"I'd put my money on the bird." I crossed my legs and leaned back, cat in my lap. "He's a cockatiel. I've had him forever, so he's got a little attitude."

"What's his name?"

"Don't laugh. Promise?"

He crossed his heart solemnly. "Promise."

"Rico Suave."

Of course, he laughed. "Oh my. You have had him for a while."

I heard April's key in the lock. "April's back."

"I guess I should go, then." Beck glanced at the door. April stepped inside and put her purse and coat on the rack.

"How are my babies," she rubbed her hands together.

"We're fine." I winked at her. "Did you get something nice to eat?"

"Kayla met me, and we shared a pot pie at Yasha's place."

"That sounds pretty tasty. I have white chicken chili in the Crock-Pot at home. I should probably head out."

"You walking?" Beck asked without actually looking at me.

"Because if you are, Callie and I are heading home. You're on the way, right?"

"Yeah. I think a walk will clear my head." I held my kitten out for April. "April, Beck's kitten—"

"Blanche," he supplied.

"Blanche has conjunctivitis. I took a sample, but my money's on a bacterial infection. Keep an eye on the others."

"Sure thing. I'll make sure she gets drops." She stepped past us and looked at the cages where we normally kept animals that needed monitoring overnight. They were currently empty.

"There's nobody here?" She turned to me, and her face fell. "Oh no. Digger?"

I shook my head. "Tough decision for the family."

"So that's three?" I nodded grimly, and she gasped.

"Three what?" Beck asked.

I took my jacket off the coat rack. "Let's go. I'll tell you on the way."

"Okay." We gathered our things and left out the back. I listened for the deadbolt that signaled April had locked up. She'd have turned the alarms on as well.

The parking lot was empty except for April's car, an older model white Mazda. Because we left from the back of the clinic, I crossed the alleyway to get to Church Street. It was a little less busy. Together, we turned away from the beach for the walk home with Callie sniffing ahead like a scout.

For a while, I forgot the thing I was supposed to tell Beck. Maybe it was the alcohol making my head fuzzy. Maybe I just wanted to forget.

"Three what?" he asked again.

"I euthanized three animals today." That felt too much like ripping off a Band-Aid. My ex Nick would have been shrill with me if I'd said that to him. He always complained I lacked the finer feelings. Who has time for those?

Beck glanced my way as he stepped over the curb, still

59

graceful despite carrying his backpack and guitar. "You had to though, right?"

"I couldn't help them anymore, and they were in pain." I tried to rub the day off my face, but my fingers just irritated my summer-dry skin. "The families decided to let them go."

"It's kinder that way, isn't it?"

"That's the story I'm sticking with."

He blinked up at me, his fathomless blue eyes wide and worried. "Isn't it, though? Better than keeping an animal that's in pain?"

"How should I know?" I said irritably. I regretted it immediately, but the words just poured out. "It's not like we can ask them, is it?"

"No," he said softly. "If only, huh? And if only we let people go when it was their time instead of prolonging lives even when—"

"I didn't mean to take you back there."

"Everything takes me back." Anger clipped his words. "Going forward takes me back."

"I'm sorry."

"When my biodad died, it was bad. I really loved him, and it was a work accident. He went quick. My mother had already remarried, and I hardly had time to grieve. Right on the heels of that, Bryce got sick, and I sort of realized it's not like were on a train heading for a destination. We're just...made of transition, and the only thing anyone can count on is this one moment right now." He glanced at Callie. In the streetlight she was nothing more than a glossy shadow, like a seal or an otter, with rich amber eyes. "That's probably depression talking. Obviously, I don't see my therapist anymore either."

"Do you need to? We can make that happen."

"Don't be silly. I'm fine." He hitched his pack to shift the weight.

"Well, I'm still sorry I started us down that road."

He laughed. "I've been travelling that road a long time. That's why you were drinking. You hate having to put a pet down."

"I don't hate it." In my line of work, hating euthanasia didn't make any more sense than hating surgery or vaccinations. It was all part of the job, and also, in some cases, the only responsible thing to do. Would Callie forgive me if I had to put her down? Would Beck? Animals in pain are all eyes. They often hide how sick they are. Their stillness is haunting as I push the drugs that relax them enough for me to administer the one that will stop their hearts.

"It's okay to feel *ambivalent* about that part of your job."

"What I hate is standing there like a moron when some adult introduces their child to the concept of death." I don't know why I confessed this now. I'd never said the words out loud. "It's unbearable when children cry."

Beck reached over and gave my shoulder a squeeze as we walked. He couldn't have said anything more eloquent than that brief, comforting touch. In fact, if he had spoken, it would have made things worse.

It was his empathy—his quiet kindness—that made him so good with Callie. I liked that about him, and I liked him, despite our age difference. I felt more in tune with him in that moment than I had with anyone in a long time.

"Are you hungry?" I ignored the warning voice in my head. *You're getting too involved. You don't really know him. Someone his age ought to be off-limits, even as a friend. Especially someone as attractive and wonderful as Beck.* It didn't seem to matter what my brain thought; my heart overrode it. "I have dinner in the Crock-Pot. I planned to make a salad to go with it. There's plenty for two."

"I could eat." He glanced over shyly. "Are you sure you have enough?"

"I always make a ton more than I need and freeze it for lunches."

"Okay, yeah. Thanks. If you're sure it's no trouble."

"C'mon." Neither of us spoke as I led him to my house, which did nothing to assuage the guilty feeling I had that I was ignoring basic common sense.

What if he gets the wrong idea? Or the right one?

What if he knows exactly what's been on your mind?

You're playing with fire.

We made our way up the street that eventually led to my house, and I stopped.

"This is me."

He took in my little craftsman house with its wide, well-lit porch and wicker chairs and charm and said, "Nice."

I smiled. "Thanks."

Through friend and real estate agent Ken, I'd purchased the place from a family trust. Whoever had lived there before hadn't changed a thing since the fifties. I'd gutted the place and given it a clean contemporary look by opening up the walls between the kitchen, dining, and living rooms. The décor was a little on the nautical side. I took some ribbing from my friends over that, but my tiny bungalow-by-the-sea suited me perfectly.

I unlocked the screen door and let Beck and Callie inside.

The minute I turned on the light, Rico Suave came to life with what—for him—was an explosive cry. "You ruin *everything!*"

To say Rico was unusually gifted was an understatement. In my experience, cockatiels enjoyed mimicking sounds more than saying actual words. But Rico could and did talk often. I put his talent down to his first owner, a Hollywood animal trainer. I'd gotten Rico when his owner went to prison for trafficking exotic animals on the black market.

I sighed. "This is it. Home sweet home."

CHAPTER EIGHT

"HOME SWEET HOME," the bird echoed. I let him out of his cage and put him on my shoulder.

"This is Rico. Watch your fingers. He'll bite or scratch the occasional newcomer for no apparent reason." I offered Beck a tiny bowl of seeds. "If you want to hedge your bets, you can try to give him a seed. Hold it in your palm at first until he gets used to you."

Beck picked up a few and held them out, palm up. "Oh, you're a pretty boy, aren't you?"

Rico eyed him before carefully taking a seed. Then he went in for another. I stayed still and watched as Beck charmed him enough to get him muttering conversational nonsense.

"That's right," Beck offered every so often. "You're so right. I always say that."

Rico said, "Home sweet home."

Beck laughed. "He sounds like a robot that's trying to sound like you."

"Yeah. Parrots are much truer mimics, and they say a lot more phrases and words than Rico can. Cockatiels get a few words right, but there's always that kind of mechanical hum to their speech. They're quieter too."

Rico had a few phrases he said often. He liked "Pretty boy," "Hello, gorgeous," and "Boop," For whatever reason he most loved to mimic my ex Nick—especially during an argument. Nick had been gone for years, but Rico held onto his words and his tone of voice like a feathered limpet.

Privately, I suspected Rico was a drama queen.

"You ruin *everything!*"

I glanced at Beck sheepishly. "That's one of his absolute favorite things to say."

"Harsh." Beck frowned. "That doesn't sound like you."

"That's because he didn't learn it from me."

"Oh." He gave Rico another seed. "Sick burn, Rico. Be nice."

"On the other hand, not everyone has a comedy cockatiel."

"Trust you to have one, Doctor Doolittle." Beck glanced around the living room. "Should I leave Callie on her leash?"

"No, of course not." I motioned toward a basket where I kept blankets and pillows. "Grab a blanket from the hamper and set it on the floor by the chair there. Have a seat. It won't take long to get supper ready."

He set his things in the corner and made a spot for Callie. "Anything I can do to help?"

"No, it's mostly done. Did you feed Callie at the office?" Beck had taken to feeding her at the same time he gave the kittens their bottles. "If not, I can get her something."

"She ate."

"I'll set up a water bowl for her in the kitchen. Just relax while I finish things up."

I slung a towel over my shoulder before transferring Rico to my nondominant side, then washed my hands. Rico liked to perch on my shoulder and mutter in my ear while I got supper ready. He was actually pretty good company when I didn't want the human variety.

"Do you have any food allergies? Oh, and do you like cilantro?"

"No to allergies, and yes to cilantro. I'm not picky."

"Good to know."

I added two types of cheese to melt in the chili while I made a quick salad. Rico needed leafy greens every other day, and I sometimes slipped him a little fruit. I gave him a spinach leaf while I worked, and it kept him busy for a bit.

Callie sat on the blanket with her jaw resting on Beck's knee. I knew the minute Beck spotted my guitar. He tensed like a hunting dog. I half expected him to point.

"You play guitar?"

"Not at all." I didn't even know why I kept the thing. Maybe because it made me look cooler than I am. "I know like...three chords."

"That's all you need, right?" He glanced over his shoulder. "Three chords and the truth."

"Ha, ha."

"Mind if I take a look?"

"As long as you don't judge me. I haven't taken that guitar out of its case since college."

I had to turn my back to get plates, and when I heard him give it a tentative strum, I shuddered.

"Dude." He winced like he'd bitten a lemon. "You need new strings."

"I meant to get around to that. There are some in the case."

"Oh. Awesome. Got a dishtowel or a microfiber cloth?" As if he couldn't help himself, he laid the instrument on the coffee table like a surgical patient.

"Yeah." I tossed him a clean one from the drawer where I kept them. "Need wire cutters?"

"I have tools in my case." He hopped up to get it. "I hope I do anyway."

"I didn't know to check."

"We're...good. Thanks." He seemed relieved as he got his tools and began the work of restringing my guitar.

"I think you're to guitars what I am to stray animals."

"You have to make sure they're in working order?"

"Something like that." I cut an avocado and added that, along with diced tomatoes, canned beans, and sweet corn to the salad mix then tossed it with a simple lime vinaigrette dressing.

Since Beck was consumed with his work, I took the time to heat some bread sticks.

When everything was ready, I set the table for two with water for both of us. Rico went back to his perch in his cage. I half expected him to complain, because I often ate with him perched on my shoulder like some tragic, lonely pirate. Instead, I put his cage on the other end of the table and left it open so he wouldn't feel left out.

When Beck was done winding all the strings on, he glanced up. "Hey, you should have told me you were ready. I can tune it after we eat."

"It's okay. I like watching you work. You obviously know your way around a guitar."

"I've changed hundreds of strings. Thousands, maybe, because I always did it for the posers at school."

"Like me, you mean?"

"Nah. Are you?"

"With a guitar? Yes. Yes, I'm a total poser."

He laughed. "It's not for everyone."

"The problem is guys like you make it look so easy."

"Ten thousand hours. Isn't that what they say?" He came into the kitchen to wash his hands. Callie followed and found the water dish.

Beck leaned over the Crock-Pot. "Mm. Smells so good."

I picked up the ladle and poured some chili onto a clean spoon.

"Try it. Does it need more salt?"

He caught my hand to steady it, and when he sipped from the spoon, our gazes locked. Everything around us disappeared, just like the first day on the beach when I'd watched him take food from Tug's hand. His obvious enjoyment caused my heart to race and my groin to tighten—except this time the person feeding him was me.

Why, oh why did the act of feeding him smash all my boundaries?

Was it an unexplored kink?

Had food play always lurked there in the background, waiting for the right guy?

I would never have considered feeding Nick. The idea would have seemed ridiculous to both of us. But with Beck, I felt nothing weird at all, nothing out there or taboo. The contentment of feeding him—of nourishing him—was why I cared way more than I should about him.

Wait. Was it some paternal-type yearning? God no.

If it was, then I had to be the most fucked-up human ever.

I could totally envision him opening his mouth for my cock in the same way he opened for the spoon—sweetly, almost reverently, and with that implicit trust.

I gasped and let the spoon clatter to the floor between us.

"You okay?" he asked.

If I was embarrassed before, I was mortified now. "Yeah. I just realized...I forgot something at work."

"Oh." His gaze dropped to Callie and he laid his hand on her neck. "Okay."

"We should set the pot on the table and serve from there if you don't mind being informal. Can you take the salad in while I get a trivet?"

"Sure." He picked up the bowl and carried it out with Callie plodding along after. I followed with the chili.

"This is nice." He waited while I dished us up two big bowls.

"It is nice," I agreed. "I don't get a lot of company."

"Why's that?" He took a sip of water.

"A lot of my friends live in Southern California, and I guess I've developed a habit of meeting my St. Nacho's friends in town for drinks. I don't have a lot of free time."

"Boop," Rico said.

Callie didn't pay much attention to him when he was loose, but she was interested now. She had to sniff all around his cage, and he wasn't too happy about it.

Beck said, "Stop, Callie."

"She can't hurt him while he's in his cage."

"I don't want her to freak Rico out." He told Callie to lie down and she immediately went to her haunches.

"You'll know if Rico's worried. He'll fluff himself up to twice his size and chatter like a monkey. He's okay with her." I held my hand out to his cage and he came to nibble my finger. "See? It's all good. You should relax too."

"Okay." He stuck his spoon into his bowl with a chuckle.

Neither of us talked much while we ate. It wasn't tense or anything. I didn't feel like I had to field interesting small talk. It felt nothing like a date. Except...I was aware of his every move. Every noise he made, every clink of glassware or scrape of his spoon. And I watched him—his hands were fucking amazing. He had the most delicate wrists.

He had pushed the sleeves of his henley up to reveal pale forearms, one of which was covered with bracelets made of leather and strings with beads and a mishmash of little symbols.

They were cheap junk really, but they made his arm beautiful. I couldn't imagine anything finer—his arms would look good in elegant watches and thick gold chains, but folk art and talismans made him seem...magical. He was spellbinding, bursting with music and kindness and so, so pretty.

It was as if he wasn't part of the world. Just traveling through.

"Something the matter?" he asked.

"What?" I swallowed. "No."

He brought his napkin to his lips. "You're looking at me funny."

I laughed, but it sounded odd to my ears. "Funny haha? Or funny weird?"

"Weird."

"That may be my natural state," I said. "Resting weird face."

He hid a smile. "Maybe."

"Would you like another breadstick?" I offered the basket.

"Please." He took one, dunked it into his bowl, and bit the end off. He hadn't quite finished swallowing before he said, "This chili is really delicious."

"Glad you like it." I was captivated by his lips—or rather by a crumb of bread that hung there for an eternity until he thumbed it off and licked his thumb.

A zing of desire hit my groin and my cheeks burned like fire.

No, no, no. This could not be happening.

I wasn't some horny old goat who got hard around guys half his age. I dated mature men. I didn't date anyone twice. I loved my life the way it was, so why, oh why, could I not simply feed this stray young man and release him back into the wild.

What was it about him?

"You know what?" he said suddenly.

I answered numbly. "What?"

"I'm going to teach you to play guitar."

Oh no. "I beg your pardon?"

He snorted. "You've got a guitar. When I'm done with you, you won't be a poser anymore. I'll teach you. It's easy."

"Right." I didn't believe that. Nobody would believe that.

"No, really. I promise. You'll be able to play something good when I'm done with you. That way, when someone asks about your guitar, you'll have something to show for the space it takes up in this room."

Because I wanted anything he offered, I said, "All right."

"You know, an instrument is like a pet. If you share space with it and neglect it, you need to rehome it with someone who will take better care of it."

My God, I thought, *he's right.*

CHAPTER NINE

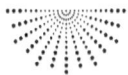

BECK USED my phone to tune my guitar, then he played scales on it like a virtuoso. I watched his fingers move with more dexterity than I could claim, even in my surgery suite, with a sigh.

"Okay, first things first." He sat on the coffee table with my guitar in his hands. "Put your hands out and let the guitar get your scent."

"Fuck off." Beck could be silly—another thing I liked about him. I took the guitar from him and assumed the position.

"Which chords do you know?"

"G, E, and D reliably."

"That's a start. Play them."

Embarrassed as all hell, I did what he asked, strumming each a couple times like a rank beginner.

"I hate this," I whined.

"Why do you suppose that is?"

"Well, Dr. Freud," I said sourly, "it's probably because I hate doing anything I'm utterly crap at, especially in front of other people."

"I see." He stroked the tiny scruff of his beard. "That's stupid."

I gave him the look that deserved. "All right. What next?"

"You, my impatient friend, are going to learn some exercises. This will help build the strength in your fingers and improve dexterity."

"And possibly drive me mad."

His eyes sparkled. "It's probably too late for that, huh?"

Probably was. "What do you want me to do?"

"Let me demonstrate." He got his guitar from its case and did some complicated moves on the neck without strumming. "Spiders. Think of spiders. It's not easy to learn to move the fingers independently. You try."

I tried to do what he did. My fingers moved like lazy caterpillars when they moved at all. It took way more effort than I imagined. I had to think about each finger the whole time, move these two fingers first, move these two next—like patting my head and rubbing my belly at the same time. It was maddening.

Rico squawked, "Couldn't be bothered."

"Does he tell all your secrets?" Beck asked with a laugh.

"Only the embarrassing ones."

"You think you'll remember that exercise? Will you do it?"

"How often?" I tried to imagine doing something this frustrating daily.

"Um. Maybe a few minutes, three times each day?"

"I think I can handle that." Although it was seriously going to cut into my brooding time.

He showed me how to make sure the guitar was in tune, and then sketched out a rudimentary chord chart for a song to practice. "Twinkle, Twinkle, Little Star" as it turned out.

"Do you know how idiotic I feel doing this?"

"You know the saying about old dogs and new tricks?"

I nodded. "That's total bullshit, by the way."

"Right. It's harder for older people to learn things, not

because they can't, but because they're resistant to the idea that they're ignorant."

"Are you calling me ignorant?"

He blanched. "Of course not, I—"

"I'm kidding. Obviously there are things I don't know."

"Everyone wants to be an expert on the first try. That's human nature."

"And you absolutely can teach the oldest dog new tricks." I championed all dogs, but seniors had a special place in my heart. "If you can't, that says a lot more about you than the dog."

"Exactly."

"So. Say I'm treat-oriented. What do I get if I do this?"

His eyes widened. "The satisfaction of building a new skill?"

"Nah. There's got to be something better. Brownies?"

He lifted a brow. "Are you supposed to eat sweets at your age?"

"You little shit." He fell out laughing over his joke, and Callie ran over to join in the fun. Rico chattered excitedly.

"You have to practice to improve. I'll know if you're not doing your part. How about if you work hard, we go out for coffee and pie."

"Friday night is my pie night."

"You have a pie night?"

I shrugged like it was no big deal. Like *doesn't everyone have a pie night?*

"All right." He held out his hand to shake on it. "Friday night we can do a lesson and have pie."

I shook with him. "You're on."

"I expect to hear you play that song."

"'Twinkle, Twinkle, Little Star'? I think I can handle it."

"I'll write something a little more challenging and drop it off at the clinic. You have to like the music you're learning at least a little. My dad used to give me one classical and one pop piece to learn each week."

"This is your biological father? You said he passed away?"

"Yeah. He was my first teacher." Beck's gaze fell.

"He'd be so proud if he could hear you now."

"Maybe." Beck rubbed his hands on his jeans. "Although all things considered, I think he'd be pretty amused that I fucked up my life like this."

"Don't say that. You're only getting started."

"I think he'd laugh his ass off. I'm *stubborn* as fuck, just like him. My stepdad got in my face about Callie and I walked away. It's not that I regret taking care of her, but...you're probably right. She's not a baby. She's a dog, and I could have seen to it that she had a loving family to care for her."

"I wouldn't second guess myself now if I were you." I'd have bet my last dollar that was the first time he'd admitted that to anyone, himself included. "You were in a really bad place at the time. Grieving doesn't start and stop. It comes at us like big waves. You lost your dad, and then later you lost your half brother. Maybe holding on to Callie was the best way you knew to handle all that emotion."

A single tear slipped down his cheek. "You're sure being nice when I know you believe it was a piss-poor decision."

"It wasn't my decision to make. I don't have the right to judge."

He shifted. "But you do."

"I try not to," I admitted. "I've done things I regret—things that weren't smart or healthy. The thing is, that's what makes me the man I am today. I didn't see it coming then, but I'm pretty content now."

"You're not listening, Doc. I don't regret my decision. I lost Bryce, and it really hurts. Callie lost the focus of her entire world. We needed each other. She's the one thing I don't regret. Never will."

I wanted to kiss him. How many times had I seen animals abused, thrown away, abandoned, neglected? Beck had a bond with Callie *I* envied. I wished I could bottle it and spray it on the rest of those assholes with a fire hose.

"I'm on your side, Beck. Do you have a plan for going forward?"

"I like it here." He spoke quietly. "St. Nacho's, I mean. It's not just the beach or the businesses."

I knew what he meant. "Jim at Nacho's Bar calls Santo Ignacio the Island of Misfit Toys."

A light, bright smile flitted across his lips. "I'll fit right in."

"Can I get you anything else? Coffee? Tea?"

"No. I should be going, probably." He eyed me but made no move to rise.

I noodled around with the guitar some more.

I didn't want him to leave, that was clear enough. I liked having him in my house—liked the sound of him breathing close-by and Callie's nails clicking on the floor when she left for the water dish I set out.

Beck watched her. "She's making herself right at home."

"She's always welcome here. I like having a dog around."

"But you don't have one."

I shook my head. "Rico only needs a mirror to keep him company. A dog needs more than that."

Beck nodded slowly, and I sensed we were heading into dangerous territory. "People too. Is that why you're not with someone? You work long hours? Volunteer your weekends?"

"Mmhmm. Pretty much. How'd you know about that?"

"While you were cooking, I noticed your scrapbook." He tapped his finger on the book my mom had made about the things I'd done with the CAVMRC—California Veterinary Medical Reserve Corps.

I wished I could sink into a hole.

"I wasn't prying."

"No, it's okay. I leave it out. I guess I'm an egomaniac or something."

"It's really interesting. I never knew there was a vet corps. You work long hours at your clinic, and then you go and do that. Were you at the Camp Fire?"

I nodded. "And the Tubb's Fire."

"Do they only rescue pets or wild animals too?"

"I'll take on any animal I have the skill to treat. Mostly companion animals, goats, pigs. I don't treat cattle or horses, and I'm not an avian vet."

"Is it only fires you go to?"

"There have been floods. I've been to earthquakes. Mexico, mostly."

"I don't get it. You run into fires to treat animals, and yet—"

"It's not as heroic as Mom's ode to me makes it sound."

"And you live alone."

"Well, that kind of goes with the sixty-hour workweek." It felt like we'd gone from talking about him to diving unabashedly into *my* personal life. I wasn't ready to go into all the reasons I didn't have someone.

"This ex who said you ruined everything…what's that about?"

"I'd rather not talk about him."

"Okay." He moved next to me on the couch. "Let me teach you a chord you don't know. You know A minor seventh?"

"I don't think so." He took my hand and placed my fingers between the frets to form the chord.

"Strum."

I did as he asked. "That it?"

"Mmhmm." He didn't let go of my fingers.

"Is it warm in here?" With his body so close, heat flooded my face and sweat stung my forehead. "I could open the slider."

"I'm not warm, but I'm nervous. Are you?"

"No, of course not. Why would I be nervous? I mean, unless you're a serial killer. Are you a serial killer? Not that there's anything—"

"No."

"Good." I breathed a sigh of relief before getting up and leaving my guitar with him. "That's good."

"Are you?"

"Nope. Haven't killed anyone." Then suddenly I remembered the awful day I'd had and why. "Oh God. Not people anyway."

"What would you say if I told you that you make me nervous?"

"Me? I'm…" I had no idea what to say to that. "I'm harmless. Mostly. You're completely safe with me."

"Oh, Doc." He laughed softly. "You have no clue, do you?"

"What are we talking about?"

"Everyone in your office says you're oblivious. I didn't really believe it, but—"

"Oblivious? To what?"

"I shouldn't have to be the one to tell you this." Beck's fingers moved automatically along the neck of my guitar while he picked out arpeggios by rote. "You're the total package, Doc."

"*I* am?" I asked, incredulous. "You're joking."

It was the perfect moment for one of Rico's zingers, "You ruin *everything*" or my personal favorite, "Not that you *noticed*."

Of course, the bird stayed silent.

"Okay, wow." Beck laid the guitar aside. "Guess they were right. Don't you know how hot you are? And nice? Wow, are you nice. This. Dinner. Sitting here with you. I'm—I guess I don't know what I'm supposed to be doing."

"You don't have to do anything."

"But I want to. You live here all alone. You eat with a bird and read from a scrapbook your mom made. You don't have to do that. You could have anyone you want."

My whole body got cold because he was singing my song, and I didn't want to admit it.

"No. Don't do that."

"Do what?"

"This." For the first time, I simply didn't believe him. It made me look back on how easily he'd worked his way into my life. Into my business and now my house. What had he learned from Tug, who I was certain had seen me as someone to manipulate and squeeze for cash and whatever else he could get? I'd avoided him because he couldn't hide it. What if Beck could? "I'm not that guy. You don't need to play me for me to help you out, okay?"

"What?" As if I'd struck him, he asked, "Why would you even think something like that?"

"Because I'm not a tool. I'll feed you dinner. I'm happy to help you. You don't have to flatter me for that."

"That's what you think? I'm flattering you, because...why? Because I want stuff from you? You already paid for my guitar. You said I don't owe you. Oh wow. I didn't think I could feel any worse than when Tug stole my shit." He snapped his fingers and Callie immediately molded herself to his side. "C'mon girl."

"Beck, look—"

"No, you look." He whirled to face me. "You did what you did with the guitar, and I—I'm really grateful. But it makes things complicated and weird for me too. I don't even know why you did it, and if you don't trust me to be nice without an ulterior motive, then I don't trust you when you say you don't want anything in return."

"I don't. It wasn't just me, you know. Cooper and Shawn helped too."

"They're just helping me because you asked them to." He slipped on his backpack and packed up his instrument.

"That's not true."

"I thought you saw me. *Me*." He made a fist on his chest. "Not the fuckup or the dirty homeless guy. The rescue dog and his hapless human pal."

"I—I did. I do. And you don't need to act like I'm some...I don't even know what. Some old guy who's buying your ass."

"*Tug* sold his ass. Not me." He clipped Callie's leash on and walked her to the door. "Never me."

"I'm sorry—"

"You're not oblivious. You're fucked up."

I opened my mouth to reply, but it didn't matter because he went out and shut the door between us. I wouldn't have known what to say anyway.

I overreacted, maybe.

Oh, Christ. I did.

I couldn't imagine someone as delightful as Beck—as gorgeous, as talented, as young—could want me. There. I said it. How could someone like Beck see me as anything more than a...a sugar daddy. I'd spoon-fed him for God's sake. That wasn't me. That was just...needy and creepy and...*of course* he was playing me.

He'd hurt my feelings by trying to make me believe otherwise. He'd wounded my pride, and I'd lashed out at him for it. Good for me, not taking that shit from someone half my age.

Good for me, not letting myself be taken for a *trick*.

Because I was right. I had to be right.

But if I was wrong...oh my God.

If I was wrong, I'd regret the things I'd said forever.

CHAPTER TEN

THE NEXT MORNING, it took me a minute to remember what had happened the night before. With a sinking feeling in my gut, I got ready for work, wondering what kind of day lay before me.

I'd been at a low ebb the evening before, distressed by patient outcomes and nervous about my absurd attraction to a man so young I could conceivably have been his dad, and I'd panicked. I'd acted out. I'd given free rein to all my insecurities, and now if I wanted to explain what I'd done, I had to get clear on what those insecurities were.

If I was right and Beck was being unnecessarily flattering, that warning might be the end of it. But if I was wrong…

I really didn't want to be wrong. Or *right*.

I got to work later than my usual time and discovered Lena already sitting at reception. April was in the back, and when I asked about the kittens, she told me Beck had already been in to feed them and was gone again.

That turned out to be the pattern for several days.

Each morning, Beck slid in and out of the clinic before I got there. Every other time he helped out, he managed to come while I was with patients or after I'd gone home for the day.

It soon became obvious that my staff might have been helping him to avoid me. "April, can I talk to you for a minute?"

She slipped her hands into the pockets of her lab coat and leaned against the wall. "Sure, boss."

"Has Beck said anything to you?"

"'Bout what?" Her eyebrows lifted in studied nonchalance.

"Well, I haven't seen Beck around at all, but I know he's been here. Has he said anything about avoiding me?"

"Why would he?" Her arch tone signified something was up.

"Is he or isn't he avoiding me?"

"He might have mentioned that he'd prefer not to come in while you're here."

"Are Travis and Lena in on this too?"

"In on what, Captain Queeg? It's not a mutiny."

"What reason did he give for avoiding me?"

Her eyes widened. "I think you need to ask him that."

"April, this is not Ridgemont High."

"What's that?"

"Never mind. Can we get back to Beck? This is my place of business."

"Well, then act like it. You're the one who says 'no chismes' all the time."

"Fine." I let her see my annoyance. "I'll ask Lena."

Lena turned out to be less forthcoming than April. Even before I reached the front desk, she said, "Nuh-uh. Don't ask me anything. I just work here."

"Are you kidding me?"

She pressed her lips into a thin line and turned away.

"All right. Jeez." I found Travis in the staff room, readying the cot.

"I suppose you're going to ask me about Beck." He spoke over his shoulder. "Took you long enough."

I sat in one of the folding chairs. "Has he really been avoiding me?"

"Yup."

"Did he tell you why?" I didn't want the answer anymore, but I asked.

"Nope." He sat, smoothing the fresh blanket out to each side of him.

That wasn't any help at all.

"But if you ask me, knowing you, you probably said something stupid."

"Thanks for the vote of confidence."

"That's right. I have absolute faith you'll stick your foot in it if you're out of your depth with someone. Tell me what happened."

I opened my mouth to speak but thought better of it. I didn't like what was going to come out. My attraction to Beck. Inviting him for an intimate dinner. Accusing him of flirting with me to get something. I didn't even know what I was accusing him of trying to get but...something.

Put like that, it was pretty obvious why he was avoiding me.

"I can answer my own question. Thanks."

"C'mon," Travis cajoled. "Confession's good for the soul. What did you do?"

"Let me ask you. Do you think someone his age could see something in a guy like me?"

His eyebrows shot up. "Like what?"

I thought about that. "Hypothetically speaking, do you believe it's possible someone his age might, uh, enjoy spending time with me...and not just...because of economics or status or whatever."

"Seriously? Are you asking if I think Beck *likes you*, likes you?"

I winced. "Don't do that."

"All right." He leaned his elbows on his knees. "For real? He probably does like you. And he's probably a little in awe of what you've achieved here."

"He said some things"—I glanced away—"I took as empty flattery. I told him he didn't have to do that. That I'd look out for him whether he flattered me or not."

Travis sat back. "Ah."

"I meant to simplify things between us."

"But now you see that you called him a liar."

"Yes," I admitted. "If he meant the things he said, I called him a liar."

Travis wrinkled his freckled nose. "Dude. Fix it."

"It might be best if I don't. Don't you think? If I make a big deal out of what I said, then what?"

"Then you're not a dick." Travis shook his head. "This isn't like you, Doc. This kid is under your skin like…burrowing deep."

"You're right." I closed my eyes. "Way too under."

"Is that what it is? Are you afraid something might happen?"

Was I? I could control myself. Nothing had to happen unless I wanted it to. But as to that…"I'm old enough to be his father."

"Barely."

"I'm not in the market for a boyfriend my own age, much less one with half my life experience."

"But don't you see? Maybe that's exactly what you need. Someone you can nurture. Someone who you don't compete with. Someone who takes you out of yourself."

"Nah, Travis. Beck's a sweet kid and a superb musician. I'd love to help him find his footing in life, but anything more is just impossible. I'd always feel like I was taking advantage."

"Funny how you accused him of that in order to push him away."

"All right, Dr. Phil. You should open up a practice."

"I should open up a world-class barbecue joint."

He should. "I'd be first in line if you did."

"Until then, why don't you order food in. You owe us for creating a hostile work environment."

I got up to do just that. "I don't know why I put up with you."

"Who else is gonna feed stray cats twenty-four seven with you?"

"You have a point."

"Fix it with Beck, Doc. That's me talking, not Dr. Phil. I don't think you could handle breaking that kid's heart."

"But no pressure or anything," I muttered as I entered my office. Didn't Bistro sell smoked brisket sandwiches? I picked up the phone and ordered enough sandwiches with all the extras for the four of us, plus a couple more in case Beck stopped by.

If I pictured myself hand-feeding it to him, nobody had to know, right? If I imagined what it would be like to have him lick barbecue sauce off my fingers...Christ.

Lena buzzed my office phone, and I answered.

"Got Mr. Henson here. He thinks Tiger might have—in his words—'piles.'"

"On my way." I slipped on my lab coat and went to greet my walk-in.

I waited a while before leaving the office that evening, but there was still no sign of Beck. I'd put the food I'd ordered for him into the refrigerator and left a note on the kittens' crate that told him where he'd find the food if he was hungry.

Outside, I took a breath of the salt-tangy air and let the bright breeze flow through my soul. Looking west, I could see we were in for rain.

I could go home and remonstrate with Rico again, or I could search out dinner and drinks at Nacho's.

I chose the latter because I thought Rico was probably tired of hearing me whine.

Jim perked up when he saw me. The crowd was a little thinner, not just because it was a Thursday night but because of the incoming storm. Already the sky had darkened to an ominous bruised purple, and lightning flashed over the sea.

I got a table by the window to watch the show. Jim joined me a few minutes later. We ordered carne asada street tacos.

"How're things?" I asked. "Cooper not playing tonight?"

"Shawn's doing a thing at the college, so Cooper went to provide muscle and support."

I envied Cooper and Shawn, sometimes deeply. If any of my relationships had ever been like theirs, I wouldn't be so determined to stay single. But what Cooper and Shawn had was different, elemental. They were air and fire—they fueled each other—whereas all too often, my boyfriends accused me of being some kind of wet blanket. I literally put their fire out. Did that make me water?

What did water do? Water smothered people. Water drowned them.

Wow. Maudlin much? "I think I'll have a whiskey, Jim. Double."

"That bad, huh?" Jim motioned our waiter over and gave him the order. "What's eating you?"

"I'm just tired, I guess."

"Heard you and Cooper been looking out for that kid. You got his guitar back?"

I shrugged. "Found it in Salinas."

"Brownie points." Our server brought our drinks, and I'm ashamed to say I knocked it back before he left.

"Same again."

Jim stared. "Oh, dang."

"What?"

"Seriously, what's going on with you?"

"Nothing." I turned back to the window. "No. Well, I think maybe I hurt Beck's feelings."

"The kid?"

"He is an adult, I guess. Voting age, not drinking. But yeah.

The kid." I tapped my foot impatiently. "Let's just say for the sake of argument, I was a dick to him."

"Mmhmm."

"If I don't have any interest in anything more than just mentoring him, or—I don't know—being nice, should I go out of my way to apologize? Wouldn't that make things worse?"

"I'm not sure I get what you mean."

"If I don't want him to get the wrong idea about me. About whether I'm—"

"Oh, ho. You *like* this voting-age-not-drinking-age adult whose feelings you hurt." Jim grinned widely.

"I don't—" I knocked my water glass over. "Shit."

On the way with my second drink, our server made a detour for a bar rag. "Here. Let me."

I scooted my chair back and let him clean up my spot like I was five years old.

"Thank you." I managed a weak smile.

Jim nodded at his employee and gave him a wink. "Thanks, Salazar."

"So." He waited a few seconds before speaking again. "Just now, you pretty much confirmed any suspicions I had."

"I did not." Salazar put a new plate in front of me, another roll of silverware, and a fresh napkin. "Thanks again."

"It's okay, you know." Jim nodded at Salazar who melted away. "There's no crime in recognizing beauty."

"If that was all it was, it'd be easy."

He sat back. "What else?"

I shook my head, unable to say.

"You know, I've been with Alfred forever. But good-looking servers come and go and the muscle boys on the beach are always pretty. There's temptation everywhere. I've learned to isolate what attracts me and acknowledge it. There's no point in fighting my feelings. I always have the choice whether to act on them."

"That's just it. I didn't recognize I was that attracted to Beck until it was clear to both of us, and then I—I overreacted and pushed him away. It's my problem, not his. I see that now. But if I explain, I'm afraid I'll only dig myself in deeper."

"You probably have to talk to him about it. You'll figure out the right thing to say eventually. Don't wait until he's moved on, or you'll regret it."

"I won't." I sipped at my drink, less anxious to slam it back. Confession was good, indeed. "He's been avoiding me."

"Poor kid. Think he had a little crush?"

"I doubt it. As you say, there are a hundred better candidates within throwing distance."

"Yeah. And we become invisible at thirty if we're not billionaires."

Perhaps Jim hadn't meant to, but he'd made my point for me. "It's probably best if I leave things alone."

"Sure. I mean, you have to do what makes sense to you. Just think things over carefully." Jim and I talked while I finished dinner. By the time I left the cantina, the sky had opened up and rain was lashing down. Typical. Nothing happened halfway when it came to rain in California.

Before I got into the car, I did a gut check on whether it was safe for me to drive. I'd eaten a full meal, sipped my second drink slowly, and spent enough time chatting with Jim afterwards that I felt comfortable behind the wheel. Possibly I'd gotten an assist from the cold. My arms had goosebumps when I started the engine, and I was shivering before I'd gone far enough to warm up the heater sufficiently.

Traffic was light. The usual beachgoing jaywalkers were all safely tucked inside. I drove up Main Street, passed the clinic, and planned on making a left turn at the light. That's when I saw a couple of rain-drenched bodies huddling under the awning of the local florist shop.

One of them was dark brown, shaggy, and four-footed. I'd recognize her biped companion anywhere.

Huh. Best laid plans and all that crap.

I made a quick U-turn and pulled to the curb in front of them. Rolling down the window, I asked, "Need a lift to the clinic?"

With both hands, Beck swiped water from his face and hair. "We've just been there."

"I can take you back to Cooper's if you'd like. Get in."

He glanced up and down the street. "Thanks anyway. It's okay. This rain won't last."

As if in answer, lightning cracked the sky and thunder boomed almost immediately after.

"Come on, Beck. It's coming down frogs."

He glanced up and down the street again. Whatever he said next was lost to the wind.

"What?" I shouted over the *shush, shush,* of my wipers and the constant drumming of rain. "I didn't hear what you said."

He rolled his eyes. "I forgot my keys and got locked out. I was heading *back* toward the clinic."

Exasperated, I shouted, "I'll take you wherever you like, just get in for God's sake. My seat's getting soaked."

He must have made up his mind because he dashed forward, opening the back door first for Callie and then slipping in next to me with a squelch. He slammed the door against the rain. I rolled up the window, thankfully silencing most of the outside noise.

"You want to go to the clinic?"

"I guess." He didn't look at me. Christ, had I hurt him that badly?

"I can take you to the clinic, or you're welcome to come to my place. I know from experience my house is warmer."

"Th-thank you." His lips were alarmingly pale. "The clinic's fine."

"The hell it is." Frowning, I made an executive decision and spun the wheel in preparation for another U-turn. "You need a hot shower, a hot meal, and a roaring fire, none of which can be found at the clinic."

"You're k-k-kidnapping me?"

"Yes." I handed him my phone. "Phone the authorities. You don't need to unlock it to dial 911."

He turned away, but I thought that was to hide his relief.

When we got to my place, I pulled into the driveway. "Only a few feet to shelter. Make a run for the porch. I'll catch up."

He slipped out and opened the door for his dog. "C'mon, Callie."

I grabbed a towel from the back and wiped up as much water as I could before running to the porch to open the door.

"Wow, the rain is fucking icy tonight."

"N-not the rain. It's the w-w-wind." Lips that had been pale before were now positively blue. I led him to the guest bathroom and motioned him inside.

"Towels are under the sink. In you go. When you get out, there will be dry clothes on the counter. I'll dry Callie off and start a fire." He hesitated. "Go on. You're safe here."

He turned on his heel and opened the glass shower door to turn on the water. I closed the bathroom door between us with a sigh.

I told myself Beck was safe with me. His heart would be safer with me than it was with his own family.

I didn't ask myself how safe my heart would be.

CHAPTER ELEVEN

I LEFT a pair of sweats and an old band T-shirt on the sink for Beck while he showered. On the way out, I locked the bathroom door.

My awareness of him—that he was naked behind the billowing clouds of steam condensing on the door seemed to permeate my entire being.

That was normal, right? I was a gay, human male, so it was entirely normal to respond to the presence of an attractive male in his prime. It was nothing more than simple biology. If I could only look at it like that—as stimulus and response—I wouldn't have to feel so...awkward about things.

I toweled the rain off Callie and made her comfortable before changing out of my work clothes. I opted for a worn pair of sweats, a T-shirt, and a hoodie, although I knew I'd probably steam like a dumpling inside it once I had the fireplace going. It was surprising how efficient the little fireplace was in warming the great room. From the front window to the kitchen, its cozy flames took the chill out of the air and fragranced my home with earthy wood smoke. The fireplace was the reason I loved the house so much. I'd always preferred my bedroom cool, so despite living near the beach I rarely needed the forced-air heater.

After I got a good fire going, I nuked food I had in the freezer. It was the perfect night for a hot bowl of chicken tortilla soup, and I had the stuff for cornbread—a mix of course—and all the extras on hand.

I was just putting the cornbread in the oven when Beck slipped into the kitchen on cat feet, like Sandburg's fog. Why was he trying to be invisible? It didn't seem very like him. Did he not even want to be around me? Well, duh. Probably not, because—to use Travis's most recent accusation—I was a dick.

"I want to say one thing—" I began, but he started talking at the same time.

"Look. You don't know me—"

We both stopped. Then I said, "You're right. Go on."

"You don't know me, so I forgive you. But listen to me now. I'm not the type of guy who flatters people to get something from them."

"I'm sorry. I may have—"

"And even if I were that kind of guy, there's nothing wrong with that. Lots of guys spend their whole lives just being charming." He poked my chest. "And plenty of men like that. Especially old men."

"Oh, *ouch.*"

He gave me a little shove. "I'm not talking about you. I'm talking about the truckers who like to tell a story while they're letting you hitch a ride. So what if they want to talk about their glory days in some war? It's better than hitting me up for a blowjob."

"Right." This was the heart of the matter. "So you tell them what they want to hear whether it's true or not? What do you care? You'll be in someone else's truck in a few miles anyway."

"That's not it. I've learned to listen to what people don't say too, you know? I'm trying to be nice and maybe fill a void in someone's heart. You only want to paint me in the worst possible light."

Rico took that opportunity to talk. "Like *you* noticed."

Beck stopped by Rico's cage to say hello.

"You can take him out." Rico had been a little subdued, which was normal for him when it rained hard, but Beck soon brought him out of his shell. Rico sat on Beck's shoulder and mostly postured while they chattered.

"Boop," I called out.

"Boop," Rico echoed.

I had to admit, if I hadn't been so socially out of my depth with Beck, if I hadn't been expecting some kind of angle, the things he said about filling voids might have warmed my heart. How often had I talked simply because someone seemed interested in what I had to say? I thought I filled conversational voids, but maybe the void had been inside me all along.

"You're saying that you like to make people feel good about themselves?"

"Don't you?" he asked defiantly.

Did I? "I confine most of my efforts to animals."

Beck called Callie to him, knelt, and rubbed his cheek against hers. To Rico's dismay, Callie then spent considerable time sniffing around him. I tensed, but nothing happened.

"You're terrific with animals," said Beck. "Who made you believe people can't be trusted?"

"Nobody had to *make me believe*." I used air quotes. "People lie. Animals don't."

"Don't they?" Beck narrowed his eyes. "Or do they just lie for different reasons?"

Who was the vet here? "No, of course they don't."

"Animals play dead. They avoid contact if they're afraid even when they really want company. They hide their pain."

He had a point. "That last one's reflexive. Prey animals' lives depend on appearing healthy and in control."

"Right, because the weakest is easily picked off. But it's a kind of lie, isn't it?"

"Okay. I concur. Dogs do not always say what they mean."

"Ha, ha. Please listen to me. Animals lie to *protect themselves.*"

God, he was right. All animals lied to protect themselves. And if he knew that, and had spotted me doing it...lying was pointless, wasn't it? How long had it taken for a man half my age to teach me something I should have learned long ago?

Still stuck in my head, I got place settings but put them on the counter instead of the table. We could eat casually that late at night. I put bowls of corn chips, shredded cheese, chopped onion, and sour cream out so he could doctor his soup however he liked.

"Shawn says people should learn to listen with their hearts. That's how you hear what the animals tell you, isn't it?"

Hmm. "Shawn is very wise."

"He's amazing," Beck agreed happily. "Him and Cooper both."

I turned to face him. "I'm sorry I hurt your feelings, Beck. I don't know what to do with compliments. I might have over-reacted."

"That wasn't so hard, was it?" His lips curved into a dazzling smile.

I turned away in order to ladle soup into our bowls. Also, I had to catch my breath.

Beck watched me carefully as I picked up my bowl and added handfuls of extras. He didn't touch his bowl.

"That's how you like it?" he asked.

"*This* is the only way to eat chicken tortilla soup. Here." And there I was, gathering a spoonful from my bowl and offering it to him. Did I want him to take it or tell me to stop acting like we were in some skeevy soft-core porn film? As he had before, he opened his mouth and let me feed him.

A sensual explosion began in my cock and ripped through

me, heating my entire body.

God, I really did have a new kink. One I'd never even considered before. Or if I had, I'd never acted on it in my life. This was a revelation of the ambiguous variety. Was it a good thing or a bad thing discovering so late in life that hand-feeding someone turned my crank so hard?

Beck swiveled on the stool, knees going to one side and then the other while he licked his lips with slow precision. I couldn't take my eyes off him. He was…adorable.

"You like feeding me," he announced with a wicked grin.

I couldn't speak, so I settled for staring at his lips like some demented sociopath. I'd already said I wasn't awesome with compliments. Maybe I wasn't awesome with the bare-naked truth either.

"You want to know a secret?" His question sounded rhetorical. He didn't give me time to answer anyway. "Tug's a goddamn genius at figuring out other people's kinks."

I cleared my throat. "Is he?"

"I'm sure that's how he always knew how to spot a mark. I know you think that's what I'm like, but I'm not. I didn't know about things like this before I met him either," Beck said. "Kinks."

I lowered my gaze to his lips. "That's…unusually perceptive."

"Tug is exactly that." He gave a thoughtful downward twist of the lips. "But I don't think Tug is interested in sex or kink at all except as currency."

I felt for Tug—he'd obviously been on his own for a while. He was an addict. He needed help. I almost felt bad until I remembered how completely he'd betrayed his friend. Beck had grown subdued.

"I hope he gets the help he needs."

"I hope he lands somewhere good." Beck continued to swivel on the counter stool, back and forth, back and forth. Was that nerves? "As long as he's chasing a high, he won't."

"Did he figure out my feeding people kink and tell you?" I supposed it was inevitable given the amount of time I'd spent looking at Beck's mouth—in public, no less.

"No. Um." Beck glanced down. "He figured out mine?" Said like a question, the words had me scrambling for the answer. What? What did that mean? "May I have more, please?"

Bright spots of red bloomed on Beck's cheeks, but he licked his lower lip again and opened his mouth. Stunned, I gave him another spoonful of soup, taking care to get chips and sour cream and cheese on the spoon with it. He took hold of my wrist and licked the spoon clean before letting me take it back.

"Holy shit," I whispered.

"If you think it's weird—"

"Nope." I hit the land-speed record answering him that time. "Honestly, I had no idea. About me, I mean. I can't think it's weird if we both like it."

"Oh really?" he teased.

"It's not like I've gone around feeding people like this. I mean, kids, yeah. Babies. Animals. But that's totally different. There was never any...um—"

"Hope not." His gaze dropped to the evidence of my obvious enjoyment where it tented my sweats.

"Yeah, well. But—"

"Oh, here it comes," he said unhappily.

"That's probably why I lost my cool the other night. Because of this...thing—" I motioned between us. "I'm completely uncomfortable with taking advantage of someone so much younger."

His lips pursed delightfully. "Oh. Okay."

"Okay?"

"Sure." He sighed. "If you push me away without being a douche canoe, that's okay. I get it."

Well, that was easy. *Too easy?* It sure as hell was.

"I really am sorry about last time."

Z.A. MAXFIELD

"I said I forgive you." He took his bowl of soup and started adding things to it. "I wasn't so sure about things between us either. I mean, you're what? My dad's age?"

"If he's thirty-eight." Was my voice unnaturally tight?

"Oh. Well, no. My biodad was older when he passed, and my stepdad is way older now. Must be why I don't think of you the same way."

"Here's hoping it's a little more than that." I clenched my fingers around the spoon.

"You know what I mean." He scooped a bite of soup with a chip in it and chewed it thoughtfully. "You haven't started losing your hair yet."

What? "Thankfully."

He gave my hairline a squint anyway. "And you haven't let yourself go or anything."

"You're doing this on purpose, aren't you?" I dug out a spoonful of soup and ate without tasting it.

His eyes went a little dreamy. "I imagine having all those animals to play with and feed makes up for a lot when it comes to younger guys, though. Does it? Do you find they're able to overlook the aging, or is it like they say? Gay men over thirty turn invisible."

"Enough already." I had to admire his needling. "Brat."

"That might be one of my kinks too," Beck offered slyly. "I love being a brat."

"Do *you* love wearing soup in your hair? Is that one of your kinks?"

His eyes lit up. "Let's find out. Do it."

I blinked, at a loss for words, until he covered his face with both hands and laughed like a hyena. Now there was an animal with a bad reputation. Sure, they make a cackling sound, but it communicates fear as often as excitement. Hyenas are rarely amused.

I studied Beck with what felt like entirely new eyes.

Was this joking and laughter his way past the embarrassment—the anxiety—of rejection? Was I finally listening with *my* heart?

"I do wish things could be different." I admitted the truth because I wanted him to know. "You...challenge me, make me laugh, brighten my days, fill my nights with thoughts I frankly shouldn't have about anyone your age."

Telling him this made me dizzy as if I were on a high wire, looking down at how far I was going to fall. *Way too late*, said my conscience. Maybe my dick chimed in there too. *Way, way too late. You're already in pieces at the bottom.*

"Now what?" he asked.

Rico squawked. "You ruin *everything*."

I glared at the cage. "Shut up, clown chicken."

Beck smiled. Maybe I did ruin everything, but even my ex would be surprised if I ruined this chance, this God-given opportunity to test the theory that I could come just from feeding a beautiful young man who looked at me like I was everything.

"Clown chicken has a point, you know." Beck said softly. "Age is just a number."

"It's so...so much more than that if you're the um, elder statesman in the equation."

"I like elder statesmen." He moved closer. "What if that's one of my checkboxes?"

Checkboxes? What did that mean. A preference? A kink? An option like *E. All of the above?* "Is it?"

He licked his lips. "Mmhmm."

"Oh."

"I like mature men." He leaned so close I felt his breath on my lips. "You make me feel safe."

I swallowed audibly because I'm just that smooth.

"How about it, Doc? Do you want to pick up your spoon and explore this epic chemistry? Or are you gonna punk out?"

CHAPTER TWELVE

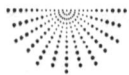

I picked up my goddamn spoon, all right.

I was thinking with my dick. Or maybe I wasn't thinking at all. It was as if a chyron behind my closed eyelids scrolled the words, *Beck likes older partners. You're well and truly older. Ergo...*

Not a ringing endorsement, I know, but I wasn't that confident.

My boyfriends had all pretty much dropped into my lap, either at school or at work. We'd been equal partners, knew the same jokes, listened to the same music, had all the pop culture references in common. All that, plus chemistry, brought us together, but mutual affection never lasted.

It seemed I was all spark and no fire.

With someone Beck's age *spark* was all that mattered—at least, I kept telling myself that while he made yummy noises around my spoon.

Beck's lips were a religious experience for me as was the way he closed his eyes to savor food. Instead of letting him dab with a napkin, I leaned in and licked away any stray bits with my tongue. Eating and kissing became one and the same thing.

I felt his smile when we kissed, and the tension in my gut

grew into a cataclysm in my balls and cock. I brushed his lower lip with my thumb.

"I could come just from watching your mouth when you eat."

Face flushed, eyes bright as stars he said, "I could come from you feeding me."

Like puzzle pieces, I thought as I captured his hand and laced our fingers together.

He took in a deep breath, and I let out a sigh. We smiled at the same time. He was starshine, and I was utterly content to reflect all that bright beauty back to him until I positively glowed.

We ate our entire meal holding hands like middle schoolers —no words, no drama—with only companionship and fierce affection to guide us.

I wanted to lead, but that role had been taken from me the second I'd seen him licking an ice cream cone on the beach. I was way out of my depth. I got the feeling he knew it. I got the feeling I amused him, and he liked that—in the same way all the great *fatales* like the affect they have on others.

I was his to play with, to enjoy. I was his, and the tiny satisfied smile I'd seen playing over his mouth all night told me he wanted me, and he was going to take me however he liked.

It was kind of freeing now that I acknowledged it.

"What now?" It felt unbelievably stupid to ask. "Um. Dessert? I have ice cream."

"Maybe later." He cupped the side of my face with calloused fingers. "Have you been practicing your guitar?"

The segue caught me off guard as if the ground had moved beneath my feet.

A flush rode high on his cheekbones. Maybe he needed to slow things down. I was overwhelmed by his nearness. By his interest. By everything about him. It was probably good I let him set the pace.

"I'm shit at it," I whined.

That got me a smug smile. "Everyone has to start somewhere."

"I might have reached the age where I only like doing things I'm good at. Like that old dog we were talking about."

"So?" There was no pity in him. "Get good."

"Must I?"

"Depends on what you want." He swiveled on the stool again. "Do you want to play guitar?"

"I don't want to *not* play guitar," I equivocated.

He snorted and pushed me toward the living room. "Go. Get your instrument."

"Let me just clean up here first." I stalled by rinsing the dishes and putting them into the dishwasher. "Did you feed Callie?"

"At the clinic." He brought her water dish to the sink. "I'll top this off, though."

Finally, I had no excuses. I went to the living room, picked up my guitar, and carefully removed it from its case.

He held out a hand. "Give it here. I'll tune it."

"I tuned it yesterday."

"The change in air pressure from the storm can ruin that." He strummed and made minor adjustments. "Humidity plays havoc with guitars."

"Now that you mention it, I've heard Cooper say that about his violin. But I'll be honest, I can't hear much difference."

"You will eventually. It takes time to learn." He handed the instrument back. "Show me the finger exercise I gave you."

I kept my mutinous thoughts off my face while I "spidered" my fingers across the guitar's neck and back.

"Faster," he demanded

"I can't." I could move a little faster but not accurately. Beck's spiders were an exercise in frustration and impatience. He told me to be accurate.

"Try." I did so as Beck watched. "Good." He nodded. "I see some improvement. How does it feel?"

"Pretty ridiculous," I admitted. "Can't you just teach me to fake something at parties?"

"*Fake* something?" His appalled expression made me laugh. "Okay, okay."

"You want to *fake* something?"

"I said okay." I wasn't going to give him the satisfaction of calling him a brat. Not then, anyway.

He stood over me. "Play the music I gave you."

Dutifully, I played "Twinkle, Twinkle, Little Star." It did not survive.

As I haltingly changed finger positions for the fourth try, he shot out of his chair.

"Okay. No. Relax. Here." He took the guitar from me and sat in my lap, facing away. "Give me your hands."

"I'm supposed to relax like this?"

"Mmhmm." He positioned my left hand on the neck of the guitar, and I brought my right hand around him to rest on the strings. He was slim enough that it was actually easy to reach.

"You need to eat more." He felt light as air in my lap, and it was very distracting. Especially when he squirmed up my thighs to rest his buttocks snug against my belly.

Predictably, my cock tried to punch a hole in my sweats.

"Sorry about the—

"It's fine." He shifted around to torture me. "Now, position your hand like this. Tips of your fingers centered between the frets. Make each note as crisp as you can. Reposition as slowly as you need to for accuracy."

I strummed.

"Wait. Remember positioning."

I cleared my throat. "Believe me, positioning is all I can think about right now."

He turned his head and kissed my cheek. "Focus."

My spine melted. "What were we doing again?"

He tried unsuccessfully to hide his smile while I played and played. I'm sure actual stars went supernova during the length of time it took to get marginally better, but eventually I earned his approval.

"That was...adequate." He seemed pleased, though.

He wrested the guitar from my cramped, nerveless fingers and leaned back against me to play a bluesy chord progression. Not a song, specifically—he played the *feeling* of sitting with a beautiful boy in my arms, listening to rain on the roof. He played the wind in the evergreens. The sound of our breaths. Our hearts beating in time.

His head dropped onto my shoulder, and I automatically lifted my hand to stroke the wild mop of hair off his forehead. It felt softer than I expected. When he lived on the beach with Tug, his hair had always looked salt-stiffened and a little dirty.

As he nuzzled into my neck now, it felt soft and smelled like coconuts. I'd never smell coconuts again without thinking of this perfect moment with him.

"Are you comfortable?" I asked.

"Perfectly." He pressed a kiss against my neck. "You?"

"Never better."

He finished by playing the seventh chord he'd tried to teach me. It hung in the air like a question. *Do you want me? Are we going to do this? Is this real or are we dreaming?*

I already had my answer, but it turned out I had some questions of my own. I didn't know how to ask. *What if this is all we have? What if I'm not enough, or too much, or wrong?*

How will I ever let you go?

He rose and put my guitar back in its case. When he came back, he straddled my lap, facing me. I made the sort of sound a vinyl cushion makes. He deflated me, in more ways than one.

"You are something." His bits-and-bobs bracelets creaked and jingled when he brought his hand up to thumb the arch of my eyebrow. "You look very kind. If PBS needed someone to play a veterinarian, you'd be perfect."

"Thank you."

"What about me? What am I like?"

"Trouble." I kissed his forehead. "And light. Lots of both."

"I'm no trouble."

"I thought you wanted to be a brat."

"I want to be *your* brat." He lowered his lashes coyly. "What would you do with me?"

"Hmm." I pretended to think about it. "Probably the same thing I'd do with a misbehaving dog. I'd try to catch you doing something I wanted you to do and reward that."

"I see." He bit his lip. "But what would you do when I'm naughty?"

"I give naughty dogs, especially puppies, the best possible chance to be good."

"How?" His lips trailed from my neck to the skin under my jaw, making me shiver with need.

"I...um...make their environment safe, for one thing. T-take away any attractive nuisances and replace them with things a puppy can have. Reward, reward, reward."

"I've been pretty good. How would you reward me?"

"I'd reward you very well and with alarming frequency."

"Okay, then." He smiled and it lit his whole face. "Let the rewarding begin."

I trailed my hand up his arm. Just that touch was exquisite. His pale skin was soft and cool as I drew my fingers up and over the sleeve of his T-shirt and around his shoulder to rest at the back of his neck.

Our lips met for a kiss as sensual and slow as the music he'd been playing.

"Mm." He opened, letting me slip between straight teeth that seemed too perfect and white for someone living rough. I imagined his family faced with the cost of orthodontia on top of what must have been massive medical bills and wondered again how anyone who nurtured a child—educated him and straightened his teeth—could let him walk away.

In the corner, Rico fluffed his feathers loudly and chittered as he settled in for the night. Callie dozed peacefully at our feet.

I wrapped my hands around Beck's hips as if I could pull him closer when there wasn't space for a mote of dust between us.

He shifted, rubbing his cock deliberately against mine.

"Okay if we take this to the bedroom?" I asked hoarsely.

His smile widened. "I thought you'd never ask."

I probably wouldn't have if the entire evening hadn't felt like a fever dream, if it wasn't exactly what I'd wanted since I'd first seen Beck on the beach.

He lifted off me, and there was no hiding his arousal. His hilariously tented sweats were soaked with precum. Mine were in no better shape. My spine popped audibly when I rose to my feet.

Beck grabbed hold of the strings of my hoodie and pulled me to him. "Where?"

"This way. Let me cover Rico."

"I should take Callie out before bed." He went to the door where he'd hung her leash.

"My yard's fenced. Just let her outside."

"Her majesty won't get her feet wet unless I go." He tapped his thigh and she followed him to the back door. She was laughably reluctant to leave. It took both of us walking her out and waiting, shivering in the rain while she did her business.

"C'mon." I ran back inside and grabbed towels from the laundry room. He followed inside with Callie, who lashed us with icy water when she shook. We had to get more towels.

I thought about leaving our damp clothes there, but I wasn't ready to parade around naked in front of Beck. I wasn't sure I'd ever be ready, but he dropped his sweatshirt. The luster of him astounded me all over again. I lifted my arm, he fit himself underneath it, and we walked to my bedroom together, followed by the silent, amiable Callie.

At the foot of my bed, I turned to him. "I could still take you back to Cooper's place if you'd rather. They're probably home by now."

"I don't want to go," he whispered. "But I should probably call, huh?"

"Yeah, they might be worried." I took my phone off the charger and unlocked it. "Here. I'll give you a minute."

What am I doing?

I'd be lying if I said I didn't have second thoughts as I washed up and brushed my teeth. Even then, I could tell Beck was no hookup for me. I had no precedent for what he made me feel, but I had a pretty good idea what it meant.

But I had no idea what he wanted it to mean.

I came back out to find my phone on its charger and Beck stripped all the way down.

He wasn't the hairless boy I'd imagined, thank God, but he was too thin and very pale. His chest and arms were covered in gooseflesh. I needed to keep the room warmer for him.

I used my phone to adjust the thermostat—first time since December.

"You need anything?" Again, I stalled. "Want a bottle of water?"

He shook his head. "You?"

He was laughing at me, but not unkindly.

"What?"

"You need anything?"

Oh God, yeah. My God, I did.

I needed *Beck.*

I needed and wanted and didn't know what to do with *Beck.*

I pulled off the duvet and stripped to my boxers.

Beck slid between the sheets, completely naked.

"Nice." He swam around in the luxury bedding like a happy tropical fish.

I shivered with the need to touch him and the desire to pull him beneath me and rut like a goddamn stag. I wanted to be on him, over him, inside him.

I wanted to nail that slim sweet body through the mattress again and again, yet I couldn't move. I had to remind myself we were both consenting adults. I had to give myself permission, even after he'd consented in no uncertain terms and said he wanted me.

I had to let go of my rational mind. Let go. *Let go.*

"Let go of what?" he asked.

"Did I say that out loud?"

He chuckled. "Mmhmm."

I turned to him. "I need you to tell me this is okay."

"It's okay." He sighed and stroked my cheek. "Are you always a dork?"

"I'm afraid so." I scooted a little closer and wrapped a hand around his hip. Our cocks nudged against one another or rather, his met the cotton of my boxers.

"What about this? Still okay?"

"Get rid of the boxers." He was laughing at me again. "Why are you like this? Wait. Have you ever done this before?"

"Shut up."

"Treat me like any other Grindr hookup. It's not that complicated."

"It is complicated," I said. "Because it's you, it's complicated."

"This is such a drag." He flopped onto his back unhappily. "It's because you think I'm too young, right?"

"No." I wrapped my hand around his neck and turned him to face me. "It's because you're important."

"Really?" His eyes widened.

"Yes. You're important to me."

He smiled and reached for me at the same time I reached for him.

This was happening. We were happening.

I didn't know how to start. I didn't know how it would end. But like the music he'd ended with that portentous major seventh chord, my questions hung in air full of promise, and we were about to search for answers.

CHAPTER THIRTEEN

GO SLOW. I squeezed the taut globes of Beck's tight ass with both hands, holding him to me so with every move our cocks strained against each other. Heat built in my groin, rippling outward, down to tighten my balls, and up my cock until it was hard enough to hurt.

He wrapped his arms around my shoulders as I cupped his face in my hand. We kissed as if kisses were both the journey and destination, the means and the end, a rondeau of passion and purpose where he and I existed without numbers, without neighbors, without judgment or the world we left behind when we slipped into my bed together.

His kisses became my breath—the air I needed to survive. His slippery, cool skin against mine an ocean of sensation to swim in.

One minute, I pulled him over me to squirm and laugh and smile down like a sullied angel, and the next, he rolled us, serious purpose written over his lovely, luminous features as he wrapped his legs around my hips.

"What do you want?" I asked.

"Fuck me." He lifted his hips invitingly and nipped at my

fingers. Sucking one into his mouth, he drew off with a *pop*. "I want you inside me. I want to come on your cock."

Jesus. That was unambiguous. *Young people today, huh?*

I kissed him one last time and left to open my nightstand drawer where I felt around for lube and condoms. Throwing those on the mattress next to his hip, I knelt between his legs.

"You're sure?"

"Guh. Yes, I'm sure. Fuck me." *Impatience, thy name is Beck.*

I slowed down even more. "I'm sorry. I didn't hear you. What did you say?"

"Please, please, fuck me."

"What was that? That last bit?"

He curled up and blew a raspberry in my armpit.

"*Aargh.* Stop. You win, you win." I ran both hands over his belly, thumbed the indents below his hip bones, and tangled my hair in his curly bush. No manscaping there. He was beautiful. Natural. One of Caravaggio's naughty youths come to life for me to pleasure.

I leaned over and licked my way from his collar bones to his navel. I dipped my tongue inside while he thrashed feverishly. I traced the lines where his legs met his torso and blew hot breath on his balls.

"Touch me. Please. Touch my goddamn cock, or I swear I'll—"

"You'll what?"

"Die." He panted. "I will die of sexual frustration in your bed. Is that how you want this to go down?"

"Since you mentioned it..." I gave his shaft teasing flicks of my tongue, keeping the pressure up all wrong so it was never enough, never the right place, never the thing he wanted so badly. All he could do then was writhe and moan and curse me out. Only when I was ready did I pull the whole of his cock into my mouth, right to the back of my throat where I worked my muscles around him.

"Christ," he shouted.

I pulled off. "It's Lindy."

"Oh God, do that again."

"Mm. Can't hear you. Must be—"

"Please. Please, Lindy. *Please*."

I swallowed around him again and again, gorging myself on his sweet cock until my throat was sore and he begged me to stop.

"Please, Lindy. Please. I need you. Need your cock."

I took time preparing him. He was tight and nervy. He jumped at every sensation, rolling his head from side to side.

"I'm opening you to take my cock, sweetheart. I'm going to tease you apart, first with my fingers, then with my dick."

"Yes," he cried. "Do it. Fuck me."

"Oh, I plan to. Relax for me, baby." Slipping one lubed finger inside him took time and patience. Then he begged for a second and a third. I stuffed him so full of my fingers he tipped his head back and precum leaked in sweet, silvery strings from the tip of his cock to his stomach. When I deliberately slid across his sweet spot, his whole body tightened with shock. I couldn't wait to feel him around me. Removing my fingers, I lined up my cock at his softened hole.

"Is this still okay?"

"Oh my God. Now, please. I want to come on your cock, Lindy. Please. Now. Now."

Lifting my gaze, I made sure our eyes locked before I started to push in. His eyes fluttered shut.

"No you don't. Look at me. Let me have those beautiful eyes, Beck. Let me see what you feel right now. I've been dreaming of this."

"It's"—his Adam's apple bobbed—"so much."

"Too much?" I slid out an inch before nudging back inside him.

"No!" he grunted. "Keep going. Want to feel you."

"You'll feel me."

"Want to feel you...next week." He lifted his head to brush his lips over mine, and it changed the angle of our bodies.

"God, Beck." I slid all the way home. "God."

"Just Beck."

"Another fucking clown chicken."

He lifted his hips. "Ah, Jesus."

"Your body's so *sweet*." I kissed every part of him I could.

"More." He lifted his hips to meet my every thrust. Beguiling. Demanding. "More, Lindy. Harder."

Lifting his legs over my shoulders, I spread him wide and pushed back into him.

"Yes. Oh, Lindy, *yes*." The smile I found so charming played over his lips as we raced to the finish line. He gasped each breath between thrusts. His hands slid up and down my sides, his fingers squeezed my hips with bruising pressure. "Yes, that's it. There, there."

He went over slowly, awkwardly, like a log on the brink of a waterfall. He froze and clenched and then arched and let go. Semen burst from his cock, painting his chest and belly with creamy white strings of cum.

I gripped his shoulders, and within three deep strokes I melted into him, the pressure of release so powerful that I saw black spots in my vision for several seconds while I held Beck immobile. My orgasm went on and on until I felt empty and spent and almost too tired to slip out of him carefully. I grabbed a tissue and wrapped the condom inside it then tucked him close.

"You're amazing." I kissed his cheek.

"No, you are." He let out a shuddering sigh.

Pshaw. "I'll get a damp towel as soon as my heart stops racing."

His lips moved against my neck, but I didn't hear his words.

"Hm?"

"Thank you." I pulled back and looked down. His eyes glistened in the faint light. "Thank you. That was...so nice. You were so nice, and—"

"Shh." Discomfort with compliments lit a fire under me. I got a damp cloth and came back to find him staring at the ceiling.

He grinned. "Wow."

"Wow?" I teased. "Is that like five stars, I'd orgasm here again?"

He bit his lip. "Maybe four and a half. Got to give you room to grow."

"I'll grow all right. Just give me a minute. We're not all twenty."

I cleaned cum off his stomach and swiped the cloth between his legs. Discreetly, I checked to make sure I hadn't done any damage to his pert little hole. It was red. He'd definitely feel it tomorrow, not next week, though."

Casually, he reached over and grabbed my cock. "So, this is nice."

Despite its recent workout, my dick tried to rise to the occasion. "I've always thought so."

"Well, you would, wouldn't you?" Good grief. Was he going to be a talker? He shot me an imp's grin. "How long before I can play with it again?"

"Don't worry." I slid in beside him and crawled over so I could spoon his pretty backside. "You'll be the first to know."

SOMETIME LATER, something woke me. I opened my eyes to find Beck kneeling at the side of the bed, chin propped on his forearms, watching me.

I startled. "Oh shit. What are you doing?"

"Had to piss." Beck narrowed his eyes. "You've got eyelashes like palm fronds. Anyone ever tell you that?"

I rose to a sitting position. "Only my mother. I tell her envy isn't a good look on anyone."

"I was trying to let you sleep because I know you need it at your age. You awake now?"

"Ya think?" What a *brat*. If he thought this sort of thing would get him rewarded, he...was probably right. "Did you need something?"

"Um. Define *need*." He smiled with his eyes. That was smizing, right?

I smized back. "Did you *want* something?"

"Now that you mention it." He crept onto the bed and straddled my lap. "I have this idea for a great game."

"Oh yeah?"

"Mmhmm. It's called 'guess why I woke you.'" He leaned over and kissed my cheek, my nose, my eyebrows, and finally my lips. "Go ahead. Guess."

"You want me to practice the guitar?"

He arched against me. "Yes, but not right now."

"You want to do a little night shopping online?"

"Hm. Not really." He grinned. "But if there is a late-night package delivery, I hope it's for me."

I let him squirm around a few more seconds before taking his cock in my hand. "You amazing, infuriating, beautiful—"

His eyes narrowed. "If you call me a boy—"

"Brat."

"Oh yeah. Mmnh. I'm a naughty, naughty brat." He kissed me again. I reached over to get some lube.

Soon we were jerking each other off, trading kisses and moans and sighs. Compared to what we'd done earlier, it felt kind of silly and tame, but there was no denying my orgasm when it finally hit me or his when it painted my chest.

He slumped against me, and I put my arms around him. We

lay like that, with his arms around my neck and his head on my shoulder, dripping with cum.

He asked, "Are you happy?"

"I've always been a pretty happy guy." It was nothing but the truth. In the midnight stillness it was impossible not to say the words. "This feels like something else. Something better."

Something better and breathless and frightening and so wonderful I wanted to run towards whatever it could be full tilt.

He took my hand and placed it on his butt cheek. "Can't quite put your finger on it, huh?"

"Your turn to get a cloth. They're in the second drawer on the right side of the sink."

Reluctantly, he peeled himself away. "Okay, but after, I'm spooning you because you, sir, snore."

"You do too, you know."

"But my snores are musical perfection." He kissed his fingers *muah* and left, shaking his head. "Every note is a gem."

AFTER WE CLEANED UP, I fell into a dreamless sleep. Maybe I was *problematically mature,* in the sense that I wasn't really up for all-nighters like I had been when I was Beck's age. But when he reached for me a third time, I was ready to give him the blowjob of his life.

It crossed my mind—as I sank onto my haunches between his legs and nuzzled into his ball sac—that I didn't have a clue where he'd been. What he'd done. If he'd been tested. The thought stopped me from losing myself in the act, but it didn't stop my enjoyment as I licked up his surprisingly long, full cock.

I took him in, giving him my throat again, but I drew off, and sank back down, and breathed in the essence of him. He smelled like the ocean, and man funk, and sweat, and semen.

My mind told me I was keeping him, and my body concurred as I rubbed my hands up and down the furry lengths of his thighs.

He dug his hands into my hair, and writhed, and made absurd, helpless noises until his cock thickened against my tongue.

"Gonna." He covered his eyes with both hands.

I pulled off before he let loose and massaged cum into his stomach with both hands while he went boneless beneath me.

And now it was my turn to clean us up.

It had been a long time since I'd considered getting a box of popup wipes for the bedside. As soon as I thought it, I nixed the idea. I lumbered into the bath with the certainty that preparing for a night like this one was the best way to ensure it never happened again.

Beck was spontaneous and sweet. A great lay. For whatever reason, I was the one he'd chosen that night, and it was so good he'd probably ruined me for life. A quick glance at my reflection in the mirror told me *problematically mature* men shouldn't look gift horses in the mouth. Even if they're vets.

At that point, there might have been a tiny, catastrophically ungrateful part of me that hoped I'd be able to sleep for the rest of the night. And there was another, truculent part of me that argued I could sleep when I was dead.

I returned to the bed and cleaned the cum off Beck's snow-white skin. Except it wasn't anymore. There was a blush to his whole body, love bites on his neck, and finger shaped bruises shadowing his hips where I'd held him too tightly.

I ran my finger regretfully over one such mark, and he rolled over and smiled at me.

"You freak. I have battle scars."

"Sorry, sweetheart. I should have been more gentle."

His eyes widened. "I love them. I'm sorry I can't just walk around naked announcing my good fortune to all and sundry.

Behold, I am totally marked because Dr. Lindy finally fucked my ass. Huzzah."

"Did you eat my ice cream when I wasn't looking?"

"If you mean am I wired with sugar, no. This is normal for me. I'm a night owl."

"Awesome." He wrapped both arms around me. I discovered I didn't hate it. "You be the one to tell Mrs. King why I can't do her poodle puppy's surgery in the morning."

He squeezed me. "I'll tell her you drank from the fountain of youth and you're still recovering."

"You really are a goddamn brat." Though even my lips could barely move, it was enough to hide my laughter. Beck tucked his face into my neck, and before long, his chest rose and fell slowly. Evenly.

Beck fell asleep, and I followed him into dreamland gripped by the worry I might follow him anywhere. Everywhere. And that once there, I'd find myself alone and lost. Forever.

It changed nothing. Wherever this took me—us—I wanted to go.

CHAPTER FOURTEEN

My alarm went off at the usual time. I blinked slowly awake only to discover I was alone in bed. My first emotional stop was confusion but, as if I were running bases in the worst sandlot game ever, I rounded the corner to disappointment and waved myself on to despair.

I rose and put on a robe before padding out to see if Beck might still be around. He'd made coffee, which was pretty handy. He sat on my redwood patio table watching Callie sniff around the bushes in the still damp, misty garden. He had on my boots, one of my best dress shirts, and my cashmere scarf. Nothing else. He held a mug of coffee. I got myself a cup and joined him.

He resembled an elven prince in the chill air. Cool and a little bit frightening. But maybe all I feared was how I felt about him. I kissed him on the neck and enjoyed the little shiver he gave when he turned to meet my lips. The kiss stirred my senses, and my cock thickened in anticipation.

"I just found another new kink," I said.

"What's that?"

"You wearing my clothes."

"That's good, because I like them." He held the mug to the side to give me the full view. "I make them look good."

"Aren't you cold?"

"Little bit, but it's so nice out here. You can hear the waves."

"C'mon inside. I'll make you breakfast, but then I have to get ready for work."

"Okay. What can I do to help?" He followed me in and watched me start oatmeal. I kept hard-boiled eggs in the fridge and precut fruit. I opened the container, found the most delicious looking strawberry, and held it out for Beck.

He smiled and bit into it so juice dripped over his lush lower lip. He tilted his head toward me, inviting me to take the other half. Our lips met around the fruit, and when we pulled away, I was fully erect again.

He blushed. "That was hot."

"Mm." I kissed him again. "You're going to kill me."

I had to turn my attention to the oatmeal because I didn't want to scrape it off the stove. "I don't have food for Callie, but you can tide her over with a hard-boiled egg."

"I fed her. I always keep enough kibble in my pack for emergencies."

"But not a change of clothes?"

Flushing, he glanced away. "I wanted to wear something of yours."

I wanted to say that he could, any time, but in the cold light of day, I wondered what the hell I thought I was doing here. I didn't really date.

Last night, it seemed utterly impossible that someone like Beck could even want anything more than a night or two with someone like me. I put his lack of restraint down to the mutual scratching of a chemical itch.

But now…now I wondered what it all meant. I liked him. I wanted to feed him, fuck him, let him wear my clothes. I wanted what we had that morning—his smile when he turned and saw me—every morning.

"What are you thinking right now," he asked.

"Me?" I startled guiltily.

He gave me a sarcastic slow blink of the eyes. "Yes, out of all the people here, I meant you."

I turned my attention back to the oatmeal. "Do you like cinnamon and dried fruit?"

"Yes." Beck moved across the room and uncovered Rico's cage. "Hello, pretty bird."

Rico chattered amiably.

"Does Rico need anything?"

"You can give him a bit of fruit if you want. He likes melon."

"Can I take him out?"

"Sure." Could I be that lucky? Was he going to let it go?

"Now that you've had a chance to relax. About that look on your face..."

Uh-oh. "What look?"

"Like you were trying to decide how best to get rid of me."

I pulled the oatmeal off the fire. "That's not—"

"Oh, please." The words were almost amiable. "Get over yourself. I liked what we did. I like wearing your clothes. You can feed me anytime. Don't get any ideas, though. You're my dad's age."

My mouth dropped open. Outrage didn't begin to cover it. "You said—"

"Gotcha. I'm hungry." Beck grinned at me. With Rico on his shoulder, he took a seat at the counter. "Whatcha gonna do about it?"

Minx. I got bowls and ladled oatmeal into them. I sat down beside him and picked up a spoon.

"This is super hot. You'll have to blow on it."

"I thought of something else I can blow while we're waiting

for it to cool." He slipped off the stool like an otter and sank to his knees.

"Oh Christ."

He parted the fabric of my robe and hummed while he took me in hand. "I didn't get a very good look at your dick last night."

"Thoughts?" He licked the spot that sinks my battleship. "Oh shit."

When he wrapped his lips around me, he lowered the stool. It stopped at the perfect height for him to take me so deep his nose nuzzled my pubic hair. He hummed, and the vibration of his throat made my whole body tighten.

"Not gonna last," I warned. He slid wetly up and down my cock a few times, tongue tickling all the right places. He didn't let up until I yanked his hair. "Stop."

He pulled off, and in two twists of his hand, I came, spattering my shirt and scarf with ribbons of cum.

I stared at the ceiling, catching my breath. I was boneless. Wordless. I stayed that way with my mouth hanging open for far too long to look cool.

Eventually I cleared my throat. "Holy cow."

He slipped onto the barstool beside me. "That was pretty quick. Think my oatmeal had time to cool down?"

"Only one way to find out." I looked into his mirthful, sparkling eyes before scooping up a spoonful.

My God, I was done. Kill me now. I thought I could handle whatever Beck could dish out, but it turned out I was a fucking babe in the woods.

I'd followed the trail to his gingerbread house and stuffed myself with gumdrops and icing, and I didn't even care if he was trouble. I wanted him. I wanted all of him. Anything he had to give me.

"I need to go to work." I drank my last sip of coffee.

"You know where to find me." He smiled.

Yes, I thought. I'd find him at the edge of the known world. My edge, at least, with the wreckage of my ordinary life behind me. Was that a good thing or a disaster?

What happens now?

"WHAT THE HELL HAPPENED TO YOU?" Travis looked up from where he was feeding the kittens with Beck. To his credit, Beck didn't even blink. "Were you called out on an emergency?"

"No, nothing like that. I was up most of the night." *Let's see how expressionless you can stay now, brat.*

"Oh, shoot." Travis's concern for me grew. "For what it's worth, my mom says melatonin is a miracle."

I smiled at both of them. "Good idea."

April assisted me in the removal of Duke's benign tumor. He was going to be far more comfortable with it gone. Things went well, and he was able to go home with Mrs. King right away.

Fridays were half days. We accepted clients until two, and then spent the rest of the day cleaning, doing paperwork, and reviewing how the week went. I didn't anticipate anything difficult until a very sad tricycle versus cat collision required me to set fractures on both of the cat's hind legs late in the afternoon.

The cat in question had been terrified and uncooperative, and the tension was made worse by the inconsolable crying of both its owner and her little boy, Georgie, who'd accidentally run him over.

"You know," I told Georgie, "accidents happen to people and animals. They're called accidents because they're nobody's fault. Stripes knows you didn't mean to hurt him."

My words didn't seem to help. Probably nothing would until Stripes was back on four paws again. Georgie's mom and I talked things over, and we decided I should keep the cat overnight, but it was hard for them to leave without him.

"That was a tough one." Travis turned the sign to *Closed*. I shut the blinds. We both breathed a sigh of relief.

"Kids kill me." Stretching the knots out of my neck, I dragged off my lab coat. "I hope Stripes pulls through. He's a senior. He might not have been able to get out of the way fast enough because of it."

"He still has a few good years left in him."

"Let's hope so." I hadn't liked the amount of time it took him to come out of the anesthesia.

For Georgie's sake, I truly hoped for a good outcome.

Lena grabbed her purse and was ready to leave just as another call came in. She answered but held up a finger so I wouldn't leave. "Call for you Doc, line one. Your mom."

"I'll take it in my office. Have a good night." I sat at my desk as I answered, "Hi, Mom. Everything okay?"

"Of course, dear. Why?"

"How come you called me on the work line?"

"I left a message on your cell, but you never called back."

I checked my phone, and sure enough, I'd failed to turn it back on. "I was in surgery and left it off. Sorry. I'd have found your call eventually, you know."

"I know. I just didn't want to miss you before you left. How are you?"

My mom could be so weird. "Just fine. How are you doing?"

"Excellent. It's horribly hot here, though. The jet stream seems to be all wibbly wobbly these days. And before you blame my generation—"

"How's Dad?" When it came to climate change, it was better not to let her get wound up.

"He's doing very well. The good news is his doctor took him off the metformin. He doesn't need it anymore."

"That is great news."

"Apparently he's lost enough weight, and the exercise regimen is helping. His blood sugar has been very stable."

"Remind him that those two things are now his daily medicine, will you? If he stops doing them, he'll be right back in the same boat."

"I do. I'm quite the harpy these days. You wouldn't recognize me."

I wisely didn't agree with that. "Something up? I was planning on calling tomorrow morning like usual."

Though our Saturday ritual had started for my mother's peace of mind when I was in college, lately it had been more for mine. My parents weren't getting any younger. They would never ask for anything, even if their need was great. The calls were a little subterfuge where I listened to what they said and what they omitted, hoping to discover anything I really needed to know.

"No, no. I was just so excited I had to call. You'll never guess who I ran into last weekend."

"I can't imagine. Is this person about my age, successful, available, and gay?"

"How did you ever guess?"

I sighed. "Who is it?"

"Remmy Kendall's son, Dylan. You remember him? He's an orthodontist."

"I didn't know he was gay. Didn't we go to his wedding? There was a bride as I recall."

"Nobody knew until his divorce. He says even he didn't know."

"Right." I took people's word for things like that, but I didn't know how they missed it.

"Apparently it was an amicable split, and the children are over the moon about their mother's new husband. There's even a baby on the way."

"That doesn't sound awkward at all."

"My point is, Dylan lives in San Francisco now. And he drives down all the time to see Dana and the kids."

"Ah." I thought I knew where this was going.

"I told him you were right there in the middle of the coast. He's dying to see your clinic."

"Mother." I gathered my patience. "Please don't matchmake. There hasn't been one time when your victim didn't end up horribly disappointed."

"They're not my victims."

"Well, they're not *mine*. I don't give them any sort of false hope."

"How can hope be false? You won't want to play the field forever. You know you won't. Sooner or later you're going to want a partner. Someone to come home to. Someone to share your life."

"Not necessarily." Unbidden, the image of Beck's inky blue eyes popped into my mind. Oh shit.

"You say that now."

"Mother, I'm nearly forty."

"That's a couple of years away. A lot can happen in that time."

"I know what I want. There's no point in sending all these very nice men on a fool's errand."

"Oh, you are the most frustrating person."

"I am." I took after my mother. "Now, are you still planning to come up for the Fourth?"

"Yes, we're looking forward to it. It's so nice to watch the fireworks over the water."

"Let's hope they don't set the pier on fire this year."

"On the other hand, the Santo Ignacio Fire Department has some very fine-looking firefighters. Have you tried—"

"I'll tell Cam you said so."

"Do that. He is such a doll." Dad said something in the background, and she gave a low-voiced reply. "Dad wants to know how Rico is."

"Ornery. He still says, 'You ruin everything!'"

"Couldn't you at least get a dog?"

"I'm never home," I reminded her yet again. "A dog would die of loneliness."

"You could take him to work. Besides, I'm worried you'll die of loneliness."

"Mother."

She sighed audibly. "All right. We'll talk more next week. You're off the hook for tomorrow morning."

"All right. Take care. Love to you both."

"And if Dylan calls you, at least be nice. You can never have too many friends."

"I'll be a good boy, Mother."

"I know you will. Kiss, kiss. Love to Lena, Travis, and April from both of us."

"I'll tell them."

I hung up feeling slightly more existential dread than usual. I rested my face in my palms, eyes closed, and tried to shrug off the day.

My phone chimed. *Oh no. What now?*

Unknown: It's Friday. Pie day. Ready for your next lesson?

Me: You got a phone? How'd you get my number?

I added his contact info.

Beck: Truck stop bathroom wall. How do you think? Cooper and Shawn.

Beck: So? Strum, strum. Guitar's not going to play itself.

Me: I'm exhausted. I need to sleep. Somebody kept me up all night.

Beck: Sleep's overrated, Boomer.

Me: Say that to my face.

My office door opened with a squeak, and Beck stepped inside. "Sleep's overrated, Boomer."

My eyes blurred when I tried to focus. "What are you doing here?"

"April and I were feeding the kittens." He frowned and closed the door behind him. "Are you all right?"

"Oh, yeah." I sighed. "It has been a long, long day."

"I heard about the kid's cat. That sucks."

"Look, would you take a rain check for tonight? I really don't think I'm up to a guitar lesson." *Or anything else, actually.*

"No, I can see that. Go on home and get comfortable. If you want, I can pick up something for you to eat, then get out of your hair."

"No, I don't want you to go to any trouble."

"But Doc, we both have to eat."

"Okay. In that case, I'd love to have dinner with you." My brain came back online. "Wait—it's silly for you to get food on foot when I have my car. I'll order online, and we can pick up dinner on the way. What do you like?"

"You really don't need to—"

"I always get one of Yasha's cottage pies and a Caesar salad."

He ran light fingers up my arm. "If you're sure you don't mind."

"I wouldn't have offered if I minded."

"All right. Thank you. I'll have the same."

"Good." I made the order. "I just need to look in on Stripes, and then we can go."

When I opened the door, I found Callie waiting patiently outside my office.

"Madame, how do you do?" Callie's ears perked up, and Beck chuckled. "You two can head to the waiting room. I'll be out in a minute."

"All right." He took off with Callie, and I stepped inside the kennel room where April was checking on Stripes's progress. "How's he doing?"

"He's subdued. I really thought he'd be fussier by now."

"Is he interested in food at all?" I checked my notes and Travis's addendums.

She shook her head. "Not yet."

"Give him his pain meds at eleven. I'll check back at

126

midnight." I put my hand into the cage and stroked his fur. Stripes simply stared, eyes groggy.

I feel you, Stripes. It's the years and the mileage.

"Maybe a little wet food on your finger will make him realize he's hungry?"

"I'll try it."

"I'm heading out, but call if you need anything."

"Pie night?" she asked. "What are you getting?"

"I thought I'd depart from tradition and have chocolate mousse."

"I see we're living on the edge these days."

"You could say that." *The edge of the known world.*

I picked Beck up in the waiting room and we walked to my car.

He glanced at me hopefully. "I could drive if you're too tired."

"I'm not too tired for that."

He snickered. "I'm sorry I kept you up all night."

"I'm not. But there wasn't enough coffee in the world for me today."

"You can make it an early night."

"You're very kind." I gave his arm a nudge. "Thank you."

I found a space at the curb in front of Café Bêtise. I'd paid for our order online, so Beck ran inside and was back before too long. He slid in beside me carrying a large brown paper shopping bag that smelled divine.

"That place is amazing," Beck said appreciatively. "I wanted everything in the bakery case."

"Yasha's the pastry chef. He's tremendously talented. St. Nacho's is very lucky to have him."

"So, it's pie night, but you got chocolate mousse. Doesn't that ruin the spirit of the thing?"

"No, because I got cottage pie."

"What even is *cottage pie?*"

"It's like shepherd's pie, only beef."

"I thought shepherd's pie *was* beef. That's how my mom always made it."

"That's a common misconception. Shepherd's pie is made with mutton. That's why it's called shepherd's pie."

"That's…weird." He turned to me. "Aren't shepherds there to keep sheep safe?"

"Ever heard of a cowboy steak?"

He rolled his eyes. "Yeah, but I thought those were made from *cowboys*."

"Ha, ha." I turned down my street and immediately noticed there was already a car in my driveway. "Oh bother. I really hope that's not what I think it is."

"What?"

"God, I am so tired." The man sitting in one of the wicker chairs on my front porch looked suspiciously like Dylan Kendall. What little I remembered of him. "And I would have gotten away with it if it weren't for my meddlesome mother."

"What's happening right now?" Beck asked warily.

"Oh my God. You don't want to know." No wonder my mother called me at the office today instead of waiting until morning. She knew Dylan was coming. Wait until I talked to her next.

And *of course* I was with last night's hookup, planning some kind of living room picnic.

This was all my fault for deviating from my self-imposed rules, which were there for a reason, goddamnit. A good reason. The best reason. It was so I would never put that look of disappointment on anyone's face ever again.

"Look, I'm really sorry about this. I think I need to ask for a rain check again. You can take the food."

"So, I guess you have a date? No big deal."

"It's not a date. My mother—"

"It's okay for you to have plans, Doc. I know old people are forgetful." Was he teasing me?"

"I didn't have plans. I had no idea this was happening."

"Oh my God. Don't have a cow. You know this is why people my age don't date, right?" Beck unlatched the door and stepped out. Callie squeezed between the front seats and jumped down to join him. "Whatever this is, it's not my circus."

I picked up the Café Bêtise bag. "Beck, here. At least take—"

"No, you need your food. You have company." He made a circling motion that encompassed me, the food, and the man on the porch. That little shit. He was *enjoying* this. "It's okay, Doc, but this is all you. You've got this. I believe in you."

He blew me a kiss, closed the door behind him, and strode away with Callie at his heels.

"Shit." I wanted to bang my head on the steering wheel for a while.

Instead, I stepped out and dragged the bag of food to the porch.

"Sorry." Dylan's confusion had turned to irritation as he watched Beck and Callie saunter up the street. "Did I interrupt something?"

"My guitar lesson," I lied. "Mom didn't know."

This mollified him. "Your mother's such a peach. I couldn't believe it when she told me you moved here. She said it was a midlife crisis."

"No, I think that only started recently." *How long before I can throw you out and go to bed?*

Because I could not wait to do just that.

CHAPTER FIFTEEN

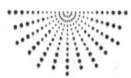

My EVENING BECAME MORE uncomfortable from there.

Not because I was so invested in having dinner with Beck and then falling into bed alone. But having to entertain a virtual stranger—sent by my mother, no less—made the ball of fatigue in my belly tighten to anger.

"You didn't know I was coming," he said flatly as I unlocked the door.

"No, I'm sorry. My mother only called a few minutes ago to broach the idea, and she never said—"

"Oh God. I'm mortified."

"No, don't be. We're all playthings on Mom's game board. Can I interest you in some dinner?"

"What about..." He glanced toward the street where Beck had disappeared around the corner. "That really looked like a date I interrupted."

"We were going to have dinner tonight, and he's teaching me guitar." Not a lie, but also not the truth. The least important fact about Beck was *he taught me a few guitar chords.*

"I'm so sorry for disrupting your plans."

"Never mind. I have enough food for two. Are you hungry?"

"Yes, thank you. The drive down the coast took longer than I thought."

He preceded me into the kitchen. That's when I noticed he had a bottle of wine.

"I brought this for you, uh..." He flushed. "Now it seems a little forward, me coming here like this. Are you certain—"

"It's good to see you after all these years, Dylan. Make yourself comfortable while I change. You can do the honors if you like. Corkscrew's in the drawer next to the stove."

I left him to open the wine while I hopped into the shower and rinsed off the day. After I toweled off, I put on jeans and a button-down and joined him. He was standing in the hallway, examining the pictures on the wall.

"This is how I remember you." He pointed out a picture of me and a man I dated briefly with our arms around each other. That was college. "You haven't changed at all."

"Liar. But thanks." I looked him over. "You look fit."

He shrugged. "Thank you. The kids keep me young."

"Is that what it is? I should have tried it." For some reason, that made me think of Rico, so I went to his cage. "Boop."

"Boop." Rico sidled over so he could hop onto my wrist.

"Hey, pretty boy. How's things?"

"Boop."

"We've got a guest, Rico. Meet Dylan." I turned to introduce Rico, but one look at Dylan's horrified face stopped me.

"Oh my God, you have a bird. Your mom didn't say."

I backed away slowly. "Probably didn't cross her mind. Rico's harmless. He's well trained. Just don't reach out for him."

"No chance of that. He's...a bird."

"That's right," I gave Dylan the same talk as when I took Rico to visit the elementary school. "He's a cockatiel. Nymphicus hollandicus. They're native to Australia."

"But he's a *bird*." Very astute was our Dylan.

"Yes. He is a bird. I keep his wings clipped so he doesn't fly.

He's used to that because he's had his wings clipped since he was a chick."

"That's awful, keeping him from flying."

"Well, since he was born and raised in captivity, it's a lot better than what would happen to him if he flew out the window and got lost."

Rico ruffled his feathers. "Hello, gorgeous."

Dylan shivered, visibly pale now.

"Dylan, are you afraid of birds?" Because while I'd never met anyone who didn't like Rico, I'd seen enough adults behave this way around snakes and tarantulas to know the signs of a phobia.

"No. Well, maybe." He clung to the wall as far away from us as he could get. "They're feathered dinosaurs with Jurassic looking talons and sharp little beaks."

"Okaaay." I silently apologized to Rico by stroking his breast before putting him back in his cage. "He's back inside the cage. No problem."

"It's not that I don't like the *idea* of birds. Outside. Flying around."

"Just the face-to-beak interaction?" If he said some of his best friends were birds…

"In trees or something they're fine. At the park. Except pigeons. I can't do pigeons ever."

"I apologize for assuming. Most people really enjoy the chance to interact with him. He's the perfect pet for me because I don't have a lot of time to spend at home. His mirror keeps him company while I'm at work. He adores looking at himself."

"You ruin *everything*!"

"What?" Dylan jumped. "Was he talking to me?"

"No. My ex used to tell me that. He just likes to remind me." I bit my lip to keep from laughing. "He doesn't know what he's saying. He's just a mimic."

"You ruin everything!"

Dylan scowled. "Because it really did sound like he was talking about me."

"He's not conversant in English. He's a parrot." I called, "Boop."

"Boop." Rico ruffled his feathers again.

Dylan shivered.

"So, dinner? I picked up food from Café Bêtise. It's pretty delicious." I went to the table where I'd left the bag and started pulling out the containers. "I got cottage pie. Do you like it?"

"Well..."

"There's Caesar salad, and this"—I held the smaller bag out —"is the holy grail. Chocolate mousse. Yasha pipes it into a hollowed out orange half with the pith carefully removed so all you get is a burst of orange zest. So, so delicious."

"I am going to be the worst date you've ever..." Dylan trailed off, mouth half-open. He snapped his lips together and glanced away.

"What?"

"I'm, um, vegan."

"You're from Vegas?" I asked in jest.

"San Diego. You know that. We're *vegans*. My wife and I both stopped eating meat because the girls wouldn't, and it just—"

Understanding dawned. "You can't eat a single thing here, can you?"

"It sounds delicious. Really. But yeah. No. Nothing." He grinned winningly. "Seriously, though. You should try going vegan. I feel a thousand times more vibrant. More strength, more stamina, better digestion. Better sex...Have you ever considered it?"

"I haven't really." Not even for a single second.

"Oh, you should. There are so many wonderful vegan recipes you'd never even miss meat."

"I do meatless Mondays sometimes, but going vegan doesn't sound like my kind of thing."

"That surprises me." And disappointed him too judging by the look on his face. That was probably a speed record for me. "I'd have thought you of all people—someone who has dedicated their life to caring for animals—wouldn't go around eating them."

"I'll just see if there's anything you can eat in the fridge." I turned and opened the refrigerator door.

Not looking at him gave me time to think. Fortunately, he'd left a glass of wine for me on the counter. I was going to need it. In the fridge, I found some fruit and hard-boiled eggs. Nope. Eggs were on the no-fly list, so I put them back.

Dylan closed the distance between us. "I really don't want you to go to any trouble for me."

"It's no trouble at all. I have fruit and lettuce and"—I opened the freezer—"Thai vegetable gyoza from Trader Joe's. Can you have that?"

"Ooh, sounds delicious. Let me read the label." He took his time. "This is perfect. Thank you. If you hand me a frying pan, I'll make it myself. Go eat your dinner."

"Are you sure?"

He nodded happily. "Of course. You have a lovely kitchen."

"Thanks. Long day on my part."

I got him what he needed, took my wine, and sat at the counter.

"So, my mother said she thought we'd hit it off, but I don't really do long distance relationships." Or any relationships.

"Well, she's a doll. She was so understanding about the divorce. Wanted to know all about how my girls are doing."

"Your girls? How many kids do you have?"

"I have three daughters, Emily, Andrea, and Dylanne with two *n*'s and an *e*. She's the baby. But I call them all *the girls*—my ex, Dana, included. My girls."

"That's nice you can still have such a good relationship."

"Yeah. I'm lucky. I probably don't deserve it, but I am."

"Mom said Dana remarried?"

"Oh yes. Her yoga instructor. He's wonderful with my girls. It's a shame he isn't poly. We could live as one big happy family."

Yeah. If having a relationship was beyond me, having one with multiple partners scared me as much as Rico scared him. I guessed I was not a good fit here.

"What my mom doesn't seem to understand," I broached the uncomfortable subject, "is that I'm not interested in a relationship. At all."

He waved that off. "She said you think that, but you just haven't found the right man yet."

"Um. No, actually—"

"It's okay. It's like being vegan. Everything has it's time. When you're ready, you'll be ready. There's no point in pushing yourself into a relationship until it's right."

He poured a small amount of water into the pan and lidded it. Steam built beneath the clear glass lid just as it was building inside me. At least he knew how to make pot stickers.

"As long as you understand that nothing is going to happen here." I truly wasn't even interested in a one-night stand.

"Really? Nothing?" He picked up his glass and stalked over to join me at the counter. "Are you so sure already?"

I was sure that to anyone else, the move would have seemed sexy and a little sweet. I put down my glass, curious to see what he planned to do. After the night before, with Beck, there was nothing he could do to interest me, but I let him wrap his hand around my neck and draw me in for a kiss because...because I was afraid Beck had ruined me for anyone else.

I was right. Beck had obliterated me.

Dylan was a good kisser. Not spectacular. His reaction to Rico may have colored my perception of him. His kiss tasted like the delicate shudders I'd seen him give every time he glanced in the direction of Rico's cage. Also, I hated his reaction to my cottage pie, which he very discreetly pushed out of smelling distance.

"Yeah," I said. "No. I'm sorry. I've had a terrible day after a rough night." He didn't know the half of it. "I really just want to go to bed."

"That can be—"

"Alone."

Dylan's eyes lost their sparkle, but it hadn't seemed sincere anyway. Not like Beck's, which came from all the light he carried inside him.

"All right." Dylan sighed. "I had to try. You're a catch, Doctor Davies."

"I'm not, though. I'm happily single. I'd chew my leg off to get away from a relationship right now if it became necessary." I hoped it wasn't, or that maybe Beck hadn't noticed my inconvenient *feelings,* and it wouldn't become necessary for him to chew his leg off.

Dylan went back to the stove. "My pot stickers are probably done."

AT MIDNIGHT, I called April at the office. In the background I could hear the kittens mewling. She must have been feeding them.

"How is he?" I asked after Stripes.

"Better. He's awake and alert now. Curious about the kittens."

"Eating?"

"He nibbled a little food off my fingers."

"Glad to hear it. It would kill me to have to tell Georgie his pet died because of their crash."

"You old softie. Me too. Go back to sleep. I've got it covered."

I blew out a breath. "I doubt I'll be able to sleep. I have a guest."

"Really? Who? I saw you leave with Beck—oh my God—"

"It's not Beck. My mother set me up with someone I used to know, and things just—" Irritation bled into my voice. "He said he was too tipsy to drive. He's in the guest room."

"Oh. It went bust, huh? That's what you get for letting your mother set you up."

"I didn't let her. She called before I left work to tell me she'd met someone we used to know, and I found him on my doorstep when I got home."

She giggled. "Your mom is a hoot."

"Her motto is better to apologize than ask permission."

I heard more kitten mewling. "I guess."

"Anyway, I imagine he'll be expecting breakfast. I have barely anything here." My mind immediately went to that morning— or was it yesterday—when I'd fed Beck spoonfuls of hot spicy oatmeal and berries by hand. "I'll take Dylan to Bistro. Expect me at around eight thirty tomorrow unless something goes south. If you need me for anything, call."

"Get some rest, Lindy. You really looked awful today."

"Thank you so much for that observation." I might have looked awful, but I had felt infinitely better than I did now with Dylan in the next room. I certainly felt happier. "Night, April."

"Night."

THE NEXT MORNING AT BISTRO, Dylan perused the menu for vegan items while I drank my first two cups of coffee. Fortunately, Bistro had several good choices for him.

I ordered a French toast combo with eggs and hash browns and plump homemade chicken-and-apple sausages. Dylan ordered the Mediterranean tofu scramble with dry toast and fresh fruit. Yum.

Jeremy, the perennially smiling waiter whose table I always hoped to be seated at came by wearing a name tag that said "Jeff." Had I gotten his name wrong? Wow. Usually I did better than that with names and faces. *Jeff* brought the check. Dylan's meatless meal cost more than mine. Not that I *noticed* as Rico would say.

It was bittersweet saying goodbye to him. On the one hand, my relief was absolutely palpable. On the other, once again, I was made aware of what an absolute asshole I was sometimes. Anyone would want to date Dylan, wouldn't they? He was handsome, bright, charming. Willing to cook his own meal, which was an obvious bonus since he wouldn't be super easy to feed unless I turned vegan too. And okay, there was definitely nothing wrong with being vegan. Vegans were helping a world dying of several preventable diseases and might be mitigating climate change one uneaten methane producer at a time.

Dylan had a good career and managed a great family life, even through divorce.

There was nothing wrong with him.

I simply didn't want him or anyone like him. I didn't *need* him or anyone like him cluttering up an already good life, making demands on my time, waiting for me to realize I'd wanted to be vegan all along. He bored me to death. *Dating* bored me to death.

Plus, he had the great misfortune of not being Beck. *Aw, shit.*

We said goodbye with a kiss in the parking lot. He went all in, I thought, maybe trying to ignite hidden physical chemistry. There could have been some. *Might* have been, but if so, it barely registered. I felt nothing for Dylan, and I wanted to put it down to being satisfied with my life. I wasn't twenty anymore after all. But that wasn't it.

Beck had destroyed the fun of fucking guys I barely liked.

Okay. Well. Work beckoned. I had to find out how Stripes was doing.

Dylan got into his BMW and backed out of the space, waving to me as he left the parking lot. Jeff exited Bistro's back door with a bag of trash, which he jettisoned into the dumpster near the alley.

He wiped his hands on his jeans as he walked toward me.

"He was hot," he acknowledged. "But I don't trust vegans."

"Why?" I asked. "You know they won't kill you for food, anyway."

"But they might kill you over food," he pointed out. "God forbid you forget gelatin is a no-no or you make the hash browns in the same pan you use for the sausage. Beatrice, my roommate, is a vegan. She's mean as a feral cat when dinner's late."

"That sounds like stereotyping."

"Nah, the word hangry was invented for Bea. My advice? Keep a ripe avocado on you at all times. Keep two, one in the house, one in the car. And hide your last avocado for when the worst happens."

"Word." You had to love Jeremy/Jeff. If I was interested in younger men, I might have hit that like the fist of an angry god. Wait…oh my God. What the fuck was wrong with me? I was only interested in one younger man, and now I had to see him after blowing him off for some guy my mother tried to hook me up with.

How was I ever going to face Beck?

CHAPTER SIXTEEN

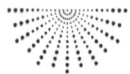

I ENTERED my clinic through the back door and slunk down the hall to my office. It felt more like a walk of shame than anything I'd done in years, but why? I had disappointed yet another man, but that man was Dylan, not Beck.

Beck had left in an awful hurry the night before, but he'd been laughing at me at the time.

Lena poked her head into the office. "You've got a walk-in. Lab might need some stitches."

"I'm on my way." I knocked ashes off an imaginary cigar. "Just let me get my Lab coat."

She glared. "You make that joke every damn time."

"Because it's a jewel, and I have so little in my life that amuses me." I slipped into said lab coat and, as nonchalantly as I could, asked, "Did Beck come in this morning to feed the kittens?"

She nodded. "He and Travis are back there now. Do you need him for something?"

"Not now. How's Stripes doing?"

"April said he looked good when she left."

"Good. I'll check on him and call his family when I get done with the Lab."

The morning went quickly after that. I saw Beck in passing, but he left while I was suturing Jake the yellow Lab, who had gotten the worst of a collision with a broken fence. He was going to be just fine, and he'd have a snazzy scar to show off to all the lady Labs.

Later on, Georgie and his mom picked up Stripes. Despite two awkward casts, he seemed to be doing well. As she left, Georgie's mother mouthed, "Thank you."

"My pleasure." I did love my job and not only because I made a good living. Reuniting Stripes and Georgie made my day in a way no amount of money could.

After they left, I slipped Stripes's chart into the stack for Lena to file, then turned to find Travis staring at me with an odd expression on his face.

"What?"

"Your mother sent someone to your house?"

I gave him a nod as we walked to the staff room. "It was a total shitshow. Did Beck tell you about it?"

"He said he went there for pie night, and the dude was just sitting on your porch."

I took off my lab coat and went behind the curtain to change my scrubs. "He was. And you know what? Dude's deathly afraid of birds. He called Rico a feathery dinosaur. I had to talk him off the ledge."

"No."

"And there was Rico, squawking, 'You ruin everything!' Dylan actually took it personally."

"I'd pay good money to see a cage match between Rico and any of your hookups."

"It wasn't a hookup. Mom set me up."

"So why was his car still in your driveway this morning?"

"You saw that?" I got tangled awkwardly in my undershirt.

Travis helped me out and handed me a clean shirt. "I picked Beck up on the way to work. We both saw. That's when he told me about your 'date.'"

"Great." Oh my God. Did Beck think Dylan and I slept together?

"Your mother's hilarious, but she's not going to stop until she has you married off."

"She warned me he might call, but I had no idea he'd be at my house."

"Was he at least a good fuck?"

"How should I know? He used the guest bedroom."

"You're shitting me." He widened his eyes. "Beck said he was hot. Don't tell me you turned down a perfectly good man?"

"I don't just fuck everything that moves, Travis. He wasn't my type."

"Since when do you have a type? Besides temporary, I mean."

I stopped in the act of washing my hands. "Do I really give that impression?"

"That's the impression I get. You're the guy everyone calls if they've got a friend in from out of town for a weekend. Haven't you noticed no one ever tries to set you up with anybody local? I just figured you were the one-and-done type."

"I am."

"So what was wrong with the guy your mom sent?"

"You said it. My mother sent him. You know she'd never let it go if she thought there was any chance between us. Believe me, there wasn't."

I gave him dinner, such as it was, and a bed for the night. I handed him a stack of clean towels, bought him breakfast, and walked away. I couldn't make oatmeal for him because then all I'd think about was feeding it to Beck.

"What's wrong?" Travis asked. "You look like you forgot to turn the oven off."

"It's nothing. Just wondering how to tell my mother to quit her fucking matchmaking."

"She loves you. Let her have her fun."

"But her timing was perfectly awful. I have to call her now and disappoint her. If Beck comes back in at lunchtime, can you have him come into the office?"

"Sure." He grinned. "Guitar lessons, huh?"

"I am so shit at it."

"Well, he's pretty patient. Maybe he'll be able to teach your ancient ass a couple songs."

I tossed a damp paper towel his way. "I'll show you an ancient ass."

"Whoa, not my type, Doc." He lifted both hands. "Don't know why I keep having to tell you that. Is this what they mean by harassment?"

"Oh God. I'm sorry." I felt sick. "Did it sound like it?"

"No. I was totally kidding."

"But—"

"Shut up, Doc. Go call your mom."

I called Mom from my office while Travis got the exam room ready for the next patient. I was kind of glad he wasn't my type either. We worked well together. The last thing I wanted to do was screw that up too.

THE PHONE RANG TWICE before my mother picked up.

"Sweetheart. So nice to hear from you. What's new?"

"Mom. Couldn't you have said Dylan was going to be waiting on my porch when I got home from work?"

"Well, how would I know such a thing?"

"He said you told him to stop by."

"I didn't say when." She sniffed. "He's a very handsome man, isn't he?"

"Yes, he's very good looking." If you didn't mind that he stole Tony Robbins's outsized smile.

"And he's got a very successful practice. You two would make such a cute couple. Did he tell you about his girls?"

"Yes, he did. Mom, I told you. I'm not looking to be part of a couple. I don't have time for that."

"And I told you, you'll make time when you find the right man."

I sighed and glanced at the ceiling. There was no winning with my mother. She was absolutely certain she knew what was best for me, and she was not going to give up.

"If you're going to send guys my way, could you please make certain I don't have plans for the evening?"

"You had plans?" She latched onto that idea too quickly. "Is he nice? How long have you been seeing him? Will you introduce us to him when we come up for the Fourth?"

"It's not like that." I had to slow her roll. "I have guitar lessons on Friday nights now. I had dinner planned with my guitar instructor, and then I was going to turn in early. Yesterday was hard. I was worried about this cat named Stripes."

"I'm sorry the timing was bad." She really sounded sorry.

"I just wish you wouldn't try to spring things on me. My life is busy. I have routines that I really like. I don't want surprises."

"But, darling, sometimes surprises are wonderful." She never listened. "And besides, I honestly had no idea he'd just present himself like that. It does seem rather desperate, doesn't it? Of course, he said he had a little crush back in the day."

"It was excruciating. Please don't do that to me again."

She hesitated. I could hear her gears whirring. "In future, I'll only give out your number, not your address or any other identifying information. I promise."

"That's gonna have to do, I guess."

"I love you, sweetheart. You're my favorite."

"You too, Mom."

"I heard that." In the background, Dad said, "You told me I was your favorite."

"I'm sorry, but today it's Lindy."

"You'll be my favorite parent if you keep Mom's match-making in check."

"Will do."

Mom said, "Oh, hush, Doug" before she hung up the phone.

I loved my parents. I missed them. But I wondered if my move to St. Nacho's wasn't the thing that kept us from killing one another.

A tap on the door made my belly clench. "Come in."

Beck poked his head inside. "Travis said you wanted to see me?"

"Oh, yeah. Sit down." I straightened papers on my desk unnecessarily. Beck took the chair opposite mine and slouched in it with an insouciance I worried was a front.

"I wanted to apologize for the way I handled last night."

His eyebrows rose. "What about it?"

"Well, I promised you dinner."

"No worries. I ate. We can catch the lesson some other time."

"I guess what I mean to say is, we didn't get much of a chance to talk about what happened between us, and then the very next night, there was a man on my porch—"

"That wasn't your fault. What'd you tell your mom?"

"I told her to knock it off with the matchmaking. I guess she didn't know he'd drive down like that."

"Guess not." He glanced around and saw the mini fridge. "Do you have a water in there? I'm parched."

I said he could take whatever he liked. He tore the cap off a bottled water and drank half down. The slim column of his throat worked, and he thumbed stray drops off his lips before he took another breath.

"Thank you. Was that all?" he asked.

"Well, I guess we should talk about...things, don't you think?"

Confusion showed in his lifted brows. "What things?"

"Um, I guess we should start with the fact that I had a really good time with you the other night."

"Oh." He smiled. "Me too."

"And while it was amazing, it's not really something I do. Or rather, I have these pretty strict rules about how I do them."

"Like, bondage rules? Safe, sane, and consensual? Should you have given me a safeword?" His expression showed only polite interest as he took another sip of his water. "Maybe I should have said. I use red."

"No. That's—" I raked my hand through my hair. "I don't want you to think I just blew you off for another guy."

"Whatever," he said. "You didn't know he was coming, and your mom sent him, so you couldn't just tell him to leave."

This was not going the way I expected it to at all.

I gathered my patience and tried again. "I want you to know that what you and I did was wonderful—"

"Oh, man. I was hoping this wasn't going to turn into a thing." Beck stared at his hands. "Because as nice as you are, I'm totally not the type to latch on after one good night. I mean, it's nothing personal or anything."

"Thank heavens," I said through clenched teeth. "We're on the same page then."

Beck wiped imaginary sweat from his brow. "Phew."

"But I still want you to know nothing happened between me and Dylan."

"Oh, shoot. Wasn't he into you? Was it the age thing? I thought he looked younger."

"No, he was totally into me. I said no."

"Wait. Travis and I saw his car this morning. Did he totally friend zone you and still stay the night? Brrr. That's so cold."

"It wasn't actually like that."

"It must have been so embarrassing getting turned down like that. I won't tell anyone. I promise." Beck lip-zipped and threw away an imaginary key. I caught that twinkle in his eyes with a sigh. "I hope he at least liked my dinner. You owe me, by the way."

"He's vegan. He couldn't eat any of it. If you want it, it's still in the fridge."

"I could eat," he glanced at his phone. "What time?"

What just happened here? "I'll be done here around three."

"Great. I've got some dogs to walk—paying clients—but I'll meet you at your place at four." He stood. "I wrote out some new songs for you to practice. I figured the Beatles would be good. They're from your generation, right?"

I sagged. "Thank you."

"And don't worry." Beck held onto the doorjamb as he turned back. "You'll get to an age where your mom gives up on trying to find you a man soon enough. Enjoy her meddling while it lasts."

He left the room and closed the door quietly behind him.

I may have thrown a thick stack of Post-it notes at the place where his head had been.

CHAPTER SEVENTEEN

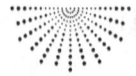

THIS TIME when I made it home, there were no cars in the drive and no men waiting on the porch.

No Beck either, although I'd had a last-minute walk-in and stayed to talk to Travis and Lena for a few minutes.

I picked up my mail, let myself inside, and freed Rico to make up for the night before when he'd had to stay in lockup.

"Hello, gorgeous," I said.

"Boop."

I strolled into the kitchen and opened a beer. "Boop."

"Boop."

I sorted my mail and threw away the junk before opening my guitar case and settling down to practice. Rico was still a little suspicious of all the new sounds. He decided to hop off my shoulder and edge along the back of the couch to get away while I played.

"Everybody's a critic." I wondered if I could get him to echo that. "Say it, Rico. *Everybody's a critic.*"

"Not that you *noticed.*"

We'd have to work on that.

I did spider exercises until my hand cramped. Four came and

went, and I dutifully continued practicing. At four thirty, there was a knock on the door.

I left Rico to eye the instrument while I went to answer it.

"I heard you. Not bad."

"'For Twinkle, Twinkle, Little Star.'"

Beck and Callie came inside. He held his arm out for Rico, who sidled up it and perched on his shoulder. "Everybody's got to—"

"Start somewhere. I know." I wiped my hands on my jeans. "Are you hungry?"

He strolled over and picked up a few seeds for Rico. "I am, yes. I just walked about four miles. I could really use some water."

"I have iced tea too."

"Water's fine."

I got him a bottled water and took the previous nights' takeout from the refrigerator to heat it while he sat at the counter. "I guess you can start with the salad."

He took it and the fork I gave him and dug in. "Mm. Why couldn't your guy last night eat this?"

"First, he's not my guy—"

"Figure of speech." Beck waved his fork.

"Caesar dressing has anchovies and eggs usually."

"Really? You can't taste them."

"The anchovy is mostly for the salt and umami and the egg gives it a creamy richness. My guess is Bistro makes theirs fresh, which means raw egg yolk, so if you have any immunity issues—"

"I don't."

I hesitated. "When was the last time you were tested?"

He glanced down at his plate where he stirred the lettuce around. "Before I left home."

"Maybe it'd be a good idea. There's a clinic here in town."

"I will." He speared a crouton and popped it into his mouth. "I've been thinking about doing it anyway."

I debated offering him money to expedite that, but it was truly none of my business. If he asked, I'd help out, but offering seemed like I was trying to line up future fucks when I absolutely positively wasn't. Even though watching him chew still made my dick tighten.

For the first time in my life, I wished I had someone to talk to about sex. I mean, could you really reach my advanced age without realizing that feeding someone by hand was your bulletproof turn-on?

No rationalization I could come up with made me want to feed Beck any less. No personal shame over perving on someone his age made me want *him* any less.

Comparing him to Dylan was so unfair, but Beck came out the winner every time. I enjoyed his company. I loved his body. And I didn't feel required to prove myself to him.

Was that it? Was our obvious inequality driving this bus?

Did that make me a total douche canoe?

"What?" He glanced at me, and God, his eyes made my heart squeeze.

"Did I say—"

"Yes." He studied me. "Why are you a douche canoe?"

"I should"—the microwave timer beeped—"just get that cottage pie."

I picked up oven mitts and pulled the steaming container from the microwave while I got my head in the game. The other game.

"So you picked up some dog walking clients? Any one I know?"

"Do you know Mrs. Roberts's boxer, Claudius?"

"I do. He's a little skittish, but a total bro once you get to know him."

"Yeah. I like him. I also walk James Callum's standard poodle."

"Doctor Watson."

"Yeah. Callie really loves him."

"He's a smart boy. Poodles are typically intelligent, but he's really something."

"I'm going to go see some guy about a pair of bichon frises too. Their owners might need someone to house sit while they're on vacation."

"Do you mean Ajax's dogs?" He nodded. "Oh. They're new around here. You'll love their house. He and Dmytro live on the bluff. They have one of the best views in all of St. Nacho's."

"Awesome."

Don't ask, don't ask... "Does this mean you might stay around here for a while?"

He bit his lip. "I might."

"Oh." *Don't say it, don't say it...* "Then maybe getting a checkup might be a good idea. The clinic's nice. And if you stay around, you'll be here long enough to...collect the results and all."

"Boop," Rico said.

"Boop," I echoed automatically.

"Boop." Beck glanced at his cottage pie. "There's plenty for two here."

"I had a late lunch," I lied.

"Come on. Get a fork. I'll feel weird eating this with you just standing there."

"All right." I thought maybe I should *taste* it anyway. Make sure it was still good. That it was warm enough. I got a fork and sat beside him at the counter.

He waited until I took a bite, blew on it, and then ate it before he gathered his own bite.

It was even better than the night before—chopped beef in a thick gravy of garlic and onions and Worcestershire sauce topped with creamy garlicky mashed potatoes and parmesan cheese.

"Oh. Mm. That's amazing. Is it a special thing, or do they have it all the time?"

"They always have a variety of sweet and savory pies. Yasha uses locally sourced seasonal ingredients so they change from time to time." There was a reason Friday was pie night, and it sat right there between me and Beck.

It was good to share Bêtise with him. I was glad I wasn't able to share it with Dylan the night before.

He licked his lips. "I could eat this every night. It's so good."

"But then you'd never be able to eat their chicken pot pie or their empanadas."

"Oh God. That sounds good too. How do you even choose?"

"Sometimes I don't," I admitted. "Sometimes I order all of them."

"Really? How do you stay fit?"

"I freeze leftovers. And I inherited good genes."

He sat back, and Rico took the opportunity to hop from his shoulder to my arm. He scooted up and nipped at my ear.

"Boop."

"Rico is so great." Beck reached down to pet Callie, whose snout rested on his knee. "I never really considered what it'd be like to have a bird for a pet."

"I always wanted a bird companion, so when I got the chance to foster Rico, I took it."

"You fostered him?"

"Yeah, but after his owner went to prison, he became mine."

"Lucky you. How long do cockatiels live?"

"Some live upwards of twenty years. I hope Rico's one of those."

"Callie likes him too." Beck glanced at Rico. "Although I'm not so sure the feeling's mutual."

"Callie's calm enough. He'll get used to having her around. I mean…" I backtracked. "It's just guitar lessons. He's not fond of the guitar yet either."

Beck eyed me speculatively. "Right."

Maybe he'd have believed me if I hadn't scooped a forkful of food and held it out for him. He gave me a knowing smile as he opened his mouth. Good grief, I was in so much trouble.

"Mmm." He started swiveling on his chair. "I thought you might not want to do that anymore."

"I—I probably shouldn't."

"It's the age thing hanging you up, isn't it?"

"Not just that. There's an immense economic gap. I hold all the power here, and—"

"You really think so?" The little shit licked his lips.

"I hope I'm not taking advantage the way some men would."

"You think I can't spot them a mile away?"

"Yes, you probably can. But if you were with someone your own age, you could explore new experiences together. If you go back to school, there will be new friends and parties with people who understand what you're talking about when it comes to music and—"

"You really believe all that, don't you?"

"I do. Why not? I had boyfriends in college. I'm still friends with some of them."

He frowned. "Do you think I haven't had that opportunity?"

"You said you have. But honestly, hasn't your recent life been more about survival? Wasn't Tug about survival?"

"Tug was a mistake."

"He took advantage of your inexperience."

"No, he stole my shit. We took advantage of each other for other things."

I put the fork down. "I don't understand."

"Oh, I really think you do," he said ominously.

Nerves made my skin tingle. "Tell me what you mean by that."

"Tug liked looking after me. He dug it. I was his boy, right? And he took care of me."

Was he saying…"I thought you said it wasn't sexual between you."

"It doesn't have to be sexual. That's not what me and him were about." As he ran the fingers of both hands through his windblown hair, the little beads on his leather bracelets jingled. "He wanted someone to take care of, and I wanted someone to take care of me. It's not rocket science."

The memory of Beck eating from Tug's filthy hands was enough to make me sick with jealousy. I tried rejecting the emotions as irrational, but my stomach clenched with rage each time I thought about it.

"So when he got food for you…?" *When he fed you like I do…*

"He dug it, same as you." Beck's gaze fell to my hands. "I like when it's you better."

I placed my elbows on the counter and hid my face. "Why is that?"

"Because with you it's not about being in charge as much as it's about kindness. You're a very nice person."

"I'm really not." I had to move away from him, from this idea that I was kind when really I fed him because it lit me on fire.

I watched the freshening breeze whip the ornamental grasses outside the front window while Beck went into the kitchen and puttered. I heard the refrigerator open and close. I heard the water run, and then there was silence.

"This is really freaking you out, isn't it?" he asked from right beside me, even though I hadn't heard him walk up.

In my mind, the words, "I wanted someone to take care of me," played over and over on a loop, along with the thought, *it could be me. I could take care of you. I would love that.* This couldn't be right. I'd feel horrible if I simply absorbed the life of a much younger man who had nothing but the clothing on his back, a guitar, and a dog.

Didn't he understand? For a man who really wanted to take advantage, he'd be utterly disposable. Easily replaced by the next needy young man to come along. He might think he had all the power, but he only held the winning cards until someone got tired of him, or he grew older, or—

What Beck was talking about seemed nothing like love.

If I knew anything, it was that Beck deserved to be loved.

Troubled, I picked up my guitar and asked, "Shall we start the lesson?"

He opened his mouth to say something but then shut it again. "Spiders." He sat down on the coffee table opposite while Callie settled comfortably by his side. I couldn't look at him. I did my finger exercises, concentrating harder than I ever had before.

I wasn't his worst option if he wanted someone to take care of him. But I was a poor substitute for what he really needed, what he deserved. The question became could I be stronger than my desire for him? Could I be there for him, care for him as he wanted me to, and keep myself from taking what he offered as some kind of payment in return?

I hoped so with all my heart, because if I couldn't, it could destroy us both.

CHAPTER EIGHTEEN

LATER THAT EVENING, Beck reclaimed his spot on the redwood table, played my guitar, and smoked a joint he'd gotten from one of his dog-sitting clients. I wondered which one, because I sure couldn't picture any of them getting lit.

The world was a very strange place. I couldn't offer him a beer, but for some reason watching him smoke didn't bother me. I thought then that my priorities had to be a bit skewed.

Mist shrouded the lawn around the landscape lights, which added a mystical quality to the scene—also to the music Beck seemed inspired to play. I didn't think it was too cold to enjoy the sea-scented air, but Beck had asked to borrow one of my jackets. My insides tightened pleasantly again at the sight of him wearing my clothes.

I recognized the piece he played but couldn't place it at first. It took me until the chorus to realize it was "Black Hole Sun." He played "Everlong" and "Sultans of Swing." Music simply escaped him into the darkness beyond reach of the patio lights. The air shivered with beautiful noise. He was the elven prince I'd compared him to before, and he had captured me in some sacred sylvan space. After a while, the rhythmic thud of his knuckles against the guitar replaced my heartbeat.

Was he truly self-taught? A boy whose parents were absorbed in the health of their critically ill child might be left to his own entertainment a lot. Maybe he'd even been left alone entirely, a latchkey kid, sacrificed to the family's need to split their time between a teen who could conceivably care for himself and a very young, very ill child.

Adolescents don't need their parents less, at least in my experience. I spent a lot of time pretending, though. I pushed my parents away, hoping they'd push right back, and they had.

I looked at Beck and wondered, *who looked after you when you needed it? Is that why you're not afraid to ask a stranger to take care of you now? Is that why you need nurturing so badly? Because you had to learn to do everything else by yourself?*

How many thousands of hours of practice had he put in? How many hours of YouTube videos had he watched, stopping and rewinding and repeating, doing it over and over again to get that good?

For the first time in my life, something beautiful hurt my eyes. The sheer complicated perfection of someone made me want to weep, and it was Beck.

Beck, who I wanted to feed, to nurture, to protect.

Beck, who I wanted to fuck, and suck, and pleasure.

Beck, who I wanted to own despite my shame. Despite my conscience.

I got myself a second beer. He took a hit from his blunt, blew blue smoke into the air, and laughed at something. Only he knew what it was. He started playing "Thinking Out Loud," and I sang the lyrics. His expression was hilarious as if Callie had suddenly broken into the chorus of an Italian opera.

"No shit?" He put his hand to his ear. "Sing it, Boomer."

That little brat.

Then I thought, why not sing? This wasn't reality. This was a fantasy. My life had turned into a contemporary musical or an episode of "Carpool Karaoke," so why not sing whatever he plays? Because things were that easy with Beck.

It was midnight by the time he put his guitar down, and by then I was thirsty for him. The silence between us begged to be filled, but I didn't know how. Beck's self-confidence, his swagger, enticed me. I wanted what he had. Comfort with the things he desired. Self-knowledge. The courage to ask for what he wanted. The ability to spot someone who might give it to him.

On the way inside, I took his hand. He shot me a smile that tried to be older than time but wasn't. He made me fifteen again. Just as unsure. Just as emotionally unproven as I was during my first-ever kiss with a boy I liked.

"I don't understand any of this," I told him.

He leaned against the refrigerator and pulled me to him by my belt loops. "Do you have to understand things to enjoy them?"

"What do you want from me, Beck?"

"Everything." He kissed the tip of my nose. "Anything."

I pressed my forehead to his. "What does that even mean?"

"What if"—he cupped my face between his hands—"I asked you to take care of me."

"Like Tug?"

"No, not like Tug," he whispered. "Everything is different with you."

"Because we fuck?"

He shook his head. "Because I want to take care of you too."

"Ah, Jesus, Beck." *I want that.*

We kissed our way from the kitchen to the hallway to the bedroom with Callie padding softly behind us.

"I could use a shower." I hesitated in the bathroom doorway with a gracelessness that was new, even for me. A disquiet, which completely sucked. For once, I didn't know how to act.

"Is that an invitation?" He eyed me. Christ, had I ever been that brave?

"Please." He was beautiful. Seeing him naked with all the lights on only confirmed that.

Of course he was smooth and perfect.

I unbuttoned my shirt and let it drop, because if my, er, *seasoned* body didn't scare him off, then maybe he really did like older guys, and if it changed his mind? Well, that was one solution to my dilemma, wasn't it?

He clucked his tongue. "You're just on fire with all the guilt and indecision you have going on."

"That fire might not be from guilt, actually."

The look he shot me was fond. "Oh yeah?"

"God, you know what you are, right?" I asked hoarsely. "Do you know how amazing, how lovely, you are?"

He lowered his lashes. "I don't think of myself like that."

"I don't know how to be the man for you, but I want to be." I qualified the statement, "Tonight, I want to be everything you need."

"That's enough." He glanced pointedly at the shower.

"Oh, yeah." I got the water going and kept my hand in until the temperature was just right. After helping him inside the oversized shower stall, I grabbed washcloths from a basket I kept on the sink, then stepped in with him. "Do you want me to wash you?"

He smiled shyly. "I'd like that."

I soaped up the cloth and began with his shoulders, having no clue how to do this. Assuming everything rinsed down, I took my cue and started at the top.

In the warm cocoon of my shower, the act of circling the soapy washcloth over his skin took on a meditative quality. I lathered the contours of his body. I circled each muscle, each knobby bone, the round sweet curve of his ass, his muscled thighs, his calves—until I reached his feet and took care with each toe. Even his feet were lovely. He held his hands out, and I worked the soap between his clever, rough fingers.

As I worked, his cock rose in the nest of curly hair around it. I cleaned between his legs, his taint. His hole.

"Under you go." I helped him rinse himself after I washed his hair. A feeling like I'd never known came over me—a rightness—when he wiped the excess water from his face and lifted his gaze to mine.

"Thank you." He kissed my cheek, then returned the favor, washing me. I sat down on the built-in bench so he could reach easily if he wanted to wash my hair.

Instead, he sank into my lap and tucked his face into my neck. It was humbling and so sweet to hold him. I didn't over-think things for a change. My heart told me to wrap my arms around him and press my cheek to his temple. My heart told me to shut up and hold him because he needed that—he needed *me*—and I needed him.

This was like nothing I'd ever done before.

It was unlike me, but I let my heart do the thinking.

I tilted my head to look into his eyes. They shimmered like blue gems under clear water, and when I kissed his forehead, tears tracked down his cheeks. He swallowed hard.

"Oh, no. Hey. C'mon. Don't cry."

He shook his head. "Sorry."

"It's okay. You're okay, Beck."

He cleared his throat. "I haven't felt this safe in such a long time."

"I'm so sorry." I smoothed his wet hair off his face. "Things shouldn't be that hard, should they?"

He shook his head.

"You'll always be safe with me. I promise."

I didn't know how I'd keep a promise like that, but it didn't seem to matter. Whatever Beck needed, whatever I had to do to make sure he never wound up homeless and scared again, I'd do it without any hesitation at all.

We exchanged salty kisses. He tasted of desperation and hope. He seemed relieved. Boneless, like melted wax in my arms. What I felt for him was so different and so much more than I'd ever felt for anyone, but I still couldn't make the idea of "love" a reality in my brain.

Or the idea of there ever being an "us."

He was too young. I was too settled. We came from different places in our lives, and it couldn't work. Wouldn't work. I didn't have time for someone in my life. I worked long hours and traveled often. I'd be as disappointing to Beck as I'd been to all my other lovers.

There would be another bitter breakup—another infamous Post-it note goodbye that went unnoticed for several days.

Sooner or later he'd meet someone his age, and the two of them would have their whole lives ahead of them, and I'd be happy for him. Pleased that he found someone who could give him what I had never been able to give anyone.

But what if it didn't have to be like that? What if I was wrong?

THE WATER WENT from hot to lukewarm. We emerged from the shower clean and quiet. I dried him off, and he went to raid my closet for something to sleep in while I saw to myself.

From the bathroom door, I watched him slip into a pair of my boxers and a well-worn UCSD T-shirt. He turned to me with a tremulous smile.

"This shirt smells like you." He smoothed the fabric down his body.

"I have a fresh toothbrush if you want it."

"Thank you." He came back to the bathroom, and we

brushed our teeth side by side. After, he asked, "Can I keep this here?"

"If you want." Why didn't that set off my proximity alarms? Beck had gotten so far under my skin. Too far.

"Your brain just melted, didn't it?" he asked.

"Little bit." I showed him how much with my thumb and forefinger. "No one's ever kept a toothbrush here before."

"I'm the first?" His eyes lit, and he seemed delighted by the new discovery.

"The first in this house. I'm not sure how it makes me feel."

"You're too serious." He chivvied me toward the bed. "Loosen up a little, Lindy."

"Beck—"

"No. Don't think so hard. Just feel."

"But—"

"Come here and stop talking." He pushed me down and lay beside me. "Just be here with me."

He drew me into kisses that were sweet and hot and silly at the same time. He smiled against my lips and teased with his callused fingers and moaned when I touched him just right.

I took a good long time preparing him for my cock, and when I entered him, he wrapped his arms and legs around me and told me to make it last.

I moved deliberately, slowly, inside him until he came apart beneath me. I lost control when it was my turn. After, I was gentle pulling out. I felt like the only person in the world who knew Beck's value and cherished him. Obliquely, I understood what it meant to be that guy, and I desperately wanted to take on the responsibility.

"Okay?" I asked when I came back with a damp cloth.

"Of course." He folded his arms behind his head and gazed up at me while I cleaned his skin. When I was done, I lay down beside him. He rolled over and laid his head on my chest.

"Thank you." I wrapped my arms around him.

"My pleasure." He tilted his chin up and kissed my jaw.

I lay awake in the darkness, long after he fell asleep.

Was this really happening? Could this be real?

I wished I had answers before sleep claimed me, but as always, Beck became more and more complicated as I tried to make sense of him. One thing was for certain. I had no intention of letting him walk away until I figured out what it was about him, specifically, I couldn't get enough of.

But things weren't any clearer when I woke.

CHAPTER NINETEEN

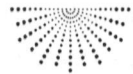

THE CLINIC WASN'T OPEN on Sundays, but we still needed to feed the kittens. Because it was such a nice day, Beck and I walked. We stopped for coffee on the way.

It wasn't my imagination that several pairs of eyes watched us closely as we sat on the patio with our drinks. The women seated at the next table—a mother and daughter last name Everly who brought their cat, Esmerelda to the clinic—said hello.

"Having a nice morning?" I asked.

"Very nice." The daughter eyed Beck like he was one of the shop's delicious pastries. "You're the guitarist, right?"

"Name's Beck." Beck preened a little. "You saw me play?"

"The other day." She nodded vigorously. "You totally shred. I'm Reese."

"Hi, Reese. You play?"

Reese glanced at her mom. "I used to take lessons, but my teacher moved."

"Beck's teaching me," I mentioned on Beck's behalf. "Maybe he could give you lessons too."

"That'd be awesome." She looked to her mother. "Can I take lessons again, Mom?"

"Oh. I don't know, sweetheart." Mrs. Everly appeared flustered. She glanced from me to Beck. "We'll have to ask your dad."

"I'm not actually a teacher or anything," Beck admitted.

"But you're so good," Reese gushed. "Think of what I could learn just from watching you play."

"I guess we could try it and see," Beck offered.

"Honey, we need to talk this over as a family first." The girl had little hearts in her eyes, and I thought that's why her mother hesitated. I hoped she didn't look down on Beck because of his circumstances.

"Here, I have these cards." Beck handed her one of the dog-walking cards Travis had made him. "Right now, I walk dogs and do some pet sitting. As you can see, I didn't even think of teaching guitar."

I kicked his foot with mine. "Until you decided I needed to learn."

He kicked my foot in retaliation. "You have a guitar just sitting there, gathering dust. I felt sorry for it."

"Well, thank you." I turned back to Mrs. Everly. "I can now play 'Twinkle, Twinkle, Little Star.'"

"You had to start somewhere." Beck reached over and covered my hand with his. Mrs. Everly noticed, flushed, and glanced away quickly, but the damage was done. Her obvious disapproval made the coffee sour in my stomach.

Jolted by her reaction, I pulled my hand from beneath Beck's none too smoothly. I didn't see his reaction, but I didn't have to. Judging by the pained look on the girl's face, I had totally screwed up.

Ignoring the emotional undercurrent, I closed my eyes and took a long drink of my too hot coffee. It burned the roof of my mouth and singed my throat going down.

That's what you get for being an asshole.

Things were decidedly uncomfortable between me and Beck after the Everlys left.

"I didn't mean to embarrass you," Beck said without looking at me.

"I—" *I couldn't lie.* "I was embarrassed when Mrs. Everly saw us holding hands. I could see her thinking I'm some dirty old man."

"Okay. Going forward, no PDA. Got it." He said this with an equanimity I didn't necessarily believe because it didn't feel right. Did he think I was ashamed of him? That wasn't it at all.

The damage was done, though. He shouldered his guitar and called Callie to him. I threw my cup in the trash and followed them to the street. At the clinic, he checked his phone.

"It's later than I realized. I need to hit the boardwalk while the brunch crowd's lining up. Tips are great on Sundays."

"Why don't you go on. I'll take care of the kittens."

"You sure?" He didn't glance my way.

"I've got it." I wanted to say more, but it didn't seem like I'd say the right thing.

"Okay, then. Thanks for the coffee." He started in the opposite direction, then turned. "Hey. If you want to come see me, I'll play your favorite song, 'Twinkle, Twinkle, Little Star.'"

I tried to laugh, to make things light between us again. "I just might."

My throat tightened as I watched him walk away. Guilt gnawed at my conscience. I even had the urge to chase after him and apologize, but the original problem remained: I didn't want people to see me as a guy who chased after men Beck's age.

Until I could get over my discomfort, I had no business leading him on, not just in public.

I had to either pull my head out of my ass or walk away.

INSIDE THE CLINIC, nothing stirred. No one had stayed overnight, so you could hear a pin drop. It was rare that I spent any time there absolutely alone. Between the techs, Lena, the clients, and their pets, there was rarely ever a dull moment, but now…it was too quiet.

I mixed formula and put it into tiny bottles then took the kittens from the cage where we'd stashed them, along with water and a blanket to curl up in. They were growing so fast. One—Rose, maybe—tried to bite me with her sharp little teeth. She clung to the fabric of my shirt with tiny claws.

"Look at you, kitty. You're a fierce one, aren't you? You're a survivor."

She drank her milk hungrily and eliminated on cue. I moved on to the next one and the next until they were all done and ready to sleep.

My phone rang as I was closing up shop.

"Mother." I was still none too happy with her just then.

"I just got off the phone with Remmy. We're both very disappointed you didn't get on with Dylan."

"*Mother.* Listen to me. Don't set me up. I can find men on my own."

"But you don't. You're nearing forty, and you live with a bird."

"Because I *like* my bird." I tried not to raise my voice. "I'm happy living alone. Why must you persist in trying to set me up when I keep telling you I'm *happy the way I am.*"

"Because I don't believe you." She sniffed. "You're a social creature. You're nurturing. You have so much to offer a partner, and if you could only find someone—"

"Okay. What if I did find someone, and they were totally unsuitable?"

After a brief pause, she said, "What do you mean, unsuitable?"

"What if I wanted someone who was already married, or half my age, or from Peru?"

That was neatly buried.

"Do you?"

"No," I lied. "But how fast would you abandon your crusade to pair me off if you didn't like my choice?"

"Linden, who is this unsuitable person?" *I should have known.* "Are you involved with him already?"

"No," I lied again. "But you keep matching me up with the same kind of man. Older, successful, connected, metrosexual."

"And what's wrong with that, I ask? You could be describing yourself."

She was right. "Maybe I'm not looking to date myself, Mother."

"You're in a very strange mood today."

"Maybe I want to express the futility of doing the same thing over and over and expecting different results."

"There's more to this than you're telling me." She was too shrewd an observer of human nature, goddamnit. Since I was her only child, she'd had plenty of time to learn how to read me.

"There's not." This was definitely going to come back to bite me. Was I trying to break the news in such a way I had plausible deniability?

"I actually called to tell you that your father and I are coming up this week."

"Wait, what?" In the background, I heard my father say, "We are?"

"Mother, that's not necessary."

"We're not coming for you. I had a hankering for a trip up the coast, and your father's taking the week off."

"What? I am?" my father asked incredulously. "Sweetheart, maybe we should discuss this before we make plans."

"I thought you were coming for the Fourth."

"We were, but then we realized how much we hate the traffic

on holiday weekends." This wouldn't be the first time my mother heard something in my voice and decided she needed to look me in the eye to find out what I meant by it. We're close, and it's very hard to fool her. Maybe I really had been trying to start something.

"You don't have to do this," I said. "Everything's fine. I'm fine."

"Of course you are." She didn't believe that, or she wouldn't have changed their plans. "But I need a vacation."

"Look. You know I'd love to have you whenever you come, but you absolutely don't need Dad to take a week off right this minute, do you? Won't you be uncomfortable staying at my place for that long?" I had two spare bedrooms, but they only had double beds. My parents were used to sleeping on a California king, so it would be tight.

"Oh, we won't be staying with you. I need to be pampered. We'll stay at The Coastal Harmony Resort just south of where you are. What's their spa called?"

"Pure Harmony?"

"I'm going to book a service for every day I'm there."

My father said, "Judy—"

"Do you want me to book you for a massage?" she asked me.

"Sure." That sounded like a great idea, actually.

"And, Doug, you'll want a reflexology session." I could just picture my father's face as she talked. He'd retired from the navy and taken a contracting job as a security consultant, which meant he basically set his own hours. Since Mom had spent so many of my formative years handling a household and child-rearing by herself while he was at sea, he believed he owed her his time now.

That was why my mother was so determined to marry me off. They were happy. They got along great. They'd shared the same dreams, had the same memories, sacrificed for their future together. So why *didn't* I want what they had? I did. There was just no one I wanted to have it with.

"We're all set then?" she asked. "We'll probably spend a shopping day in Solvang and be up there by Wednesday."

"You haven't even made reservations yet. What if they're booked?"

"We've never had any trouble booking the resort during the week, but if anything changes, I'll let you know."

"Fine." I knew better than to argue. Mom was a force of nature. "Give me a call when you get in."

"I will. Can you dine with us on Wednesday? As I recall, the resort restaurant is quite good."

"We'll need to play it by ear. If I get finished at the clinic on time, it should work."

"Smashing. I can't wait to see you, darling."

"You too, Mom. Love to Dad." He probably needed smelling salts as well.

"I'll tell him. Bye."

The call disconnected, and I was left holding my phone between sweaty palms.

My parents were coming.

On the one hand, I really did adore them. We'd always been a tight knit family, and I'd only grown more fond of them as they'd gotten older.

My father wasn't around much when I was a kid, but now he made Mom and me feel like we were the most important part of his life. And I had learned to use humor to deal with frustration from my mom.

I knew they wouldn't be around forever, and I wanted to enjoy their company—frustrating as it could be—while I could.

Obviously, I'd raised my mother's suspicions that something unexpected was going on with me. Did I dare talk to her about Beck, even indirectly? About how my feelings for Beck were developing into something more than friendship and how confused I was by those feelings?

From the beginning, I'd made the same assumptions about relationships Mom did—that I should stick with men from the same walk of life, at the same stage in their evolution, with the same tastes, the same interests, the same likes and dislikes as mine.

My brain told me real romantic partnerships ought to be equal. That, as in my parents' case, equality was the way to mutual admiration and affection and happiness.

But my heart...said something entirely different.

My heart wanted someone to nurture. To take care of. To bathe and even hand-feed. Because despite all my misgivings, taking care of Beck was the most natural expression of love I'd ever known.

My brain said it was wrong—maybe even a little weird—but my heart wanted Beck.

I no longer knew which I should listen to.

CHAPTER TWENTY

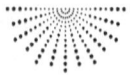

OVER THE BEACH, the sky was full of kites—figural kites, fabric kites in rainbow colors, and elaborate dragon kites. The sight of them made me catch my breath in awe. Nacho's Bar was packed and jumping. A live jazz band played Brubeck's "Take Five," the sound of exuberant horns spilling out along with the scent of delicious Mexican food.

A little farther along the boardwalk, a bunch of people surrounded a seated musician. I assumed that was Beck, playing his guitar. People clapped along, danced in time to the music. Someone drummed on an upturned Home Depot bucket.

I meant to get closer, discreetly, just to watch. He'd invited me, but as soon as I saw it was mostly people his age, I came to a standstill.

Jeff from Bistro had taken a seat on the ground next to him. Between them, there were pop bottles and bags of chips. They'd obviously struck up a friendship. It reminded me of the first time I saw Beck when Tug offered his ice cream and Beck leaned in and opened his mouth.

There was something kitten-like about Beck. Something

that made you want to pick him up, cuddle him to you, and take care of his needs.

Maybe it was his innocence or the way his eyes lit up with happiness when he saw something he wanted. Maybe it was his quirky sense of humor or the way he laughed at people with kindness and not malice.

Anyone could see he was special. Everyone could.

Who was I to think he'd seen something in me he couldn't find in someone his own age—in the same place on the journey, so much more in step, in sync, with him?

He glanced up, saw me, and gave a little wave. Callie barked hello, and I went over to greet her. Her ears were so soft, and she dug her snout into my chest to be sure she got all the scratches and rubs she needed.

A few of Beck's friends said hello. I'd met a lot of the kids with their pets at the clinic.

"Have a seat." Beck motioned toward the ground next to Jeff. "A group of us were thinking of getting some pizzas later."

Jeff leaned closer to Beck and whispered something.

Beck nodded and said, "We're getting a fire pit later if you want to come hang out."

From my experience "hanging out" meant beer and weed and sitting on the beach with the wind whipping smoke and ash into your eyes.

"I'll pass, but thanks for the invite." I wasn't going to be graceless about this. "I need to get some paperwork done this afternoon, and I'm on call at the clinic."

I was always on call, which was a wonderful excuse for bowing out of things I didn't feel comfortable doing.

"Oh, okay." I couldn't read Beck's face. I didn't know if the invitation had been serious, and I couldn't tell if it mattered to him one way or another if I went. "You have fun."

"You too." I gave Callie a final full-body rub down. "Do you want me to take Callie with me? Or are you going to a dog friendly beach?"

He glanced up, mouth open. He'd probably not given that much thought since he'd camped out with her the whole time, city ordinances be damned.

"You mind?"

"Of course not. She's delightful. I'll look after her. You can pick her up in the morning."

He met my gaze with a slight frown. "If it's okay, that might be best."

"I'd be happy to have her." I took Callie's leash from him. "Callie and Rico and I will have our own party."

"If you're sure."

"Perfectly." I stood with Callie by my side. "Have fun, Beck."

"You too." There was something odd in his gaze when he waved goodbye.

Callie and I took the long way back to my place. The more I thought about Beck, the more obvious the answer to at least one of his problems became. If he wanted to go to school, or work, or find a place and they didn't take dogs, there was no reason Callie couldn't stay with me.

Perhaps it wasn't the best solution—after all, he'd made a solemn promise to his little brother—but surely he'd let me help take care of Callie so he wasn't responsible for her twenty-four seven. Surely, he'd see that he could have a future and keep his word without either of them suffering the kind of deprivation they'd experienced on the road.

Later that afternoon, Callie and I took my car to the clinic where we fed the kittens and raided the supply room. I found a nice dog bed, some toys, and a big bag of the kind of food I gave Beck to feed her. At my place, I saw her staring at the door a couple of times, no doubt wondering when Beck was going to come for her.

"He'll be here in the morning," I reassured her.

"Hello, gorgeous." Rico tried reassuring her too, but she continued to look subdued. We binge watched *Pit Bulls and Parolees* together—Callie seemed to like that show—until I fell asleep on the couch with her big, warm body lying between my calves.

At about two in the morning, there was a knock at the door.

Disoriented, I got up and looked through the window.

Beck stood there, guitar in hand, looking ruffled by wind and altogether not dressed warmly enough.

I opened the door to let him in. "Hey. I said you could leave her tonight."

"I didn't feel right without her. And I didn't want her to think I would go and not come back."

"She's safe here, Beck. She'll get used to it if you need me to dogsit." I had my hands in my pockets, but he moved into my space anyway. He smelled of woodsmoke, and sea air, and beer, and weed, and something that was utterly, instantaneously recognizable as Beck.

I breathed him in and knew I'd never get my fill.

He set his guitar down and crowded me until I put my arms around him. "Missed you."

"Me too," I admitted. "Callie and I watched Animal Planet, but she never took her eyes off the door. Guess she missed you too."

"I'm so cold." He put his hand out to greet her from within the circle of my arms. She tried to nudge between our legs. "How come you didn't come with us?"

"Seemed like it was the local college set."

"No one would have cared."

"I didn't want to spend the night sitting on the ground." I teased, "And smoke always finds the best-looking guy. Was it fun?"

"Mmhmm." He let go and fell onto the couch. Callie jumped up beside him. They took up nearly the whole thing, so I sat in the chair opposite. "It was weird, though. It felt like being back in high school."

"How so?"

"It was as if the last year never happened. I played guitar, we drank beer, people messed around. Maybe fifteen minutes would go by, and then I'd remember about Bryce and how I got here."

"Well, that's good, isn't it? I mean, that you had that opportunity to be a kid again. You know, Callie would thrive with me, I think. If you wanted to, you could get a place, go back to school. Make a fresh start."

His gaze flew up to meet mine. "Is that what all this is?"

"All what?"

"I noticed you have a new dog bed. I see the toys." He stood and began stomping around, taking stock.

"Beck—"

"You think just because it's you it's okay for me to walk away?" He clipped Callie's leash to her collar. "Or are you thinking that if you keep Callie, that's a good excuse to keep me around? People won't think anything of it because it's about the dog."

"No, that's not it at all." I held out a placating hand. "But leaving her with me sometimes would give you freedom to work and go to school and just…be young and carefree sometimes."

"And then what? I get busy with friends my own age and everything will be okay?"

"I didn't think that far ahead." He stopped in his tracks and picked up one of the toys, a particularly resilient shark-shaped stuffy. "This is actually kind of awesome."

"Take it. Callie tried to kill it for quite a while. She likes it."

He tucked it under his arm. "I know you mean well, but you're not taking my dog."

"I never even imagined taking your dog."

"You think what matters is a nice house and a bunch of toys and food that comes out of a cupboard and not a backpack or a restaurant bag. You think only someone like you can take care of an animal, that people like me are too young and inadequate and unstable—"

"That's not it at all, Beck." I raked my hands through my hair while I searched for the right words. "I want what's best for both of you."

"And only you know what that is, is that it? Because you're so mature and wise and wonderful." He shook his head. "I should have known you'd try to run my life."

I finally shut my mouth. This could be Beck's exhaustion talking, or alcohol, or pot. He might even have a point, and I should consider learning to listen better.

It was too late, and I was too tired. I didn't want to argue.

I scrubbed my face with both hands. "I'm sorry. It was just an idea."

"Not a good one," he clapped back.

"I apologize."

He glanced away. "I'm sorry too."

"I have work in the morning, so I need to sleep now. Would you like a ride to Cooper and Shawn's?"

He shrugged. "I could walk."

"It's okay. Let me get my keys. Hang on."

I didn't bother putting on shoes. I walked him out to my car, and it took no time for me to run him home.

At Cooper's place, we sat in the idling car for a minute or two. He seemed reluctant to leave.

"You okay?"

He bit his lip. "I don't know if I can go back."

Surprised, I asked, "What do you mean?"

"Like...tonight. It was just like school, but I wasn't the same. Everybody was nice—don't get me wrong. They're all friendly and funny. But I don't know if I could be part of that group anymore."

"It's a totally new bunch of people in a new place," I said. "You only just got here."

"It's not that I don't know them. It's that I don't connect with them. They talk about popular music and what they drink and the classes they take, and I see Tug on his knees for some guy to get enough for the big box of McNuggets."

Sick at heart, I reasoned it out. "You have experiences they don't have, and you feel like they come between you."

"They can't hear anything but my music, and I have so much more to say. There are all these things I'm feeling. Stuff that terrifies me. And I don't say any of it because they're on the other side of this river of experience, and—"

"Oh, sweetheart." I took him into my arms.

"I can't find my way across the things that make us different." He spoke into my shoulder. "Taking Callie away won't make things more convenient for me. She's the only family I have."

"I didn't understand, Beck. I'm sorry."

"You didn't know," he said in a small voice.

I took both his hands in mine. "We'll figure this out. You'll see. Callie's awesome, but I'm here for *you* too."

"I did have some fun." He looked at me through lashes spiked with tears. "But I'd have felt safer if you'd been there."

"Why?" I gave his hands a hard squeeze. "Why me?"

"Because you see me. You get me."

"Yes." I cupped his face and kissed him. "I see you."

He smiled against my mouth. "Tug saw me, but he used what he knew to manipulate me. You just give and give and give. I don't want to lose that, even if you think it's for my own good. Please...don't let me go, Lindy."

Oh fuck. *Oh fuck, fuck, fuck.* What was this kind, beautiful, vulnerable *boy* doing to me?

"I won't." I wrapped my hand around the back of his neck and felt him go still. "I won't let you go."

I pressed kisses to his eyelids, his cheeks, his nose, and finally his lips, which parted on a gasp, and I took shameless advantage, slipping my tongue inside to deepen the kiss.

We pulled apart and pressed our foreheads together.

He bracketed my face between his hands. "Thank you."

"You never need to thank me. Not ever."

He nodded. "I should probably—"

"I'll get Callie. You grab your guitar."

We exited the slightly steamy SUV just as the porch light turned on. The door opened, and Cooper stepped out followed by Shawn, who had his arms crossed.

"Hey." I waved.

They said nothing. I glanced at Shawn and then Cooper in turn. Was it my imagination or did Shawn seem more serious than usual?

"Night, Doc." Beck stood on tiptoe to kiss me again before heading into the house between the two men. "Sorry if you waited up."

"No problem." Cooper gave his shoulder a pat. "Did you have fun?"

Beck shrugged. "Some."

"Get some rest, kiddo," Cooper said. "You've got dogs to walk tomorrow morning."

"Night." He slipped into the house and disappeared.

Once he left, the three of us stood there awkwardly staring at one another.

"What's up?" I asked.

Coolly, Shawn said, "I think we need to talk."

What the hell was this? I glanced at Cooper, who looked none too happy with me.

Was this about Beck? Had they seen us kiss? Was that it? Christ. Did they think I was taking advantage of Beck? How mortifying. I tried asking myself what I'd do if the situation was reversed and winced. This looked bad. *I* looked like some gross old goat.

Oh my God, what had I done? How could I do the right thing and still keep my word to Beck? I made Beck a promise. As long as he needed me, I would not let go.

Two in the morning was no time to have a conversation, though.

"Let's meet for lunch tomorrow."

Shawn nodded, then closed the door between us.

Wow. What would I do if I lost the friends that made St. Nacho's home for me?

CHAPTER TWENTY-ONE

By the time I got to Bistro, the lunch service was already in full swing. I saw Cooper and Shawn in the corner booth I normally favored, so I joined them. I sat next to Cooper, opposite Shawn, so he could read both sets of lips. Despite their physical separation, they presented a united front. I'd have been lying if I said their expressions didn't cause a guilty chill to creep down my spine.

I picked up my menu but didn't open it. "I know what you're going to say, so just spit it out."

"If you know, then why are we having this conversation?" Shawn's profound deafness had never stopped him from speaking his mind.

"We're worried about Beck, Lindy." Cooper tried to soften his words. "You know he's vulnerable."

"I know," I admitted.

"So do you think a relationship with him is in his best interest?"

Jeff came over to our table, although his name tag read "Bob" today. "Can I get you something to drink?"

"Wait." I held up a hand. "I've seen you wearing name tags

that say Jeremy, Jeff, and now Bob. Is one of those your name? I hate to keep calling you the wrong thing."

"Oh. Yeah. It's so stupid." He laughed and clapped his hand over his badge. "I lost like, three name tags my first week, and now my boss won't make me anymore. I just grab one from a box we have in the back."

"What is your real name?"

Pink crested over his high cheekbones. "I go by my nickname, mostly. People call me Epic."

"Epic?" Shawn spelled it with his fingers, and Cooper nodded. Epic answered in ASL. I sat and watched while they talked for a few seconds. Shawn appeared delighted by his communication skills. "Good job. You're pretty fluent.

"Epic's an awesome name. If it's okay with you, can I call you that?" I asked.

"I think that's why the owner won't make me another one. He thinks people will think my name is a joke."

"Well, it's not nice of him to say your name's not serious enough," I said. "But nice for me to finally know what to call you."

"I know, right? Can I get your drink orders?" We asked for water and iced tea. Epic left to get them.

Shawn continued to glare at me while Cooper talked. "The thing is, we know you. You're all about work. How'd this even happen?"

"I don't know. There's something about Beck."

"But you can see our point, right?" Shawn asked. "He has nothing, and you're...you. It's unethical to start a relationship when he's not on more equal footing. Even if he weren't so young. Don't you think?"

"Of course I think so. Do you think I don't lie awake at night worrying about that very thing?"

"So maybe let him down gently," Shawn said. "Put off a

romantic relationship until he's not homeless and dependent on you for the well-being of his pet."

Wow. Tell me how you really feel. "I don't know if that's possible."

"What do you mean?" Shawn turned to Cooper with a frown. "What does he mean?"

Cooper used sign language but spoke so we could both understand. "I think he means it's too late."

Shawn sat back. "Linden Davies. I know you know better than this."

Cooper lifted his hands. "Chill, mama bear. We understand that you feel protective of Beck, but he's not a child."

"Compared to Lindy he is. I can't believe I even have to say this. You hold all the power in that partnership. If you go forward with it, he'll always feel *less than.*"

Shawn was right. I'd thought the same thing myself. Yet on the other hand, an unequal relationship seemed to be exactly what Beck wanted from me. He wanted me to take care of him. And for my part, that was a major turn-on. The things we needed from each other meshed perfectly.

We meshed perfectly.

Was it possible that made it okay? If he wanted me too— never forgetting Beck was a consenting adult—who were Cooper and Shawn to stare me down like this? I studied the words on the menu without reading them.

"I think maybe you misunderstand," I said quietly. "It's a pretty personal subject, but you'll have to take my word for it. I'm not some predator."

"Of course you're not." Cooper patted my arm where it lay next to his on the table. "No one is saying that."

"It's the partnership," Shawn said. "That kind of inequality isn't healthy."

"Shawn, seriously." I addressed my next words to him. "Don't think I'm not listening, because I've heard every word you've said. But this is between me and Beck."

Shawn pressed his lips together unhappily. At the same time, my phone rang.

"We might have to disagree on this." I checked the caller ID. "Shoot. It's Jeanine Montgomery, and she usually doesn't call unless there's an emergency. I'm sorry, but I have to take this."

I stood and dropped a ten on the table for Epic. "If I don't come back, we'll talk later, all right?"

"Take care." Shawn started signing to Cooper before I left the building.

I answered outside. "What's up, Jeanie?"

"I just got a call from Monterrey County Animal Control. They have a big hoarding case, and they asked for my help."

Shit. "Where is it?"

"Just south of Gilroy. Looks like some kind of breeding opera-tion, but there's apparently been real neglect. The owner is older. It's bad. Nearly a hundred animals, half of them near death."

"Okay. My schedule is light this week. Let me get back to the clinic to see if I can make changes. Can you text me an address?" My phone beeped, and I pulled it away from my ear to check the message she'd sent. "It will take me two and a half to three hours to get there."

"It's gonna be slow going and sad as hell. We'll take whatever help we can get."

"Got it. I'll let you know when I'm on my way."

"Thanks, babe."

"See you."

WHEN I GOT BACK to the clinic, I had Lena see if she could reschedule patients. I hated doing it, but unless there were emergencies in town, I could help Jeanie and only inconvenience a few people. If there was an emergency, there was another vet in Cayucos, which was only a quick drive away.

"A hundred animals?" April repeated when I told her.

"Jeanie says it's grim. She'll start triaging cases as soon as she gets there."

Our organization had worked with Monterrey County Animal Control before, and we had a good relationship with them.

"Can I go?" April asked. "You'll need help."

"Of course. Can you call Travis?"

"On it." She pulled out her phone and left my office.

I headed to the supply room and found Beck feeding the kittens. "Hey."

He turned to me with a winsome smile. "Something going on?"

"Yeah. We're going to see if we can help animal control at a site near Gilroy."

He bit his lip. "That's hours away."

"Right." I pulled a duffle off the wall and started filling it with supplies. "I might be gone a couple of days."

"I'll miss you." He put the kitten he was holding down and moved toward me. "What did Cooper and Shawn want to talk about?"

"You knew about that?"

"I heard them arguing last night."

"They're concerned about you, that's all. They want to make sure you're not—" I didn't know how to put it. "That I'm not taking advantage."

"Even if you were, sign me up." He shot me a shy grin. "It's hot."

"There are some very real issues we need to talk about, Beck."

"Why didn't they talk to me about it? It's nobody's business who I fuck."

I put my hands on his shoulders. "Like I said, they're worried."

He grabbed my shirt and fitted himself close for a hug.

Travis entered the room and froze. "Um. Sorry to interrupt. I just wanted to let you know I'm here."

Guiltily, I let Beck go. "That was quick."

"I was taking a walk on the beach."

"Did April fill you in? You want to come?"

His eyes widened. "Yeah. Of course."

"Great. Start taking the collapsible crates out to the SUV, please."

I went to my desk and got him my spare car keys. "How many?"

"How many do we have?" *I should know the answer to that.* "See how many fit. Jeanie said there might be as many as a hundred animals needing rescue."

Travis's mouth tightened. "Douchebags."

"I'll get medical supplies. Beck, can you ask April to pack bone broth, food, and water?"

"Got it." Beck went to get her.

"A hundred dogs?" asked Travis. "We have nowhere near enough supplies."

"Jeanie's supervising. She'll call in favors from rescue organizations if we run out. For now, we have to get up there and see what we're up against."

Beck reentered the room. "You don't know when you'll be back?"

"I'm sorry. I'll keep in touch."

He and Callie looked a little forlorn as I was leaving. I didn't want to acknowledge his growing dependence on me, and I didn't want to admit how much I liked it. I wanted to take him with me. Maybe someday.

"I'll be back soon, Beck." I unwound my house keys from my key ring and handed them to him. "This one's for the house. Can you look out for Rico? He doesn't need much. Just check his water and feeder and tell him hello for me every so often."

"Sure."

"Thank you."

"I'll really miss you," he whispered.

"Me too." I glanced around before pulling him in and meeting his mouth in a hungry kiss. His lashes fluttered open afterward, and I wanted to believe his eyes held an intimate gaze just for me. "See you, sweetheart."

"Bye." My words left him smiling.

ONCE WE WERE on the road, Travis met my gaze in the rearview mirror. "So. Beck, huh?"

"Is that a question?" I asked.

"No. Just surprised is all."

April snorted. "Where have you been?"

"You did tell me I should go for it."

"I didn't imagine you would." Travis was driving, which left nothing for me to do but consider how deep a hole I was digging myself into with Beck. And now my staff knew. *Everyone* knew because I couldn't keep my feelings for Beck off my goddamn face.

He shrugged. "I'm just surprised is all."

"Do we have to do this?" I was a captive audience. Couldn't they let me off the hook until later?

"I always figured you were a confirmed bachelor too set in your ways to settle down with someone," said April.

"Who says I'm not?"

"Uh, your face for one." April laughed but glanced out the passenger window.

I had hoped sitting in the back would make this conversation less likely. No such luck. Travis eyed me in the mirror every chance he got, and April craned her head around like an owl.

"So. What do you want to know?" I asked.

"Are you dating him?" Travis asked. "Like...dating, dating?"

Was it throwback Thursday? "Who wants to know? Is Jenny afraid I won't ask her to homecoming?"

"Don't be snide." April pulled lip balm out of her pocket and swiped it over her lips.

"Is this a midlife crisis thing?" asked Travis

"Is this *what*?"

"You're one red convertible away from hitting the trifecta there, Doc."

"How do you figure that?"

"You've been wearing your hair longer. You're dating a guy half your age. Now all you need is a convertible, or wait"—he snapped his fingers—"a motorcycle."

"It's not a midlife crisis, and my stylist has been on maternity leave."

"But you would argue, wouldn't you, if you were actually having one?" April reasoned.

"I'm not having any kind of crisis."

"So, then what?" Travis asked. "You suddenly realized you dig younger guys?"

"Maybe it's him that I dig. It's possible I'm not shallow, you know."

"Is it?"

I sighed because I wasn't ready to answer that. "I don't know. Do I have to define everything all the time? What if I let my life happen organically and you just butt out?"

April turned back to the front. "Touchy."

"I think you mean touché," Travis said. They high-fived each other. "Don't be a grouch."

An unbelievably long three hours later, we pulled onto a gravel drive at the end of which sat a manufactured house. Animal control was already there, along with an ambulance and police. I pulled in next to a van I knew belonged to my colleague Dr. Montgomery. Three or four people who must have lived nearby stood to the side, watching and filming with their phones.

The lawn, the trees, and the bushes were dead. You could see heat scintillating over the barren landscape around the many, many kennels. The air was filled with incessant barking and black flies. The odor of feces and decomposition hung like a thick fog.

"It's bad." Jeanie met me as soon as I got out of the car.

"Is the owner ill?" I nodded toward the ambulance. The other possibility—the much worse possibility—was predation by hungry, desperate dogs. Jeanie and I had seen both.

Jeanie nodded. "Woman in her seventies. Her forty-year-old son lives here, but it looks like he's got some emotional problems. She's been ill for some time, and we think she believed he was caring for the animals. Apparently they had a confrontation this morning. A postal worker called it in to the local PD. Said he heard her screaming from the box at the curb."

"Good thing, probably."

We walked toward the kennels while she pulled on nitrile gloves. "Police came and found her unresponsive. They're taking the son into custody. Animal control needs help triaging the dogs."

"How many dogs are we talking about?" The kennels were full of listless, emaciated animals. I saw mostly Siberian huskies with matted fur. Some had mange.

"We think about forty mature animals and an unknown number of puppies."

"How the hell has she been getting away with this?" asked Travis.

189

"Big properties. The houses are well apart and set back off the street." She looked beyond him at the screen of eucalyptus trees and chain link fence that hid the property from neighbors. "She was probably keeping up with the needs of her animals until she became ill, and then she trusted the wrong person to help her."

"Where do you need me?" April, who'd remained silent while putting on protective gear, asked.

Jeanie took charge. "I'll talk to animal control and see if we can start bringing the animals out. I've got a call in to a Siberian husky rescue organization. If they can, they'll help. Better get ready."

"I'll get the supplies." Travis got the duffle bags out one by one and then hauled out the crates, which needed setting up.

"It's going to be a long day." Jeanie squared her shoulders.

"No lie." April and I followed her lead.

CHAPTER TWENTY-TWO

BECK: Thinking about you. How are the dogs?
I looked at the text and wondered how I should respond. Even in the shade, the temperature was over a hundred degrees. Biting flies buzzed all around me. Sweat dripped from my face in rivers. It got so bad I had to borrow a bandana from April to keep it out of my eyes. And every dog we pulled out was worse off than the one before. I rehydrated every hour, but it still didn't feel like enough.

On top of that, we were wading into the river Styx to pull dogs out. Skeletal, half-dead, sore-covered creatures so pitiful that even I spent most of the time fighting nausea.

This was grim, grim work, and I was loath to share it with Beck, who was made of light and music.

Lindy: It's pretty bad here.

Beck: How are you?

Lindy: Taking a ten-minute hydration break. I looked at what I typed through blurry eyes. God, could I be more perfunctory?

Lindy: You deserve a better answer. I wish I was with you on the beach. I wish I'd gone to your party and let the smoke blow in my face because...you. Sounds so goddamn good right now.

Beck: You're kind of worrying me. Are you really okay?

Lindy: This is bad. It's always bad, but this is BAD.

Beck: What can I do?

Lindy: Be the perfect elven prince I have in my mind right now. Play music. Smile. Be happy. That's what I see when I think of you. Be that. Shine, so I can find my way home.

It was a while before he answered.

Beck: You're making me cry.

Lindy: No. God, please forgive me. I'm just tired. Not making sense. Sorry.

Beck: I wish I could be there with you.

Lindy: No. You really don't.

One long day turned into two before most of the dogs were safely in the hands of veterinarians or animal control and on reserve for nonprofit rescue organizations, like NorCal Siberian Rescue, for removal and fostering.

I sometimes underestimated how many wonderful human networks there were to rescue animals under circumstances like these. Whether it was pathological animal hoarders, or puppy mills, or ordinary breeders who let greed or misplaced optimism blind them to the duty of care they had on behalf of the animals they took on, these humane organizations were still a drop in the bucket compared to the number of animals in need. The second night, I was asleep when my phone buzzed.

Beck: Lena says you're coming home tomorrow.

Lindy: Yes.

Beck: What can I do? What would you like?

Lindy: Just want to see you, shower, and sleep for a week.

Beck: It's a promise. I'll weld the doors shut and close all the blinds.

Lindy: I'm so tired.

Beck: You're almost home.

Lindy: Yes, Home and heart, here I come.

Beck: Hearth?

Lindy: No. Heart.

After the hard work we put in, we were exhausted on the return trip. Even Travis, whose irrepressible good humor I counted on, was silent and morose as we entered St. Nacho's at sundown on Wednesday.

He grabbed the gear out of the back of my truck and helped me stow it away, but he and April hardly said a word while we worked.

When it came time to go our separate ways, he said good-night and asked April if she wanted to get a drink. She gave him a smile. I wondered if St. Nacho's was working its special magic there. I'd had no hint of a budding romance prior to that moment. Maybe they were feeling simple camaraderie, or the need to avoid drinking alone, but as I watched them head to the cantina together on foot, I thought maybe...maybe I'd missed something blossoming between them.

They deserved every happiness, which of course made me think about Beck.

I finished putting away gear and made notes with regard to restocking supplies. Despite having showered at Jeanie's place that morning, I felt like I'd been dipped in a special kind of filth. I wasn't going to feel clean until I'd showered at home and donned fresh clothes.

It was a mark of how tired I was that I disregarded the unre-markable black Mercedes sedan parked across the street from my house. Instead, I pulled into my driveway and slogged up to my front door. I had little on my mind besides cleaning up and falling into bed.

My first inkling my plans had changed was the delightful sight of Beck sitting on my sofa with Callie in his lap and Rico on his shoulder. Seeing him was a cool drink of water in Death Valley.

"Hey, sweetheart." I dropped my duffel bag at the doorway and slipped out of my shoes. "This is a really nice surprise."

Only as I stepped fully into the living room was I able to see my parents where they sat on the loveseat. Their body language told me everything I needed to know about their mood.

Shit, shit, shit. I hadn't seen my mother look as angry since the election.

I crossed the room to kiss Mom's cheek and hug Dad. "I thought you were staying at the resort?"

"We are, darling." My mother sat back down and settled in, because of course she did. To Dad's credit, he looked to me helplessly before returning to his seat beside her.

"We only stopped by to say hello. Beck has been kind enough to entertain us while we were waiting for you," he said.

I glanced Beck's way. "He should have texted me you were here."

Beck cringed. "I figured you were on the road."

"We haven't been here very long," said Dad. Beck, on the other hand, looked like he'd been trapped on a deserted island with them for days.

"Long enough to get to know this very nice *young* man." Mom's emphasis on the word young could be heard from the ISS.

Awesome.

"I just came by to feed Rico." Beck looked to me for answers. "I guess I can leave now."

"No, don't go. How about you put Rico back and come with me while I freshen up?" I turned to my parents. "You'll be all right here, won't you? Help yourselves to anything I have while you're waiting. There's a pretty nice cabernet in the pantry."

"Lovely." My mother wasn't going to be deterred from an interrogation it seemed, but if she thought I'd send Beck away like the help while she had her say, she was wrong. "Your father and I could use a drink."

"Super," I said.

"Splendid," Dad echoed.

Beck followed me into the bedroom where I shucked off the scrubs I was wearing. "I'm sorry you had to go through that."

"When the doorbell rang, I figured it was a package. I opened the door to get it, and there they were." Beck looked ashen. "I didn't exactly invite them in, but they're your parents. I'm sorry if I caused a problem. "

"You could never cause a problem between my parents and me. They do fine on their own." I grabbed a towel before slipping into the bathroom. "If you want to stay, I'll be out in no time. Then we can face them together."

He frowned, and I guessed he was debating the wisdom of fleeing from me and my family. "I'll wait, but you should probably know something before we go back in there."

"What?" At his hesitation, my heart sank. "Did they say something to you? Because it's not their goddamn business who I see."

"No, it's not that." His cheeks darkened. "I just have this history of blurting stupid stuff when I'm nervous, and I may have ruined any chance of them ever liking me."

"I'm almost forty. It's not my parents who have to like you."

"I know, but—"

"It's all right, sweetheart." I reassured him without feeling at all reassured on my own behalf. I owed him that. He shouldn't feel insecure because my parents had burst in on him. No doubt Mom laid one of her perfect information gathering snares and he fell into it like everyone did. That woman could have been the head of the CIA if her life had taken a different course. I should have been here to answer her questions, not Beck. I was the one who needed to take the heat from now on.

If I'd learned nothing else from Cooper and Shawn's censure and Travis and April's teasing jabs, it was that I didn't have to listen to what they said. Or I could listen, but it was my business who I dated. Mom and Dad had no right to interfere.

"I missed you." I kissed Beck's forehead.

"Missed you too. Glad you're home." He melted into my body and stayed like that for a long time, letting me rock him back and forth with Callie happily leaning against our legs.

"Back soon," I murmured before closing the bathroom door between us.

MY MOTHER HAD POURED HERSELF, my father, and me a glass of wine, and therefore it was painfully poignant when she then set a can of pop and a big glass of ice on the table for Beck. As an opening salvo, it was a masterful stroke of passive aggression I was sure we would all laugh about someday.

"So." Dad tried to talk around the tension between the two of us as he always did. "Beck tells me you helped him out with Callie. She's a wonderful dog. Reminds me a little bit of Lady."

"Lady was the black Lab we had when I was a kid," I informed Beck.

"Oh, yes. You loved that dog so much." My mother sipped her wine. "She died when you were what, nineteen? You were devastated. You carried on as if the world had come to an end."

"Judy," my father warned.

"At that age, everything seems so much more painful, more permanent, more everything, don't you think?"

"Mom, I was seventeen, and Lady's death was permanent, and nobody even remembers that anymore."

"That's my point, darling."

"We all got your point, Judy." My father started to rise, but she turned to stop him.

"I'm not finished, Doug." She turned to me. "Have you eaten, Lindy? You must be starving."

"I'm fine. I planned on showering and hitting the sack."

"You should at least have supper. I'll go see what there is, or we can order out. Is that Chinese place still open?"

"I'll be fine, Mom." Ignoring my words, she went to the kitchen and searched through the drawer by the sink for takeout menus.

Dad stared at her with a bemused expression. Even he couldn't figure out why she was doing this. It seemed surreal as if we were in a play and nobody knew their lines.

"I really just need about eighteen hours of sleep, and I'll—"

"I've got it. Yen Chin. You still like pot stickers and Mongolian beef?"

"Mother—"

My father frowned. "Judith, please come back to the hotel with me. We can talk about this tomorrow."

"No. I'm sorry. I really need to talk to Lindy right now." She turned to Beck, and thank God, she spoke gently. "Beck, dear, you'd probably better go. Do you need a ride?"

"Mother." I loved my mom, but this was a side of her I'd never seen before—or rather, I'd never seen that maternal steel in her spine unless it related to me.

The longer I waited for her to let me have whatever she was storing up in her outrage arsenal, the more inescapable the conclusion became. She was getting ready to blast me for my relationship with him on *his* behalf.

She met my gaze, and I instantly knew who she saw as the villain in the piece.

"I think it's better if you go," I told Beck. "I'm sorry."

"I'll take you home." My father would have gnawed his leg off to get out of the coming conversation. Giving Beck a ride was a best-case scenario for him. If he stopped off for a drink and takeout on the way back, he could miss the whole ordeal.

"I can walk." Beck stood without looking at me.

"Beck, wait."

"No, Beck," my dad said. "I need to pick up our supper anyway. Is this the place with the sweet and sour duck breast?"

197

"Get whatever you like, dear," Mom said. "I'm sure it will be wonderful."

"Lindy?" Beck looked at me with concern and questions in his eyes.

I could have told him to stay—asked him, rather, because he needed to be the one to make the decision, but I was exhausted and depressed. Like an utter ass, I didn't say anything one way or another.

I knew how that made me look.

It gave my mother the satisfaction of chivvying me into her plans, and it made Beck think I wouldn't stand up for him or whatever it was we'd started building together.

If I didn't think my mother was right, that I had no business trying to fit a man his age into my life, I might have fought for him. Even a simple, *we'll talk later* would have softened the blow.

Instead, I uttered the three most dreadful words in the English language when it came to dating. "I'll call you."

A pat on his leg called Callie to his side. She snuggled up to him while he clipped her leash onto her collar. He didn't look at me again.

Dad pulled his car keys out of his pocket with a frown. "Text if you think of anything you want me to bring back."

I got the feeling he might have even been referring to Beck, and I wanted him back before he'd even left. Of course I did.

It broke my heart watching him avoid any eye contact as he walked to the door. It hurt, letting him go like this. But because we'd been close all my life, I understood exactly what my mother was trying to tell me in her unsubtle way.

You can't do this to him. He's just a boy. You'll hurt him because you always hurt everyone eventually, and because he has no one else, it will not only be painful, he will be utterly devastated.

Hurting him now will save him pain later.

Mom once told me that once you become somebody's mother, you become everybody's mother. I'd never seen her in action on anyone else's behalf but mine—yet now, I was glad she was on Beck's side.

He needed someone like her in his life to look out for him. I had no doubt that if he allowed it, she would take him under her wing and shepherd him into a much better future.

My father ushered Beck out and closed the door behind him.

"It's better this way, darling." She put her hand on my shoulder. "Don't you think?"

"Yes." God, I was so tired. Rescue and move on. That was what I always did. A cat burned badly in a house fire. A dog nearly drowned in a flood. Whether it was a hundred Siberian huskies or a much younger man, I was made to save them, not keep them.

Everybody seemed to understand that but me.

CHAPTER TWENTY-THREE

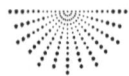

I WASN'T ready to talk to my mother about Beck.

So, obviously, she would not let it go.

"Out of all the men you've dated, that's what you want?" she asked. "A *homeless* boy half your age?"

My head was killing me. "I hear what you're saying."

"You have no right to start anything with someone in his situation. You know that. I know you know that. Despite what you're telling yourself, he has no choice."

"You don't know him."

"I know consent is a lot more than age, and so do you if you'd take a single moment to think about it."

"Mother, what are you trying to say? That I—" I couldn't say it. I couldn't believe she'd even imply it. "That what I have with Beck isn't consensual?"

"Oh, I'm sure it was." She softened. "I know he believes it was. I know *you*."

"Well, thanks for that."

"My point is someone like Beck needs protection without strings attached. He's confusing kindness, which it doesn't seem like he's had a lot of, with love. Bringing sex into that equation was wrong, sweetheart. You're old enough, wise enough, to know that."

I wanted to argue that I felt a hell of a lot more than kindness. That I'd fallen for Beck. I wasn't *using* him. I was in love with him. But my doubts were too close to the surface. My mother's voice was so much like the voice in my own head. When she said I had to protect Beck by keeping him at arm's length, it was nothing more than I'd been telling myself since I'd met him.

I don't do relationships.

I'm awful at anything long-term.

I would never forgive myself if I couldn't give Beck what he needed, and how could I? I'd never been enough for *anyone.* I didn't want to break Beck's heart. It would be far worse than losing Nick. Beck made me see myself in a whole new light. He made me feel things I'd never felt with anyone. Losing Nick had been painful, but it was inevitable. If I hurt Beck in any way, I would lose myself—at least the dominant, nurturing part of me I was just beginning to acknowledge—along with him.

"I never meant for any of this to happen," I told my mother.

"Of course you didn't."

"I don't want to hurt him."

"I know, sweetheart." She brushed my hair back. "You have a good heart."

I thought I did, but it was breaking.

"What should I do, though? He's going to be so hurt."

"Talk to him, baby. Explain that you're still there for him. Let him know that even if a relationship between the two of you isn't in his best interest, you still have his best interest at heart."

"He's never going to listen to anything I have to say again."

"He said he's living at Cooper and Shawn's place, so he has them if he chooses to go down an angry path for a while. If you're truly friends and not just"—she lifted her hands—"you know, he'll come around."

"I feel so ashamed." I lifted my glass and took a large swallow. "I knew better than to get involved with him like that, but there's just something so wonderful about him. If you only knew. He's bright, and he's funny. So smart. And he's a musical genius. He lights up a room when he walks in, but he's down to earth too. He's so kind. That's what I like best. He's genuinely kind."

"He's very sweet," she agreed. "Of course you were drawn to him. He's very much like you when you were his age."

"Why couldn't I have met someone like him then?"

"You wouldn't have known what to do with him back then," she said. "You didn't know what your future held any more than he does. You were too young to know what you wanted, much less what you'd want forever."

"No. He's light-years ahead of where I was back then."

"He might seem that way. I promise you, though. I *promise* he needs something else right now. He does not need to get involved in a sexual relationship with a man twice his age."

I winced. "It sucks when you say it like that."

"That should tell you something."

She let me sip my wine in silence for a while. It was a blessing and a curse having her for a mother. I respected her. She'd always given me good counsel. We had a track record that —except for her attempts to see me paired up and on my way to the altar with just about any successful middle-aged man— spoke positively about her parenting skills.

I listened to her. I believed that she had both my and Beck's best interests at heart. She was utterly outraged on Beck's behalf, and I kind of admired her determination to throw me under the bus. But it killed me to hurt Beck. Even if I was doing it for his own good, it still fucking killed me.

"I don't know how hungry I'll be," I said.

"Mm." She waited to weigh in on that until my father came back with food that smelled so delicious, I ate about twice what I'd planned. I also finished off the wine by myself. She and Dad helped me toss the trash and wash up the dishes.

"I'm sure you need a good night's sleep." She kissed my cheek. "We'll be expecting you to stop by after work for dinner at the resort tomorrow evening, and I've booked you a massage on Saturday morning."

"Thanks. I'll let you know what my schedule is like. I don't know if it will be possible to get up there every night." Friday was pie night after all. I ached when I thought about giving up my guitar lessons. Would Beck even speak to me if I called him?

"We'll take whatever time you have, son. We understand work comes first." Finally, Dad was able to forestall one of Mom's arguments. *Better late than never.*

"Night, guys. Thank you for dinner." I didn't plan on thanking them for stopping by unannounced and ruining my life, but old habits died hard. "Talk to you soon."

"Tomorrow." My mother crossed the threshold before my father practically pushed her out the door.

He turned to me. "Always remember, your mother has your best interests at heart, but she's not perfect."

As I closed the door behind them, I heard my mother say, "What do you mean by that? I'm not perfect? What does that mean, Doug?"

My house seemed so empty after they left.

Except for Rico, who probably slept peacefully beneath the quilt Beck had used to cover his cage. It was going to seem empty for a good long time.

I loathed the idea of going back to the old days before I had the sight of Beck's face when I hand-fed him to look forward to. He loved it when I spoiled and cherished him. His body spoke so eloquently for him every time I treated him like he was mine.

I'd miss the enjoyment he took feeding kittens, the sound of guitar music wafting in through the bedroom window, the feel of his slim body pressed against mine when he sought me out sleepily in the middle of the night, and the scent of him—coconuts and ocean breeze and that certain sweet something that was only ever Beck.

It hurt so much I wanted to cry.

THE PHONE RANG four times before Beck picked up.

"You don't have to tell me. I already know what you're going to say," he said by way of a greeting.

At first, I couldn't respond.

"Are you there?" That was a little less confident.

"I'm here," I said. "I was just trying to decide if you were right. What do you think I'm going to say?"

"That we're over."

"We're not over. We just can't keep going on like we are." I cringed because never in the history of the world was *it's not you, it's me* more true or less awful.

"Just the part where we fuck."

"I guess. Yes."

"Your Mom thinks I'm not good enough for you, is that it?"

"Not quite. My mother told me in no uncertain terms that she thinks I'm an asshole. She wants to adopt you, and I'm a dirty old man."

He chuckled. "That's rich."

"Yeah, well. That's Mom. She likes you. You could do worse than to pick her brain about getting help going back to school. She knows a lot about grants and scholarships."

"Right. Me and Callie could move into a dorm room, and I could join a fraternity and go to keggers. You're all dreaming if you think that's my future."

"School is only one avenue open to you." *I'm not your future, but you have one.* "She's on your side. We're all on your side."

"Thanks, but I'll take my chances by myself."

Alarmed, I asked, "What does that mean?"

"I don't need you on my side." He sounded like he was gritting his teeth. "I did fine on my own. I'll do fine on my own in the future."

"Except you weren't on your own, were you? You had Tug looking out for you."

"And look where that got me. I guess I really can't rely on anyone but myself."

"Beck, please believe me when I say there are people who don't want to see you by yourself. We're here for you. *I'm* still here for you."

"But you're really not. You see me as a charity case. Another rescue. Or maybe I'm just another casualty of your all-work-and-no-play ethic."

"According to who?"

"Everyone, duh. I asked around about you, you know. I didn't just blunder blindly into this. Travis, April, and Lena had a lot to say on the matter, and those are just people you work with. Cooper, Shawn, Jim, they all said the same thing. You're not interested in finding someone. I should have listened."

"So should I."

What followed was a solid minute of silence.

I sighed. "Look, I've never dated anyone who wasn't just as glad to be rid of me a couple months later because I'm a worka-holic. Work takes up my whole life, Beck. What I do—especially the volunteer work—means everything to me."

"I know that." He huffed. "You know I know that, and you have no clue how I'll handle it."

"But it doesn't matter. The work I do means I don't have anything left over to give to a relationship. You see that, don't you?" I waited, but he didn't respond. "Even if we were the same age, at the same place in life, and you had a career you loved and a home of your own, I would still have nothing to offer you because I'm too tied up in my work."

"What about what you need?" he asked. "What about what I can offer you?"

I closed my eyes. "You would always feel less than, Beck. I don't want that for you."

"Don't you dare tell me how I'll feel." His outrage was just... precious. My God, I even adored his rage. "You fucking suck."

"I know."

"I'm still feeding the kittens. You can't stop me."

"I wouldn't dream of trying."

"Stay out of my way."

"I will."

"You're a total douchebag."

"I know."

"I also might actually love you, you fuckbundle," he whispered.

His words broke something inside me.

How was I going to breathe again? How was I going to laugh, or sing, or see beauty, or listen to music again after hearing that?

Things seemed to fade all around me, and I grieved the loss of color.

"I'm sorry."

He disconnected the call.

A huge part of me left with him, so I was right all along.

Nothing would change and everything would.

I held my phone between my palms as I went to sleep, waiting for some kind of message from Beck—one that would allow me to hope for something, even if it was only a moratorium on being called a fuckbundle—but it never came.

Things between me and Beck were over. It was the right thing to do, but then why did it hurt like this?

"*Sometimes doing the right thing,*" my mother's voice said in my head, "*is the hardest thing. But the pain only lasts a minute, and then you'll see it's for the best.*"

It's been longer than a minute, Mom.

I think this is going to hurt forever.

CHAPTER TWENTY-FOUR

To say I was in a foul mood the next day would be a massive understatement. I hadn't slept well. I was still processing the work of the Gilroy case. When it came to trying to save neglected animals—or those who might be, through no fault of their own, behind the eight ball genetically due to bad breeding practices—it was an uphill battle with few victories.

I'd hurt someone I cared about. My parents were disappointed. My friends watched me with a new kind of suspicion.

I'm certain it wasn't as bad as I pictured, but at the time, it felt as though my life had taken a really dark turn.

"Lena, this is the wrong file." I didn't snap at her. No matter how it sounded, I wasn't snapping; I was tired and resigned. "This is Julia Fleming's dog, not Angelica's."

The fact that Julia and Angelica were middle-aged identical twins who still dressed alike made things difficult, and Lena was in no way deserving of my ire.

She shot me a wounded look and got up to get the correct file. As she handed it over, she said, "Maybe try decaf for a while, Doc."

I took the file and headed back toward the exam room.

Julia's apricot toy poodle, Frankie, was aging but still looked healthy and alert. He got his regular vaccinations, prescriptions for flea, tick, and heartworm medication, and I recommended she make an appointment to have his teeth cleaned.

Julia and Frankie made that appointment on the way out. The rest of my day had gone much the same. There were no surgeries and no emergencies, just the way I liked it. Healthy animals. Happy people. Two cats and a rabbit later, it was lunchtime.

I'd ordered sandwiches from Bistro to make up for my short temper, and I headed for my office with mine. On the way, I passed by the recovery room where Beck was feeding the goddamned kittens.

Because he didn't notice me, I stood behind the doorjamb for a few seconds, watching. He held the kitten with care while he talked nonsense to her.

"And then I saw a seagull eating Teddy Grahams somebody had dropped on the ground. Bet it was one of the kids from the day care center. I don't think seagulls are supposed to eat graham crackers. They're supposed to eat fish, aren't they?"

Heart tightening, I passed the open doorway quickly and shut myself in my office.

My favorite Cuban sandwich went down like sawdust.

I doubled up on coffee to stay awake, but I already knew I'd pay tonight when I tried to sleep.

Whenever my eyes closed, I imagined Beck feeding the kittens, or playing guitar on the boardwalk, or wrapping his sweet sexy mouth over a spoonful of ice cream.

We were good together. We made sense.

We had so much in common. We valued the same things.

I could honestly see myself marrying him. I could even imagine having children with him someday...

I could have something lasting with Beck, but I had nothing to offer. Only long days alone. Stretches of time when my volunteer work took me out of town, out of state—sometimes even out of the country.

Then there was the fact that my body would age and give out while he was still young and vital. The possibility that I'd let him down in the most fundamental way, simply by becoming a burden to him and not a partner, made the coffee in my stomach threaten a revolt.

I was a fool to believe that wouldn't matter. Even if I lived well and took excellent care of myself, he might still have to pay a heavy price for loving me.

April knocked on my door. "Can I come in?"

"Sure." I wiped my hands off on my napkin. "What do you need?"

"Is everything okay?"

"As far as I know." I held her gaze steadily. "Why do you ask?"

"You snapped at Lena." She wrung her hands together. "You never do that. Plus, you haven't been singing."

"Maybe some days I don't feel like singing." That was out of line. I softened my tone. "I guess the case in Gilroy bothered me a lot more than I realized."

She pursed her lips as if she wanted to argue with that, but without calling me a liar, she couldn't. "If you need to talk about anything—"

"We've handled worse situations. It just takes a while to get back in the groove. Plus, my parents are in town, so it's going to be a busy few days."

She frowned. "I thought they were coming for the Fourth?"

"They moved it up a week. Apparently Mom thinks I need special handling right now."

"Are they staying with you this time?"

"No." *Thank God.* "We get along much better when they don't."

She gave a snort and turned to leave.

"April, you're right, and I'll do better, okay?"

"Okay, Doc." She left without closing the door behind her. From the hall, I heard a low-voiced conversation between April and Travis. Lena was making phone calls, double-checking appointment times and dates. The fax machine made its own peculiar noises.

The window in my office looked into the parking lot, and beyond that there was an alley with a little river of foamy runoff moving sluggishly down the center of the street, probably from someone hosing something down or washing a car.

Every so often someone would speed by on a beach cruiser or carve a trail down the hill to the boardwalk on a skateboard.

I wasn't looking for them, but when Beck and Callie left through the back door, I went to the window to watch them until they turned the corner.

I didn't know where Beck was headed for the rest of the day. He didn't tell me, and I didn't ask. It wasn't that he'd gone silent —he answered when I spoke to him—but he had a way of looking through me now as if he was trying to focus on anything *but* me.

I never realized how often I'd felt his eyes on me before.

I never realized how hot it was to be the object of his desire until he took that away from me. I felt the loss like a physical blow. Like a change in barometric pressure—no longer presaging the excitement of a storm.

It was no wonder I'd been snapping at people.

Later that afternoon, I left the office for April and Travis to lock up and went home to shower and change. I spent a few minutes with Rico, making sure he had everything he needed and listening to him idly berate me before heading south to the resort and dinner with my parents.

I dreaded it. Mom would want to dig into what we'd talked about the night before. She'd probably try to take my emotional temperature while Dad fussed at her to leave me alone.

There was no way to avoid it, so I parked my car, took a deep breath, and walked toward the resort's elegant front doors.

We met in the restaurant, which was basically a long room with floor to ceiling windows overlooking the ocean. The sun was in the process of putting on a spectacular show, igniting layers of color—fiery red, orange, gold, and violet—over the sea.

"I hope I didn't keep you waiting too long." I kissed Mom's cheek and patted Dad's shoulder before sitting. The waiter saw me arrive and came by to pour me a glass of wine.

"We got here a little early. Your mother wanted to watch the sun set."

"Did you have fun today?"

"Oh my, yes." Mom's cheeks were flushed, and her eyes sparkled girlishly. "We rented one of those bicycle surreys."

Dad grimaced. "Once again, we forgot to turn back before we got sick of peddling. The return trip is always such a slog."

"It's a little harder going into the wind too."

Dad put his arm around her. "We made it, though. Your mom's a trooper."

"But I spent the rest of the afternoon in the spa."

"We're getting a couples massage tomorrow." Dad waggled his brows. "Poor masseuse. She'll have to rub the cycling kinks out."

"How was your day, darling?"

"It went well. No emergencies, which was nice. Plus, I didn't have any surgeries scheduled."

"That's good. I read online about the case you went on earlier this week. How is it that no one notices someone has a hundred neglected dogs until a disaster happens?"

I shrugged. "In this case, it turned out to be a legitimate dog breeder who lived on a large property. The neighbors were used to hearing barking. The neglect really only began when she got sick and her son had to help her care for the animals. He didn't, of course, for whatever reason. It only came to anyone's attention because the son had a dangerous confrontation with his mother. We're lucky someone heard that. I'm not sure how it would have turned out otherwise."

"Some people don't deserve to keep animals," Dad complained. "Aren't there laws in place that keep them from having so many?"

"The statutes vary from county to county here, and up until recently, there has been no national data base that flags serial animal abusers or animal hoarders. Even when there is, it's not always available to rescue organizations and civilians trying to rehome a pet. There's a grapevine of course. We try to keep track of the abuse cases filed in court, but that's not even taking into consideration the fly by night puppy mills who sell online or by word of mouth."

"I guess it's like any other crime," Dad mused. "People always find a way."

"I'm afraid so."

Mom patted my arm. "I'm so proud to know you're out there doing something about it."

"Rescue and release." I took a healthy sip of wine because the words had become a bitter and painful reminder of the man I'd lost. "That's me."

We ordered dinner—cedar-plank grilled salmon for me and Dad and scampi for Mom—before she decided it was time to probe into my emotional state.

"Now, I know you probably don't want to talk about this, but I really feel like we should. How are you feeling today, sweetheart?"

"I'm good." Petulantly, I picked up a piece of bread and buttered it a little too thoroughly. What did I care? I wasn't trying to live forever. "Everything's golden."

"Oh, honey. Did you talk to Beck?"

"I did, and everything's fine. He's still stopping by to feed our stray kittens."

"Well, that's good."

"I have no doubt everything will continue as if—" *I never lost my heart.* "Everything will be fine."

"Darling," she put her hand on mine. "Now, this is just a suggestion, but maybe give Dylan a second chance. You weren't expecting him, and you got off on the wrong foot, but I'm sure if—"

"No."

"You haven't even considered it."

"It's not going to happen."

She pouted. "All I'm saying is that he seems like a lovely family man."

"Lindy said he's not interested, hon," said my father. "Let it go."

"But—"

"Our son knows his own mind, Judy."

After a few minutes of silence where all three of us pretended to be fascinated by the sun's final descent into the sea, the waiter came to the table with our meals.

I wanted to love the food, but again, I barely tasted it. I had another glass of wine—absolutely my limit—and coffee with dessert.

My mother got some kind of chocolate extravaganza to share with Dad.

Goddamnit, I wanted what they had.

Sure, I was wrapped up in my work, but Dad had been too— he had been on a goddamn aircraft carrier for the first half of my life. Mom had seemed content to man the home fires and found things to occupy her mind and her time when he'd been gone. When they were together, it was delightful. They had embarrassed the hell out of me back then, displaying their affection publicly and sneaking in make-out sessions when they thought I wasn't around.

Why had I not been enough for my lovers?

Why had I been such a consistent disappointment?

"Sweetheart?"

"Hm?" I guessed I'd been holding my coffee halfway to my lips for too long. I put it down.

"Would you like to take a little walk?"

"I don't think so. I'm still catching up on sleep. I should go home." I kissed Mom goodbye. Dad stood and gave me a bear hug.

Before he even guessed what I was up to, I picked up the check wallet. "Dinner was great, guys. I'll take care of this."

"Aw, no, son." Dad grabbed for it.

"Nuh-uh. Done deal." I held it away from him. "You have a good night."

"You too." Mom blew me a kiss. "Sweet dreams. See you here for dinner tomorrow?"

"Sure." Friday. Pie day. Also, my guitar lesson, but I doubted Beck would want to carry on with those. At least not for a while. I didn't want to sit at home thinking about things I couldn't have. "I'll text to let you know when I'm on my way."

"Drive safe," Dad admonished me.

"You golfing tomorrow?" He nodded. "Then you too."

My mother snickered as I walked away. "He still says that every time."

The joke was too old, but just then I felt too old as well.

Too old for Beck. Too old for tears.

Way too old for a broken heart that felt like it would never, ever heal.

CHAPTER TWENTY-FIVE

THERE WAS a news van in front of the clinic on Friday morning following up on the Gilroy case. What had started as an altercation between mother and son and led to the discovery of the neglected animals had grown more grim because the old woman had died in the hospital.

While it had nothing to do with me, it was likely news of the case would go national now that there might be homicide charges against the son.

They wanted an in-depth interview about what I'd seen, but I gave them only the barest facts. I'd been there on behalf of some unfortunate animals, and beyond that, I knew nothing.

I was sure they'd already gotten a statement from Jeanie. She was far better positioned to give them a follow-up than I was. I'd handled the press before, so it didn't faze me, but Lena was discombobulated.

"They were so pushy," she complained. "I kept telling them I wasn't there, but then they asked what you said about it and how you felt about euthanizing animals, and I was like, nuh-uh. No comment, motherfuckers."

"Thank you. I appreciate that." The last thing I wanted was a member of my staff putting words into my mouth.

"Did they bother Travis or April?"

"They hid in back until you got here."

"Good for them. What's on for today?"

"You sound like you're doing better."

"It's amazing what a good night's sleep will do for you." Not that I got one.

After I got home, I lay in bed for over an hour thinking about things. Why was I so enchanted by Beck and not Dylan? Was it just his youth and looks that attracted me? Was I *that guy*? Why wasn't I content to stay in my own lane?

"Today looks like it's going to be slow. You've got time to get a cup of coffee before your eight o'clock comes in." She held out a file.

"Thanks." On the way back to my office, I heard Travis and April talking about the reporters. "I heard you guys hid. I was not so lucky."

"That woman died," said April. "The whole thing is so sad. Do you think they'll charge the son with manslaughter or murder?"

"No way to tell." I glanced through the file on the cat we were going to see. "Humans are above my pay grade."

"Not our department." Travis nodded. "You think the police will want to talk to us?"

"It's a possibility." One I hadn't even thought of. "If they do, stick with evidence-based fact and not supposition. We came onto the scene long after the argument, therefore, we have no firsthand knowledge that would shed light on their situation. We speak to the condition we found the animals in and nothing else."

"Got it." April jammed her hands into her pockets. "That was bad enough."

"Just another day in paradise," Travis muttered. "I need coffee."

The rest of the morning went smoothly. I got into the groove by midafternoon when we were ready to shut things down. I even serenaded Iguana Bill while I cleaned the abscess beneath his eye.

"There. All tidied up. I took a sample to see what's causing this." Bill's fifteen-year-old owner, Tilly, looked much relieved. "Lena will call you."

"Okay." Tilly beamed at me. "Thanks, Dr. Lindy."

Bill was my last patient of the day. Now I had to answer the big question. Should I go to the resort early for my visit with the folks or stick to just seeing them at dinner? Since the resort was so nice, I decided I'd like to go over there now. Besides the spa and restaurant, they had a lush, private garden that people from all over used as a wedding venue. From there you could make your way down to the beach and walk along the sand. The place was lovely, serene, and maybe exactly what I needed today.

I texted my Dad to tell him to expect me around four.

He sent a thumbs up emoji and a few smiley faces.

On my way home, I stopped for coffee. Of course, when I stepped out onto the patio to look for a nice place to relax and drink it, who should be sitting there but Beck and Callie with a pair of bichon frises I recognized as belonging to the Fairchilds.

The sight of him froze me. I must have looked like an idiot, standing there uncertain whether I should join him, but I truly didn't know what to do.

He made it easy for me by reaching out one long leg and kicking the chair opposite him with his foot to indicate I should sit there.

It scraped across the polished concrete until I took it and sat.

"Hi," I said.

"Hi." He eyed me cautiously. "Just off work?"

I nodded. "Fridays are half days."

Silence fell all around us. That might have been my imagination.

"Are those Ajax Fairchild's dogs?" I asked.

"Yeah. Well, they belong to his grandpa. You know him?"

"I know Ajax. He's the one who brought them in when they moved here. They look good."

"They just got out of the groomer." He wrinkled his nose. "They smell like potpourri."

I reached down and picked one up. "They're sweet. Don't know how he tells them apart."

Beck picked up the other dog. "This little girl has an orange collar. Yours has pink."

I set her in my lap and petted her while sipping my coffee with my free hand. "So you're dog walking for the Fairchild household?"

"Not just that. Dmytro and Ajax are taking the girls to LA for a week, and they hired me to stay with Mr. Fairchild the elder while they're gone. He's pretty self-sufficient, but they want someone around in case he needs help."

"That's cool. They have one of the best views in town."

"They do." He quirked a brow. "Have you met Dmytro and his daughters?"

"Not yet."

"He was married before. He's almost forty, and Ajax is only in his twenties."

"Is that so?"

Beck winked. "Just sayin'. Dmytro's pretty badass."

"I hope I get to meet them all sometime. They sound like an awesome family."

"They're pretty sweet." Beck turned away. "Guess some people think it's okay to live in the present instead of always thinking about what might go wrong."

Ouch. "Guess so."

"Look, it's not my business anymore, but—"

"Beck."

"No, hear me out." He leaned forward, eyes like lasers, straight to my soul. "You think I'm just some dumb kid who got caught up in a couple bad choices. You think that's why I was living rough, why I latched onto Tug, why I came on to you."

"Beck, you don't know what I think."

"No, I know you believe I'm naïve because I'm young. You've said that. But I've been through things you have no way to understand, and what I know is there are only three truly certain things. We're born. We live. And we die."

"I know you've had it hard—"

"No, listen. Everything is secondary to those three basic realities. We have no control over being born. Death is a matter of biology or bad luck. My biodad died in a welding accident. My younger brother died of leukemia. I've seen the beginning and the end, and all I want to do now is live. We're born. We live. We die. And we only really have control over one of those things."

I stroked the dog's soft white fur. "What do you want from me?"

"I want you to choose how you want to *live*. Don't borrow trouble from your future, and don't make decisions based on your past. I choose how I live now. I choose to love you because you're a good man, and you make me happy."

"Oh, God, Beck." I let the dog down and staggered to my feet. "I don't know what to say to that. What you're saying...it's such an oversimplification."

"Is it?" His blue gemstone eyes hardened.

"It feels like it. It feels like you can't always choose how to live. There are priorities, for one thing. I may want to choose something or *someone*, but my work takes up so much of my life everything and everyone else suffers from neglect. It wouldn't be fair to—"

"Please think about it, Doc. Think about it before it's too late to find a way to wedge in something besides saving all the animals. Maybe people need you too."

"I will always be here for *you* if you need me." I let my fingers trail down his arm. "Hope you enjoy your stay up at Ajax's place."

"I start there on Sunday morning."

"Good." I couldn't think of anything else to say. "Well…"

He sighed unhappily. "Bye, Lindy. Have a good weekend."

"You too."

I DROVE to the resort numb with grief. If only I believed my destiny was mine to control, it would be a lot easier to swallow. It wasn't that I didn't have choices. I had choices. But honestly, when I compared how effective I was at work with how good a boyfriend I'd been the few times I'd tried it, there was no question where my priorities should lie. I had an actual calling. It seemed wrong to let a man get in the way of that.

Of course, my brain told me Beck wouldn't begrudge me my work. My heart told me my love for him provided me with strength and healing. I could see our relationship enhancing my life in a thousand ways, not least of which was to bring us both joy.

But…I still worried it might be a big mistake. I might simply be another deluded old fool dazzled by a pretty young thing.

Who should I believe?

Dad met me in the resort lobby with a hug. "Your mom got a little more sun than she expected in the pool this afternoon, so she's taking a nap. We're on our own until dinner."

"Okay."

"I'd like to get a drink at the bar and then maybe take a walk if that's okay with you?"

"Sounds great." I followed him to an elegant mahogany bar

with brass fittings, marble tables, and cane back chairs. Around the perimeter, groups of leather wingbacks made the place look like a gentleman's club. "How was your golf game?"

"Wonderful. I don't know if I mentioned, but some old friends drove up from San Luis Obispo, and we got a chance to catch up."

"That's cool."

The bartender came over. "What can I get you?"

I started to speak, but Dad held his hand up. "Your whisky is Laphroiag, right?"

"If you're paying." I nodded.

"Two," Dad told the bartender. "You got the check last night. Today is all mine."

"Thanks." We got our drinks and sat in two oxblood leather wingback chairs in the corner with a low table between us.

"Look at you." He shook his head. "Can I be old enough to have a kid your age?"

I laughed. "I hope so, or Mom's got some explaining to do."

"Oh my. Wouldn't that be something?"

I sipped my whisky. The piped-in music was Chopin. The black-and-white marble checkerboard floors shiny and pristine. I ought to have gone to the resort for drinks and dinner more often. It was delightful to spend time there.

"You know, there was a time when I was devastated you didn't follow me into the navy."

"Surprise!" I teased. "That is not news to me."

"I know." He sighed and looked out toward the ocean. "I know I gave you a hard time about it."

"You didn't push too hard."

"I didn't let you off the hook either. It wasn't until recently that I realized how disastrous that life would have been for you. In a weird way, your volunteering reminds me of some of the things I did. In your way, you serve."

"My ragtag band of veterinary mercs." I smiled behind my glass. "I'm a veterinary pirate."

He laughed. "Arr."

"You know I always wanted to be the kind of man you are. I'm just crap at doing what I'm told."

"Your mother tried to tell me that. Do not, under any circumstances tell her I admitted she was right. It will go straight to her head and then where will we be?"

"She doesn't need you to tell her she was right." I glanced up to find his eyes on me. "I'm sorry I wasn't more—"

"Don't regret anything. I am so proud of you for standing your ground and doing what you love. You're a success, despite my interference."

"I don't know about that. You're a hell of a role model."

He lowered his gaze to his drink. "Thanks."

We took our time finishing our drinks and then headed out the exterior doors for a walk.

There was a pathway through the gardens that led past statues, a fountain, and a greenhouse. The garden wasn't manicured, but it was lush and green and fragrant with a thousand different flowers.

Eventually we arrived at an open gate beyond which was a steep set of stairs leading down to the sandy, rocky shore. A posted sign warned it was too dangerous to swim. They were right to issue the warning. At low tide, I'd seen jagged rocks beneath the waves, plus the area had rip currents that would challenge even the strongest swimmers.

We left our shoes and socks at the base of the stairs and took off barefoot. I loved having cool sand between my toes again.

"What's that look?" Dad asked.

"I was just thinking how long it's been since I was in Hawaii."

"Oh, yeah. I miss tropical waters. Have you been doing any sailing?"

"No." Cold water and foam lapped at our feet. "There's a

marina just north of St. Nacho's that rents boats. I suppose I could."

"That would be fun. Let's look into that for the next time your mom and I are up here."

"Or I could come down there. Lots of boat rentals where you are."

"Plus, I know the area. Maybe so."

He picked up a mussel shell and threw it into the waves. "Been thinking about what we talked about last night."

I glanced over. "What?"

"Your boy, Beck."

"Not my boy, I assure you." I pictured him as I'd last seen him, surrounded by the dogs and looking right through me.

"I didn't want to say in front of your mom because she can be so…I don't know."

"Determined? Hardheaded? Intractable?"

"If she ever hears about this conversation, you tell her I said 'delightful,' you hear?"

I laughed. "I get it."

"I'm going to need unconditional immunity regarding this conversation."

"You have it. Go on."

"Half the officers I knew dropped their first wives in favor of some young thing Beck's age."

"This is not an endorsement is it? Because—"

"No, no. Let me finish. Most of the time when a man goes out with someone half their age it's about trophy hunting. You know it, and I know it."

I did know it. "Right."

"Thing is, I don't think that's who you are. You wouldn't pick up just any young thing to bang. I know you better than that."

My ears burned. "How?"

"You're not shallow."

"My coworkers said I'm one Harley shy of a midlife crisis."

He stared at me for a long time then shook his head. "I don't see it."

"So what, then? It's not about me. Mom's right. He's too young to fall for someone like me."

"She doesn't know that. Neither do we. It's up to him who he falls for."

"But—"

"Oh, I know. I heard all the arguments. You're both right about one thing. It could go horribly wrong."

"Well, when you put it that way, where do I sign up?"

He gave me a shove, and I lost my balance, stepping into the water with a splash that soaked the hem of my jeans. "Hey."

"Do you think it couldn't end horribly if you got together with Dylan? Or had stayed with Nick?"

"That did end horribly. Rico loves reminding me."

"That's my point." He clapped me on the back. "Even if you were exactly the same age and perfect for each other, there's no telling what could happen. Whatever you're worried about, it could happen to anyone."

"Dad, I'll be sixty when he's forty. He could end up being more of a caregiver than a lover."

"You remember your cousin Celeste?"

I winced. "Yes."

Celeste had gotten married right after college, and her husband died around his thirtieth birthday from ALS.

"Life's not predictable," Dad said.

"I know that. But shouldn't we play the odds?"

He waved his hand as if to say, fifty-fifty. "There are odds and then there are odds. From what your mother tells me, the odds of you going on a second date with anyone anymore are pretty goddamn slim. What are the odds you'll ever connect with someone else the way you do with this boy?"

I turned toward the waves. "Based on experience, not good."

"You love him?"

"Could be." Understatement of the year.

"A special someone." The hand Dad laid on my shoulder warmed me through my shirt. "Now that doesn't come along every day, does it? I believe that even if something goes horribly wrong, you won't be sorry you had your time together."

"Mom thinks—"

"*Shush.* Your mom got her say. This is mine. You're not chasing after all the boys half your age. You met one guy who happens to be young, and things clicked, right?"

I nodded. "Right."

"I'm thinking your mom reinforced the doubts and fears you already had. But what if he's your actual soulmate and you walk away because you're scared?"

"I...never thought of that."

"Well, think about it now." Dad squeezed my neck and shook me a little. "In the end, any partnership is between two people. And those two individuals are the only ones who know whether it's right or not."

"Consenting adults."

"Duh." He gave me another shove. "Your boy's twenty, isn't he?"

"Yeah."

"So. Now you know what I think. Just leave your mother to me."

"She's going to go nuclear."

"No, she won't." Dad jerked his head toward the stairs. "She's going to love anyone you love who loves you back. Full stop."

It was a lot to think about.

Was he right?

Borrowing trouble was probably the number one pastime of people contemplating relationships. After sex.

"I may have already ruined everything." I didn't need Rico to say it.

"Well, first, let's go get dinner. Everything looks better after a good meal."

"Right." As I followed him up the stairs, my heart beat twice as fast as the exertion required.

Dad's right.

Loving someone—really loving them—and walking away because things might not work out? That was just stupid. If what I felt in my heart was real and if Beck felt the same way, then we had something precious.

Oh God. I'd fucked up. Could I fix it?

And what about the naysayers—my mother's disapproval, the ribbing from my staff, and the likely censure from some of my peers? Was I so afraid they were right, so caught up in how things looked to *them*, that I didn't consider how things actually were between Beck and me?

Could I live with that? Why let other people make our decisions for us?

In order to find out if I had what it takes to reach for joy, I had to give up my ego, go all in, and make things right with Beck.

CHAPTER TWENTY-SIX

AT MIDNIGHT, I rang the doorbell at Cooper's place.

I'd walked to Cooper and Shawn's, loose from a couple glasses of wine at home but not at all drunk. What I did feel was giddy, breathless excitement, like the snap of energy you feel when you meet someone's eyes and that spark of chemistry bursts into flame.

I'd brought a wagon loaded with Rico—in his bird cage—and a wooden step stool so I could sit down while pleading my case. I'd also brought my guitar and a hastily printed Beatles song I could probably play at least serviceably. Halfway there, I realized I could sit on the wagon itself, but I was already committed.

I rang again, and then I knocked. After a few tense minutes, Cooper came to the door in an undershirt and a pair of jeans, followed by Shawn, who wore some kind of flowy wrapper, which he belted in a bit of a huff while standing behind Cooper and glaring at me.

"I won't ask if you know what time it is."

"You kinda just did, though."

"Are you out of your mind?" asked Shawn, who does not

own a stage whisper.

"I hope not." Obviously the question had been rhetorical because Cooper rolled his eyes. "I'm here to see Beck."

"You can wait until morning." Cooper started to close the door, but I stopped it with my foot.

"I'm not going home until I see Beck."

From somewhere behind Shawn, I heard Beck say, "It's okay. Let him talk."

"Okay, so…" I had practiced a hundred times so *of course* I couldn't remember what I'd planned to say. "Wait."

"Why?" Beck stepped forward wearing skinny jeans and a band t-shirt. He looked edible. Callie hugged his side as usual.

"We prepared, er…a statement." I pointed behind me, and his eyes widened when he saw the wagon. "Well, Rico's just here to watch. The statement is mine."

"You brought Rico?"

"Of course I did. He's family." I could see he was intrigued. Nobody looked like they were going to slam the door in my face anymore. "Wait. Just wait here."

"Cooper pulled a phone from his pocket. "You have five minutes, but I swear to God, if someone calls the cops, I've never met you before."

"*Pft*, good luck with that." I waved a hand. "Everybody in St. Nacho's knows me. I'm kind of a big deal here."

Beck turned a snort into a cough.

I backed away down the path toward the sidewalk where I'd left the wagon. It was pretty smooth except I tripped gracelessly over an ornamental rock and nearly took a header.

"It's okay." I smoothed my shirt. "I'm all right."

When I got to the wagon, I pulled the stool out and set it on the uneven pavement. As I was adjusting it, the absurdity of the entire moment shook me. I turned back to the house and the trio of disapproving men.

"Look, Beck. I brought a—*stool sample*."

Beck covered his face with both hands. "I guess that means we've come full circle."

"Guess so, huh?" I moved my guitar into position and sat down. I tried to cross my legs several times, but my knee was really slippery for some reason. Only when I moved to the edge of the stool and braced both feet against the concrete was I able to stay upright.

I gave a sigh of relief.

"Okay. Thank you for listening to what I have to say." To my right, I noticed a couple other neighbors had their porch lights on now. Two or three people were standing on their lawns, arms folded. "Oh, hey. Hi."

I waved.

"It's me. Doc Lindy." I glanced down at the guitar, and it was honestly as if I didn't know how it had gotten there. I was very comfortable singing. Adding an instrument had always been like walking on a high-tension wire. "You know, I'm a passable pianist—"

Oh my God, how had I never noticed *pianist* sounded almost exactly like *penis*?

"The guitar adds a whole new level of danger to courtship." I strummed a few chords, certain it was completely out of tune but unable to fix it without asking Beck for his wonderful ears.

"My dad's one of the smartest guys I know. So's Beck. They both told me I could make choices that make me happy, and...I really hope they're right."

I strummed and hummed and generally girded my loins to make the biggest fool of myself. Beck stepped toward me with Callie by his side. He still had his phone in his hand. Was he videoing this? Oh, shoot. I was going into the permanent record with this little display.

I tried to straighten my spine and nearly fell off my perch.

"Wait—Okay. So. My dad reminded me that when you have

feelings for somebody you can't start looking at the odds of whether it's going to work out."

I strummed again, and because my incessant babbling both put off having to play and gave me something to do besides wallow, it relaxed me.

"I mean between uncommitted, consensual adults, though, because anything else is...pretty problematic."

Maybe I needed some kind of legal disclaimer? Where was I?

"Wait. *Yes.* Because no matter how perfect you think things are, you're never guaranteed a happy ending." Oh fuck. I said *happy ending.* "Life isn't a sure thing. Love is a gamble. I want to be the guy who just puts his heart out there. I want to be absolutely transparent because my feelings are real and they're true, and whatever happens, happens."

Behind his phone, Beck said, "Is that so?"

"Damn right." I fiddled with the guitar as if I knew what I was doing and started "If I Fell" by the Beatles. No other song captured what I was starting to think of as the bargaining phase of love: *Is it safe to give you my heart? What will happen? Will you love me back? Will you betray me?*

Is our new love—as the Beatles so feverishly sang—*in vain?*

It took meeting Beck and listening to my Dad to make me see that it was okay to love someone without worrying about what happens after. And I did love Beck. So I sang.

It's a proven fact that my voice carries.

More porch lights came on after that. Most people seemed to think my caterwauling was of the lovable variety. No one threw a shoe, anyway.

Beck filmed the whole ordeal, and a couple of times, Rico put in his two cents—saying, "Boop," and "Who's a pretty boy," and once, everybody's all time fave: "You ruin everything!"

I had not ruined this. I saw warmth in Beck's eyes. Heat in the way he took his plump lower lip between his teeth. He blushed visibly even under the weird glow of a streetlight, hands shaking as he captured my song.

I trailed off, and there was silence once more.

"So. That's pretty much all I came here to say."

After the initial *bang,* I'd finished with a bit of a whimper.

"If you—" Beck began at the same time I said, "When you—"

He tilted his head. "You go first."

"If you want to talk about this sometime, my door is always open."

"Now." Beck jammed his hands into his jeans pockets. "I want to talk about it now."

I turned away to hide my smile. "Okay. Let's go."

Beck got his things and added them to the wagon. I waved at Cooper and Shawn, who were still trying to give me the stink-eye. Shawn wasn't really that good at it because he hid a smile too.

"Sorry I woke you," I said, addressing everyone still watching.

Some people drifted back inside their homes. Some applauded. I bet the dividing line there was between people who had pets and people who didn't.

"Come on, Captain Romance." Beck chuckled as he tugged my sleeve.

Captain Romance?

What a great superhero name for me.

It is I, Captain Romance.

"So it is." Beck snorted. "How much did you drink, big guy?"

"Wait—did I say that out loud? Just a couple glasses of wine. I'm silly but not drunk. You're too important to me to do this drunk."

"Mmhmm." I took hold of the wagon's handle and started walking. Beck stayed where he was. "Yep. Your whole ass looks good in those jeans."

"Of course it does. C'mon Callie."

Callie trotted toward me. She barked as if to say, "Let's go home."

I smiled stupidly. "Home."

"Boop." Even the bird had his say.

"Boop," Beck echoed. We ambled along as if we were already a little family.

On the way, silence built around us. Maybe that was a two-edged thing about Beck. I loved his stillness, but it could be weird too. I talked in order to put others at ease.

Repeat people's names.

Repeat their pet's names.

Ask about their day. Talk about their animal.

Find something you like about them and tell them about it.

"Is that what you do?" Beck asked.

"Goddamnit." Why couldn't I keep my thoughts to myself? Beck's eyes sparkled like gems in water. Oh, well, if he was laughing with me and not at me, that was okay.

"You really talked to your dad about me?"

"More like he pulled me aside and lectured me."

"What about your mother?"

"She'll come around." *Or she won't.* "I'm done looking for approval where my feelings are concerned."

His eyes widened. "I see."

"Well, I guess I wouldn't mind your approval."

"In that case…" He made me wait for it. "I approve."

His words made me smile like I don't know what. I wore a wide, huge, drooling grin, and I didn't even care.

Let the world see it.

I glanced at Beck, chagrinned, but apparently I managed to only think those words.

"What made you pick the Beatles?" he asked.

"It's not because of my age." I said testily. "I'm not a boomer. It just fit."

He nudged me with his elbow. "Better than 'When I'm Sixty-Four'?"

"Shut up." I needed no reminders that I'd get there long before him, thank you very much.

"Honestly, though," he said as we walked up the porch steps at my place, "forty's the new thirty, and I'm an old soul. We're gonna be just fine."

I met his serious gaze. "You think so?"

"I know so." He stood on tiptoe and kissed me without breaking eye contact. "I *know* so."

CHAPTER TWENTY-SEVEN

BECK TOOK Callie out while I put Rico's cage back.

"We did good, you and me," I told him before covering him with his quilt.

"Here, girl." Beck got Callie her water bowl and filled it. Callie nuzzled up to him.

"I love how you look in my kitchen." I wanted a picture. "How about we go into all the other rooms and see how you look there."

"All right." He unclipped Callie's leash and hung it on a wall hook. "Show me."

"All right." We started with the living room. "Stand by the mantle."

Laughing, he did as I asked.

"To your right a little." He moved, and I took the picture. "You look much better there than the Christmas tree ever did. Of course it hardly stood a chance. You're far more beautiful."

"I think I like silly Lindy."

I took him by the hand and led him to the hall. "Stand here." I snapped another picture.

"Perfect. You know what I'm going to do? I'm going to frame

this picture and hang it in the hallway so all my asshole friends can come over and say how meta it is."

He snickered, then rushed over to catch me when I overbalanced. "God, I am so tired."

Beck narrowed his eyes. "Maybe you should go to bed."

"All right, but can we continue our research into how wonderful my house looks with you in it tomorrow?"

"Yes." He kissed me again, and my head spun. I calculated how many hours of sleep I'd gotten that week and decided sleep was definitely in order.

When we broke apart, I had to gasp for air. "Ah—excellent. It's a plan."

"Come on." He took my hand and led me to my bedroom where he unbuttoned my shirt, starting at my collar and working his way down.

"I really like where this is going."

"Mm. Me too." He smoothed his hand over my pecs, my ribs, down my abs, to my belly. "You're hot for an old guy."

"That's right. And I promise you I'm never going to take my health for granted."

"Your dad still has all his hair."

"Mom's dad too."

"Well, that's good news."

"Isn't it? I'm going to be a silver fox."

Beck's hands stilled on the button of my jeans. He leaned in as if he wanted to tell me a secret. "I've got news for you."

I turned my ear to his lips. "What?"

"You already are." He gripped my jeans and my briefs and worked them over my hips. "Did you wear these jeans for me?"

"I maybe thought about how you'd like them."

"Mm." A moment later, he was on his knees, pressing his face into my cock. "You smell so good."

My dick tightened and my mouth went dry.

"I like you on your knees, Beck."

A MUCH YOUNGER MAN

He glanced up, lips pursed in thought. "Oh really?"

"How would you look swallowing my cock?"

He spread his hand over his chest. "Moi?"

"Mmhmm." Playfully, I held it out for him. "No time like the present to find out."

He contemplated me for a while, then swallowed just the tip.

"Oh, sweetheart." I let my head fall back.

It was a good thing I was close to the wall because my entire body kept going until I slapped up against it.

"Oof."

"Careful there, Doc. We don't want an unfortunate dick disaster."

I snorted. "I think the difficulty level might be beyond me."

"Standing?"

"Come take a shower with me."

"All right." Beck stood, pulled his T-shirt over his head, and skimmed off his jeans. He had nothing on underneath.

"Now that is just...*mouthwatering*."

With a seductive backward glance, he slipped into the bathroom and turned on the water.

I waited for him to leave, and when he didn't, I said, "Go away. I have to pee."

Beck smirked. "You can do that while I'm here, you know."

I flinched. "Is that one of your things, because—"

"Hell no." He eyed me. "It's not one of yours..."

"Nuh-uh. Nope. Nyet. I'm just pee shy."

He sighed and left me to it.

I washed my hands and gave him the same privacy.

While I waited, the idea crashed over me that I'd just made the first negotiation in what might actually be a *relationship*, and it wasn't so hard after all. I was feeling kind of proud of myself when Beck cracked open the door just wide enough for his hand and gave a *come hither* crook of his finger.

God almighty. Beck's fingers were especially sexy. His soapy body? Magnificent. His lips were my new favorite flavor. The way he clung to me while I worked his cock, the way he begged, and moaned, and came apart in my hands gave me peace I'd never known before.

Genuine happiness I believed would last.

I rinsed us both off and left him to stay warm while I left the shower to get a towel. I had to take good care of him after all. He was precious to me.

We cuddled in bed with Callie at our feet. Beck looked warm and sleepy-eyed. "I like this."

"Me too." I pulled him to me. "You're the very best little spoon ever."

"You're a pretty sweet big spoon yourself."

"Thank you kindly."

He was silent for a while, but I didn't sense he'd fallen asleep.

"You okay? You didn't—"

"I'm fine." I had no doubt he'd wake me when he was ready to go again.

"Are we really doing this?" He reached for me and wrapped his hand around the back of my neck.

I examined the question carefully before I answered. If there were promises to be made, I had to be clear-eyed and consider every angle before making them.

"I am. I guess you still have a choice."

"Not really. Not since I fell in love with you." I smiled against the skin at the nape of his neck, making him squirm.

"Hey, that tickles."

"I hope you'll always choose me," I said.

"I hope you'll always choose me," he echoed.

I was so proud of myself for only thinking the "but" that goes along with those words and not saying it.

I wasn't sure what I was in for. Nothing was all fun and games, but honestly, I looked forward to our challenges too.

Beck made me want to race into the future just to see what it held for us.

"I'm so lucky you stopped in St. Nacho's." I really couldn't believe my luck. "If you hadn't—"

"I'm not sure I really had a choice."

I propped my head on my arm so I could see his face. "What do you mean? You said life is the only thing where you have a choice. How did you not choose St. Nacho's?"

He gripped my free hand to lace our fingers together. "Me and Tug planned to go north to Portland, but we got one free ride after another that took us off course. A weird coincidence led us to the coast instead of I-5. Tug listened to some guy who promised him a sweet deal that led us south instead of north. Suddenly we were just here, despite our plans."

I felt him yawn, and then he must have drifted off. His breathing evened out and his fingers released their hold on my hand.

It's a marvel, sleeping with a human being in your arms. It seems crazy when you factor in the trust it takes for someone to allow you that access.

I was never going to take Beck's trust for granted. *Not ever.*

It took me a long time to fall asleep.

One last time, I worried about the clinic and how people might react to my new lover. I worried about my colleagues. My friends. About my parents. I worried about the ribbing I was going to take, but then I remembered I was part of a family at last, even if it was a boy, a bird, and a dog. We might even consider the idea of having children someday. Beck might want that.

How lucky was I that I'd ended up in St. Nacho's too?

When I finally drifted off to sleep, I wasn't just smiling with my face but with my whole heart as well.

EPILOGUE

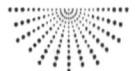

SOME TIME Later

Just before Christmas, Beck and I took my parents to the resort for dinner. On an average day, the resort was truly lovely, but at Christmastime, it was known for its number of decorated trees and outdoor spaces lit with twinkling fairy lights that illuminated the pathways and special seasonal tableaus with nondenominational messages of peace and hope for a bright new year.

We walked hand in hand behind Mom and Dad, who marveled at every little thing they saw. My mom's cheeks were flushed pink from wine and the cold, and her eyes sparkled with happiness that I knew was in part because she'd not only made peace with my decision to pursue a life with Beck, but also, because in the ensuing months, she had fallen just as deeply in love with him as I had.

"Oh, Beck, look." She pointed out a flurry of twinkly angels hanging from the boughs of a fir tree. "Take our picture, will you?"

Beck lifted his phone and captured Dad giving Mom a none too discreet smooch.

"Got it. Sending it to you now." Beck's thumbs went to work, and Mom's phone chimed.

Mom looked at the picture. "Oh, it's wonderful. Look, honey."

We left them to look at her phone and—I was certain—send the image to all their friends.

I took Beck's hand. "Oh, your hands are so cold, sweetheart. Here"—I pulled my gloves off—"wear these. I don't know why you never wear the gloves I bought you."

"Because I like them prewarmed." He lifted his eyebrows. "Feels like I'm putting on a skin suit."

"Creepy." I pulled his hand into the crook of my arm. "I have had a wonderful evening. What about you?"

"Me too. I really enjoy it here."

"How do you feel about our Christmas gift from Mom?"

"It's awesome." His eyes widened. "I can't wait to get a couples massage with you! How about you? You looked strange when you opened it."

"I'm looking forward to it. It's just that my mother gave it to me. Awkward."

He shrugged. "But nice, huh?"

"Yeah."

He looked toward the ocean, which glittered in the moonlight past the garden's edge. "I honestly never believed she'd come around."

"It just took her a minute to warm up to the idea of us enough to let you into her heart. Believe me, it was a foregone conclusion. I love you, and I'm her mini-me, ergo—"

"I'm just glad they like me because they're stuck with me."

I kissed the top of his head. "Let's walk that way."

"Okay." As always, Beck let me take him by the hand, content to follow wherever I wanted to go.

Who knew blind faith would be so precious to me?

Who knew that of all the successful, mature men I'd dated, I'd fall for a boy who, on the face of it, was neither?

Beck's old friend Tug had understood me better than I'd understood myself. He'd identified me as a sure thing—a sugar daddy to be used for whatever Beck could get—but labels weren't my style at all, and I knew what Beck felt for me was real.

I had blind faith in him too.

I indicated to my Dad that we were heading down to the beach. He knew why. I hadn't told my mother because I knew better than to ask her to keep a secret. If I had trouble hiding things from Beck, she would find it impossible.

"Come on," I said after reaching the bottom of the stairs. "There's something I need you to see."

Beck let me lead him to one of the big rocks scattered at the bottom of the cliff.

"Up you go." I lifted him so he was sitting on top of a smooth, midsize boulder. "I want a picture."

"Sure." He smiled shyly and then ruined the demure image by getting into a sexy half-reclining pose. His shining sapphire eyes seemed to say, "I'm all yours."

I took a couple of pictures, slipped the phone into my pocket, and pulled out my Christmas gift to him. There were two things, actually. He could pick one, or both, or neither.

This was his decision. I got on one knee.

"What are you—" He clapped both hands over his face. "What? Oh my God, what are you doing?"

"Beck, you mean everything to me. You're my world."

"Oh my God. Do your parents know?"

"I don't need their permission. Now hush."

He clamped his lips together.

"You're my whole world, Beck. And even though I seem to lead and you basically follow, I don't want you to think we aren't equal in this partnership of ours."

He narrowed his eyes. "That's...a little pedantic there, Doc. Where's Captain Romance?"

"I said hush."

He mimed locking his lips and throwing away the key.

"I have two things to give you tonight. One is this—"

He held out his hands, and I dropped it in.

He looked down. "Ooh. This is Jurassic technology. Wait—I think it's a flash drive. A whole terabyte? You shouldn't have." He sang, "On the first day of Christmas my true love gave to me—"

"It's more symbolic than anything, and if you'd hush like I told you to, I'll tell you what's on it."

"Please tell me it's dick pics." He grinned. "Or wait—did you record us having sex? Is that why your parents aren't here? I hope it's that time when we were in the backyard playing with the hose and you said, 'I'll show you a hose,' and then you did, right out in front of God and everyone."

"It's not that."

He quieted, cupping the drive between his hands like he was afraid of it. "What is it?"

"It's the completed paperwork laying out our new family trust."

"What does that mean?"

"You and I are now equal partners in everything."

"Define everything?"

"The clinic. The house." My knee was starting to hurt. "Everything. Can I finish?"

He nodded.

"And this," I held out the box with the ring inside. "Is a wedding ring. You can take one or both. You don't have to marry me to become my partner in every way, but I'd like it if you did."

"Oh my God." His hands shook as he brought them over his face again. "Oh my God, Lindy. You idiot. You can't just...give me half of everything and marry me and…What if I murder you in your sleep?"

"Okay." I glanced out at the water. "Out of all the possible responses to my proposal, that was not—"

"You dork!" His body hit mine with a thud, toppling me backwards onto the sand. He kissed my forehead, each eye, my nose, my chin, my ears. Finally, my lips.

"Yes," he said between kisses. "Yes. I'd be happy to marry you, except we're signing the world's most preemptive prenuptial agreement. I don't want your shit, Lindy. I only want you."

"Too bad. Cause you're getting my shit anyway."

"We'll see about that. I never want anyone to say I married you for your cash or your status. Only you, Lindy. You're all that matters."

"You matter to me too. So much."

The sound of footsteps scraping over the stairs leading to the beach came nearer as my parents made their way down to the sand.

"Hey, you," Dad called cheerfully. "Do we need a hose?"

"He said hose…" That broke Beck up all over again. He rolled off me, laughing hysterically while my Dad looked on with amusement and my mother blotted her eyes.

"If that wasn't a yes, then—"

My mother froze. "Wait. What was a yes?"

"I have news!" I got clumsily to my feet. "My beloved Beck has agreed to marry me."

She turned to my father. "You knew? *You knew* he was going to *propose*, and you didn't tell me?"

"He asked me not to."

She narrowed her eyes. "Do not think for one single second that this will be the last time we talk about this. I am not even wearing the cutest dress I brought."

"You look lovely as always, my dear." Dad kissed her hands.

"Nuh-uh. Don't even."

I'd paid the bartender to stash an ice bucket with champagne and four flutes behind the boulder before dinner, and I hoped no one else had found it first. What I found was the champagne, a basket of cookies, and four perfectly dipped chocolate-covered strawberries.

"A toast, then." Mom got out her camera. "Let's get a picture of the grooms-to-be."

I took the ring out of the box and placed it on Beck's finger. Platinum with sapphires that matched his eyes. Maybe that was the pedantic part. "I am so glad you and Callie drifted into my life. You're the best thing that has ever happened to me. I will love you for the rest of my life."

"Me too. For always." With tears flowing, Beck made a fist and thumped his chest. "My heart knew we belonged to each other. Just took you a while to believe it, huh?"

"I do believe. Now and forever."

He wiped his tears with one hand and shoved the flash drive at me with the other.

"But slow your roll, Batman. Take this back. We need to talk about it. No one is going to call me a *gold digger*. I'm getting my own lawyer, and you're not going to know what hit you."

I laughed. My parents looked shocked.

Beck crossed his arms, then switched them so he could look at the ring I'd given him.

"I said I don't want your shit, and I don't. Except this. This I totally want."

"Okay." Dad popped the cork like a pro. "Who's ready for champagne?"

"Ooh, cookies." Mom went right for a white chocolate macadamia nut.

"Truce on the trust, for now?" I asked, holding out a chocolate-covered strawberry. It was an idiot move because as soon as he wrapped his lips around the fruit, our little G-rated party got steamier. Between the ring on his finger and watching him devour that strawberry, I wanted to find the nearest bed. "You are delectable."

He chewed thoughtfully before turning worshipful eyes my way. "If you say so."

That little brat.

"Say cheese doodles!" Dad snapped a picture.

"Let's take this into the bar. I'm freezing." Mom picked up the basket, and Dad got the ice bucket, and we trudged up the steps together.

"You should have hired a photographer, honey," Mom said. "Professional proposal pictures would be so wonderful."

"This was nice," Beck muttered around a cookie. "A photographer would have spoiled the moment."

"We can always take pictures later."

"It won't be the same." She pouted. "Why didn't I have a daughter? Then I could manage everything."

"Not if she was anything like me." At the top of the stairs, I wrapped my arm around Beck."

"Have you thought about a wedding venue?" Mom asked. "Or how many people you'll want to invite? I'll bet I could—"

"No!" Beck and I spoke at the same time.

"What I mean is—" Beck started.

"It's between me and Beck what happens. Only us."

As we entered the resort, Beck said, "Give us a minute. We'll be right there."

Dad caught my mother's arm before she could argue, and they walked toward the bar together.

"That was perfect." Beck lifted onto his tiptoes and kissed me. "If your mom wants to help us with the wedding, I think we should let her."

"You don't know what you're saying. We'll end up with six hundred guests, and she'll make you ride in on an elephant."

"I like elephants."

"Sweetheart—"

"What if we give her a very firm maximum number of guests and we tell her we want to be married here, in the gardens, then let her organize the details."

"You don't think she'll drive everyone who loves her crazy?"

"What I think is, I don't see my parents coming. Do you?"

His parents had turned their backs on him. When we'd visited to talk to them, they'd been unable to look at him or Callie. I didn't know if there would ever come a time when they'd reconcile, but I was willing to work on the relationship if that's what Beck wanted. He didn't, so case closed.

If Beck chose to revisit his relationship with his parents later, I'd be there for him. I'd always be there, by his side.

"Your mom acts like she's my mom now." Pink stained his cheeks. "I like when she fusses. Don't ever tell her I said that."

"I'm a vault." The number of secrets I'd been keeping from my mom made me Gringott's. "Are you sure?"

"Oh, please." He put his hands together beneath his chin, and I died of love for him on the spot. "I would love it."

"Then you shall have it." I kissed him. "Whatever your heart desires."

"Really, all I want is you. But your family is a close second."

"You ever think about having kids?" I asked carefully. I shouldn't have thrown that out there right after the proposal, but I trusted that if it was too shocking, or too much too soon, Beck would let me know.

His hand tightened on my arm. "All. The. Time. And I'm in favor. Totally."

"Okay." I should have known. Beck was always ten steps ahead emotionally, whereas I took the lead on the physical plain. I motioned toward the bar where my parents waited. "Shall we?"

He shook his head. "After you."

I took his hand, and we started toward the future—our future—together.

WHAT TO READ NEXT?

Want more Men of St. Nacho's?
Try the next book in the series, **A Flighty Fake Boyfriend.**

All Ryan Winslow needs is a fake date for his ex's wedding. What happens when a fake date turns into real, but impossible, love?

Ryan Winslow has everything he needs to attend his billionaire aristocrat ex's wedding. He's got an out and proud A-list celebrity date, reservations at an exclusive resort in Santa Barbara, and two weeks to enjoy a vacation—his first in six years.

The drive down gives him a chance to visit old friends in tiny St. Nacho's, but that's where things start to go wrong. His workaholic, driven lifestyle takes its toll, and his date calls to say he can't make it. How will he ever find a substitute date for a formal wedding in time?

Epic Alsop waits tables, but that's not all he does. He pays special attention to people, and responds to their needs accordingly. When he meets an overworked, underfed Ryan, he offers him a healing smoothie and a little extra care. When Ryan's date for a wedding cancels, Epic offers to be his fake boyfriend.

What Epic doesn't expect is Ryan's kindness, or the amazing resort vacation he offers. He doesn't expect Ryan's patience, his wit, or his passion.

But they live in different countries, and Ryan's job leaves no room for a social life. The hunger and weariness that drew Epic to Ryan in the first place is only a symptom of the reason they can't be together.

Can fake lovers who fall in genuine love find a way to make their relationship work? Or are they destined to be alone forever?

Find out if Epic and Ryan have a chance. Buy A Flighty Fake Boyfriend today!

Want more in the St. Nacho's series? Try **Winter Solstice in St. Nacho's.**

Luke is desperate to rescue the boy he once tutored. Can a winter solstice miracle bring them a second chance at love, or will Tug's dangerous addiction destroy their happiness forever?

Librarian Luke believes "Everything is possible at the library." He cheerfully provides his patrons with whatever they need,

WHAT TO READ NEXT?

even if that means administering Naloxone when they overdose in the library bathroom.

Tug's a heroin addict. He's in the grip of a powerful addiction. He has no self-esteem. He sees no way out. When old crush Luke offers help, Tug's willing to see what he can get out of the deal. But there's a terrible cost to exploring his painful past and claiming his second chance.

Miracles happen for the men of St. Nacho's. Will Tug seize a new life and the chance to be with Luke? Or will he give in to the siren's song of a drug he can't resist?

Z.A. Maxfield pens a taut and tender second chance gay romance. If you believe a good man can find love even on the darkest, longest night, buy "Winter Solstice in St. Nacho's" for an HFN you will believe in today.

Want beautiful men willing to do dirty jobs?
Try the first book in **The Brother's Grime Series, Jack: Grime and Punishment.**

One man's tough job is a path to love.

The Brothers Grime is Jack Masterson's way of helping people in crisis after disability ends his career as a firefighter. Jack's people get to a scene long after the physical trauma ends. They don't solve crime or rescue the victims. They help people move on. The new job is all Jack wants or needs, until he gets the call about old flame Nick Foasberg's suicide.

Ryan Halloran's cousin Nick has been on a downhill slide for a long time. Despite that, Ryan does everything he knows to help. Ryan only understands part of what happened between Nick and Jack in high school, but after Nick's suicide, Ryan agrees both he and Jack need closure. They work together to clean the scene and despite the situation, heat flares between them.

Jack is keeping a painful secret and fighting his attraction to Nick's lookalike cousin, Ryan. Ryan calls himself a magnet for lost causes and worries Jack might be the next in a long line of losers.

Despite his misgivings, despite the past and the mistakes they've both made, Jack gives Ryan something to look forward to, and Ryan gives Jack a reason to stop looking back, in Grime and Punishment.

Or try something completely different. How about a series with a little more….bite?
Try **Deep Desire**, the first book in **The Deep Series.**

There's no leverage like seduction...until love takes a big bite out of Adin's plans.

As the Indiana Jones of historical erotica, there is no document Adin Tredeger can't unearth. Why he would risk the biggest coup of his career to join the mile-high club is beyond him. Nevertheless, the disarming, dark-eyed vampire Donte somehow enters Adin's locked airplane washroom and has him completely nude and coming apart, all without a whimper of protest.

From that moment, Adin and Donte engage in an international battle of wit and cunning. The prize is a priceless 500-year-old journal with illustrations so erotic the Marquis de Sade would blush.

Yet Donte's desire for the journal goes far beyond simple possession. He wrote it. And he's not above using every trick in his otherworldly arsenal—including seduction—to get his journal back.

Chemistry draws them together even as fortune tugs them apart. When a third party enters the chase, will Adin and Donte join forces to fight an enemy with a deadly goal—to erase Donte from history forever?

ACKNOWLEDGMENTS

I could not have begun this new series without a book bible for the St. Nacho's Series, which Susie Selva painstakingly created. Susie wears all the hats on the editorial side, and has done a fantastic job taking the noodles that come out of my brain and turning them into a book I can be proud of.

Without Susie, this book would not have been possible.

Also, a great big thank you to LE Franks, Morticia Knight, Belinda McBride, and Sue Brown for being my partners in Writerly Shenanigans. For all you do to help foster an environment of commerce, cooperation, enthusiasm, and community, I love and thank you!

ALSO BY Z.A. MAXFIELD

Novels

Crossing Borders

Drawn Together

Family Unit

ePistols At Dawn

Gasp!

The Pharaoh's Concubine

Rhapsody For Piano And Ghost

The Long Way Home

Home the Hard Way

The St. Nacho's Series

St. Nacho's

Physical Therapy

Jacob's Ladder

The Book Of Daniel

Men of St. Nacho's Series

A MuchYounger Man

A Flighty Fake Boyfriend

The Brothers Grime

Grime and Punishment

Grime Doesn't Pay

Partners in Grime

The Deep Series

Deep Desire

Deep Deception

ABOUT THE AUTHOR

Z. A. Maxfield is a fifth generation native of Los Angeles, although she now lives in the Inland Empire.

She started writing in 2006 on a dare from her children and never looked back. Pathologically disorganized, and perennially optimistic, she writes as much as she can, reads as much as she dares, and enjoys her time with family and friends.

If anyone asks her how a wife and mother of four manages to find time for a writing career, she'll answer, "It's amazing what you can do if you give up housework."

Look for ZAM on Social Media!

COPYRIGHT